Fergus Hume

The Mikado Jewel

Fergus Hume

The Mikado Jewel

1st Edition | ISBN: 978-3-75235-298-6

Place of Publication: Frankfurt am Main, Germany

Year of Publication: 2020

Outlook Verlag GmbH, Germany.

The Mikado Jewel

By

FERGUS HUME

CHAPTER I

A MYSTERIOUS MISSION

From the main thoroughfare of Bayswater, where the shops display their goods and the tides of life run strongly, Crook Street extends its long line of ugly dwellings to a considerable distance. Its shape suggests a shepherd's crook,—hence undoubtedly the name—as it finally terminates in a curved *cul de sac*, the end of which is blocked by Number One hundred and eleven. This is an imposing, if somewhat dilapidated mansion, standing in its own limited grounds, which are surrounded by a high crumbling wall of brick, more or less overgrown with grimy ivy. There is a small front garden, planted with stunted shrubs; a narrow passage on either side of the house, screened midway by green-painted trellis-work, and—at the back—a worn-out lawn, dominated by a funereal cedar. Beneath this, through rain and sunshine, is a rustic table and a rustic seat, where the boarders have afternoon tea in summertime. Everywhere there is a feeling of dampness.

The mansion is of Georgian architecture, square and heavy, greatly in need of a coat of paint, which it has not received for years. With its discoloured surface, once white, its cheap stucco scaling off in leprous patches, its trails of moss and soot, never to be washed off by any rain, however violent, it looks a tumbledown, ruinous sort of dwelling. Or, as an imaginative boarder once suggested, it is like a derelict hulk, stranded in a stagnant backwater of Life's mighty River. It is certainly doleful, and infinitely dreary, only securing inhabitants by reason of the unusually cheap board and lodging to be obtained under its weather-worn roof.

Mrs. Sellars, who rented this sad suburban dwelling, euphoniously called it "The Home of Art," and in a seductive advertisement invited any male or female connected with music, literature, painting, poetry, and more particularly with the drama, to enjoy the refinements of an æsthetic abode at the moderate cost of twenty shillings a week, inclusive. As the house was shabbily comfortable, and its mistress was a retired actress of cheery manners, still indirectly connected with the stage, the bedrooms of The Home of Art were generally occupied by youths and maidens, ambitious of renown. There were very few really old people, as Mrs. Sellars—although elderly herself— did not care for the aged, who had no future, but loved to gather the young and aspiring round her hospitable table. And that same table truly deserved the kindly term, for the slatternly, good-natured woman supplied far better food in far larger quantities than the rate of payment allowed. Indeed, it is questionable if Mrs. Sellars made any profit whatsoever, as nearly all the boarders were juvenile and hungry. But what they paid, together with the landlady's small private income, kept things going in a happy-go-lucky fashion, which was all that was necessary. The children—as Mrs. Sellars called her boarders—adored "Ma," as the boarders called Mrs. Sellars, and with good reason, for she gave one and all largely what money could not buy. She advised, she sympathized, she nursed, she scolded, and to her the children came with their troubles, great and small, for aid and consolation. It was no wonder that with such a blessed helper of humanity, the ruinous old suburban boarding-house was usually filled to its greatest capacity.

But full as The Home of Art was last November, on one night of that foggy month it was empty from seven o'clock until midnight of all the boarders. A third-floor lodger—the lean youth with bright and bird-like eyes—had not only written a play, which Ma pronounced magnificent, but the same was to be produced on this very evening at a suburban theatre. Of course, this was a red-letter day—or, rather, night—at The Home of Art, and equally of course, Mrs. Sellars led forth her children to occupy boxes and stalls and pit and dress-circle on the great occasion. By her advice the friends of the playwright were thus fairly distributed throughout the house so that they might applaud vehemently at the right moment and stir up the public to enthusiasm. Even the cook and the parlour-maid, the housemaid and a decayed butler, who had fallen, through drink, from Mayfair to Bayswater, put on their best clothes and departed for the night's entertainment. Already the supper—and a very good supper, too—was laid out in the shabby dining-room, and would be eaten at midnight by the boarders, when they returned with Ma and the successful playwright. And assuredly he would be successful—no one had any doubt on that point, for Mrs. Sellars had long since infected all her lodgers with her constant optimism. With Ma as the head of the house, the atmosphere could scarcely fail to be cheerful. Even debts, duns, difficulties, disappointments and suspense could not, and never did, damp the hopeful spirits of the little community. And Ma, with her unfailing good humour and helpful nature, was responsible for this happy state of affairs.

When the occupants of The Home of Art departed for the Curtain Theatre, two people remaining behind had the entire house to themselves. One was Mrs. Pentreddle, who had sprained her ankle on the previous day, and could not leave the sofa on which she lay in the drawing-room with any degree of comfort, and the other was Patricia Carrol, the out-of-work Irish governess, who had arranged to stop and look after the old lady. And Mrs. Pentreddle was really old, being not far short of sixty. She was the landlady's sister, who had come up from Devonshire on a visit six days before the exodus to the theatre: a tall, gaunt, grim woman, wholly unlike Mrs. Sellars in looks and disposition. No one would have believed the two women to be sisters had not the relationship been vouched for by Ma herself. "Martha never was like me," said Mrs. Sellars, when her boarders commented on the dissimilarity, "always as heavy as I was light. Comedy and Tragedy, our Pa called us in the old days.

3

Not that Martha ever had any turn for the stage. It was only Pa's way of talking. Martha's a killjoy, poor dear, as her late husband was drowned at sea and her only child's a sailor also, who likewise may find his grave in the vast and wandering deep. She's housekeeper to Squire Colpster, of Beckleigh, in Devonshire, and knows more about managing servants than I've ever forgotten." And, as usual, she finished with her jolly laugh.

Mrs. Pentreddle certainly was no favourite with the boarders, as her lean and anxious, wrinkled and pallid face, her hard black eyes and melancholy dark garments impressed them unpleasantly. She spoke very little, but constantly maintained a watchful attitude, as though she was expecting something to happen or someone to tap her on her shoulder. As a rule she kept to Mrs. Sellars' private sitting-room, which pleased everyone, as the dour woman was such a wet blanket. But on the night of the play she insisted upon being carried down to the drawing-room in spite of the sprained ankle, which should have kept her in bed. Mrs. Sellars remonstrated, but the sister from Devonshire had her own way, saying that the first floor was preferable to the second, as it was less dismal and more comfortable. "One would think that Martha expected something to happen," said cheerful Mrs. Sellars, when she set out for the theatre with her train, "and was afraid to be too far away from the nearest policeman!" This remark was afterwards remembered when something did happen, as emblematic of Ma's prophetic powers.

The drawing-room was a large apartment with a fire-place at one end and a door leading from the hall at the other. One side was taken up by the windows, heavily curtained, and the other by large folding doors, usually closed, which gave admission to the dining-room. Outside, a narrow iron-railed balcony ran in front of the three windows from the entrance door to the corner of the house, and below this was the basement. Within, the room was fairly comfortable in a shabby, slatternly sort of way, although overcrowded with furniture of the Albert period, which had been picked up at various sales. Indeed, the entire house was furnished with the flotsam and jetsam of auction-room derelicts of prosperous days. In the drawing-room were rep-covered chairs, two horse-hair sofas, several round tables, each poised on its shaky leg, fender-stools, Berlin-wool screens, a glittering glass chandelier, and on either side of the handsome marble time-piece which stood on the mantel-shelf, antique green ornaments with dangling prisms of glass. The walls were covered with faded scarlet flock paper, the floor with a worn red carpet, bestrewn with bunches of poppies mingled with wheat-ears, and the three windows were draped with stained, ragged, crimson curtains of rich brocade. Mrs. Sellars was very proud of those gorgeous curtains, but they were distinctly out of date—a matter of indifference to those who occupied The Home of Art, in spite of its name.

4

One of the horse-hair sofas had been drawn to the fire, and Mrs. Pentreddle lay thereon, with her hard black eyes fixed on the leaping flames. Outside, the night was chilly and damp, the air was thick with fog, and even in the drawing-room could be heard the dripping of water from the ivy clothing the surrounding wall. In spite of its being in London, the house was markedly isolated, and only occasionally did a policeman venture down the curved *cul de sac*. But within, all was shabbily warm and comfortable, and Mrs. Pentreddle's grim face relaxed into more pleasant lines. Nothing could be heard but the dripping of the water, the ticking of the clock and the occasional fall of a morsel of coal from the grate. But shortly the almost silence became oppressive, and Mrs. Pentreddle spoke in her harsh voice.

"It's very kind of you to stay with me, Miss Carrol," she said, glancing sideways at her companion; "few young ladies would do that when a theatre-treat is offered to them."

The girl addressed raised her eyes from the evening paper which she had been reading and smiled. Patricia Carrol's smile was delightful, and displayed such white teeth that her beauty was enhanced. But even when her face was in repose, she looked an extremely pretty girl, and was one of those richly-coloured Irish brunettes, who remind the observer of a peach ripening against a mellow brick wall. Her hair was bluish black, of a wavy quality which lent itself admirably to the style of coiffure which she affected, and her eyes were sea-blue, of that wonderful Irish tint which goes so well with dark tresses. Her admirable figure was clothed plainly, but tastefully, in a Prussian blue serge dress, perfectly cut, and worn with a charming natural grace. Her hands and feet were slim and aristocratic, and her whole air was one of repose and good-breeding. She was a flower of civilization, and should have bloomed amidst more fitting surroundings than the shabby drawing-room could afford. Yet she was only a poor little governess seeking for employment, and even when Mrs. Pentreddle spoke to her, she had been searching the columns of the newspaper in the hope of finding a situation.

"Oh, I am very pleased to stay with you, Mrs. Pentreddle," she said, with her charming smile. "I have too many troubles to care about going to a play. I would only take them with me, and then would scarcely enjoy the performance."

"That is true," replied the elder woman, examining the girl closely; "and yet you should have no troubles at your age and with your looks."

Patricia coloured and shook her head. "My looks are really against me," she said, somewhat sadly; "ladies don't like to engage me on that account. If I were ugly and old I should be better able to get what I want."

"What do you want, Miss Carrol?" asked Mrs. Pentreddle, abruptly.

"Fifty pounds a year as a nursery governess if I can get it," replied the girl promptly, "or even thirty, so long as I can get a situation. If it were not for dear, kind Mrs. Sellars I don't think I could hold out. She's an angel, and lets me stay here for ten shillings a week until I can get something to do. Bless her!"

"How did you come to this?" asked Mrs. Pentreddle, still abruptly.

Miss Carrol coloured, for she did not like to whimper about her misfortunes to strangers. "It's a long story," she said evasively; "all you need know is that my father was a Colonel in the army, and that when he died his pension ceased and I was left penniless. But I have had a good education, and I hope to get a situation as a governess."

"Won't your friends assist you?"

"I have no friends," said the girl simply; "when I left the world I was brought up in, I left my friends for ever."

"I don't think so; you will go back to them some day," said Mrs. Pentreddle encouragingly, although the expression of her iron face did not soften; "but, meanwhile, if you wish to earn a five-pound note—" she hesitated.

The newspaper slipped from Patricia's lap to the ground and she looked surprised. "I don't understand!"

"If you will do an errand for me I will give you five pounds."

"Oh, I can do an errand for you without taking money."

"I don't ask you to: this is rather a dangerous errand. But I think you are brave, and I know that you are hard up—"

Patricia interrupted. "I have enough money to go on with," she said, flushing.

"At ten shillings a week!" retorted Mrs. Pentreddle, unpleasantly. "Well, please yourself!"—she turned over on the sofa—"I have given you the chance."

Miss Carrol thought hard during the silence which ensued. Certainly, in her pauper condition, five pounds would be a god-send, and, as she had determined to lay aside all pride when she gave up the position to which her birth entitled her, she considered that she might as well take what she could get at this difficult stage of her fortunes. For five pounds she would do much, but— "Is the errand an honest one?" she asked suddenly with a catch in her voice. The thought had just struck her.

"Perfectly honest," said Mrs. Pentreddle coldly. "What is there about me that you should think me capable of asking you to do something wrong?"

"Nothing at all," confessed Miss Carrol frankly; "but if you wish me to go on a mysterious errand, it is only natural that I should desire to hear everything about it."

Mrs. Pentreddle carefully lowered her injured foot to the ground, and sitting up very straight, folded two thin hands on her lap. "You shall hear," said she quietly, "only I must request you to keep your own counsel."

Patricia nodded. "That goes without the saying," was her answer, and she again wondered if the five pounds could be earned honestly.

"I came up to London to go on this errand myself," explained the old lady slowly, "but this sprain has prevented my keeping an appointment which must be kept to-night. As the matter is important, I am willing to pay you the money on your return with It."

"It? What is 'It'?"

"A small deal box you can easily carry in your hand. A man will give it to you if you will stand at nine o'clock by the right-hand corner of that bridge which crosses the Serpentine. On this side, remember, before you cross the bridge. Nine o'clock, and you must hold this"—she fished amongst the cushions of the sofa and produced a small bull's-eye lantern, the glass of which was pasted over with red paper. "This is the signal."

"The signal?" echoed Miss Carrol, rather nervously, for all this mystery did indeed hint at something criminal.

"Oh, you needn't turn so white," said Mrs. Pentreddle scornfully. "What I ask you to do is perfectly straightforward. There is nothing wrong about it."

Patricia still hesitated, vaguely afraid to be implicated in such unusual doings. "If you will explain further, Mrs. Pentreddle—"

"There is nothing more need be explained just now," interrupted the other woman imperiously; "when you return with the box, you shall know all. What I am requesting you to do can harm no one, but can benefit someone."

"Yourself?"

"No! That is, in a way, perhaps. But you can judge for yourself when I am able to tell you my reason. That will be when you return. If five pounds is not sufficient, I can give you ten, although I can ill afford it."

"I am satisfied with five," said Patricia quickly, and flushing again, for even in her poverty she shrank from taking money. "I don't like mysteries, and only accept your offer as I need money very badly. But for all the wealth in

7

the world I would not go if I thought that there was anything wrong," and she looked searchingly at her companion.

"How many times do you need me to assure you that there is nothing wrong," said Mrs. Pentreddle, impatiently; "you are singularly suspicious for a girl of your years. All that is necessary is for you to receive this tiny box from the man who will hand it to you."

"How shall I know the man?"

"There is no need for you to know him at all. The red light of the lantern will assure him that you are the person who is to receive the box. Well?"

Miss Carrol rose nervously and ran her fingers through her hair, as she walked up and down the long room. Her instinct told her to refuse a mission about which she knew so little, but the prospect of earning five pounds in this easy manner was so alluring, that she could not find it in her heart to decline. After all, Mrs. Pentreddle was the sister of the woman who had been, and was, so kind to her, and in every way appeared to be an almost aggressively respectable person. It was worth risking, she thought, and at this moment, as though to clinch the matter, Mrs. Pentreddle's voice broke in on her uneasy meditations.

"I can't wait much longer," said the old woman; "if you won't do what I ask, perhaps you will telephone to the nearest office, asking that a messenger-boy may be sent to get what I want. It will certainly be cheaper."

This proposal banished Patricia's last scruple, as, if a messenger-boy could be employed, the errand, mysterious as it seemed, could not have anything to do with criminal matters. Miss Carrol picked up the lantern, with its faked red glass. "I shall go at once," she declared hurriedly, for now she feared lest she should lose the money, "but who will attend to your foot while I am away, Mrs. Pentreddle?"

"I can stay here, as I am doing. Rest is the sole thing which can cure my sprain. You will only be away an hour, more or less. It is a quarter past eight now, and the distance to the Serpentine bridge is not far. Nine o'clock is the hour. You know exactly what you have to do," and she repeated her instructions, to which the girl listened carefully.

"I am to show the red light standing on this side of the Serpentine at the right-hand corner of the bridge," she said slowly, to be sure that she knew what she had to do. "I understand. What shall I say to the man?"

"Nothing. He will simply place a box in your hand and walk away. All you have to do is to bring the box to me, and then you shall know all about the matter which strikes you as being so strange. Don't lose any time, please."

Indeed, there was no time to be lost, as it would take Patricia some minutes to get her out-of-door things on. She ran up the stairs, and assumed boots in place of slippers, a heavy cloak as the night was damp, a plain cloth toque, and gloves. She then took her umbrella in one hand, the lantern, unlighted, in the other, and descended to say a few last words to Mrs. Pentreddle; or, rather, to hear them, for the old lady gave her no opportunity of speaking. For such a grim, unemotional woman, Mrs. Pentreddle seemed quite excited, although she tried to keep herself calm. But a vivid spot of red was certainly showing itself on either pale cheek.

"Show the red light and wait in silence," she directed; "do nothing more, and say nothing at all. Then when you receive the box come back with it at once to me. You thoroughly understand?"

"I thoroughly understand."

"I am glad. Finally, let me assure you once more that there is nothing dishonest or even wrong about the errand I am sending you on."

There was nothing more to be said, and Patricia departed. When she closed the front door of The Home of Art, and found herself in the street, she became aware that the night was damp and dense with fog. The gas-lights, however, shone blurred and vague through the white mists, so there was no need for her to use the lantern. No one was about, not even a policeman—in the curve of the *cul de sac* at all events; but when she passed into the straight line of Crook Street, she almost fell into the arms of a constable who was standing under a lamp. Patricia paused to ask a question.

"Will the fog get worse, officer?"

"I think it will, miss," said the man, touching his helmet and bending to look at her face. "I should advise you not to go far."

"I am only going to the Park to see a friend," answered Miss Carrol, heedlessly; and then remembering that it was a complete stranger whom she had to see, and one to whom she was not even to speak, she regretted having been so doubtfully truthful. "What is the time?" she asked, to cover her confusion.

"Half-past eight o'clock, miss," said the constable, consulting a fat silver watch. "Best go home again, miss. You might get lost in this fog, and in the Park there are some rough characters about."

"Oh, I am all right, thank you," said Patricia with a bright smile, and passed along. All the same she now began to feel uncomfortable, and to realize that Hyde Park on a foggy November night was not exactly the place for a young lady. Only the desire to earn the coveted five pounds nerved her to do that

9

which she had agreed to do.

Crook Street is not far from the main entrance to the Park on the Bayswater side, and, as the fog grew thin further on, Patricia found herself speedily on the broad path which leads directly to the Serpentine bridge. She knew this portion of the Park extremely well, as, having much time on her hands, she frequently wandered about the grassy spaces on idle afternoons. There were few people about, as the night was so disagreeable, and those she saw moved swiftly past her. Occasionally she caught a glimpse of vague forms under the trees: but she never looked closely at these night-prowlers, but, keeping in the middle of the path, moved steadily to her destination. At last she came to the bridge and took up her station at the right-hand corner on this near side. Having come to the end of her journey she lighted the lantern.

Across the water the broad bridge stretched weirdly, vanishing into the fog, which here grew denser, like the Bridge of Life in the Vision of Mirza. Patricia had read Addison's fantastic story in some school-book, and it was suggested to her again by the sight before her. People came out of the mist and disappeared into it again: some passed, unconscious of the quiet figure at the corner, while others peered into her face. But no one addressed her, much to her relief, and the ruddy light of her lantern shone like an angry star. Then the expected happened in one moment and quite without preparation.

A man came swiftly over the bridge—so swiftly, that it might have been said that he was running. She had no time to see what he was like in looks, or how he was dressed, before he caught sight of the red light and stopped for one moment to thrust a small box into her hand. Then he darted away to the left and disappeared along the bank on the Bayswater side. That was all!

CHAPTER II

WHAT HAPPENED

For some moments Patricia stood still, with the box in her hand, and stared into the gloomy fog, behind which the man was retreating. Another man passed her swiftly, as if in pursuit of the first, but halted for one single moment to look at her. She was an indistinct figure in the misty air, but she could feel that his eyes were piercing her through and through. A few seconds later and he disappeared also, but whither he went she could not tell. The whole oddity of the episode startled her, although much that had taken place had been anticipated and described by Mrs. Pentreddle.

As the name flashed across Miss Carrol's brain, she remembered that she had yet to complete her mission by taking back the box to the old lady. Almost mechanically, and with the lantern still burning, she began to retrace her steps in the direction of Bayswater. The fog was growing denser, but by her knowledge of the path and the feel of the hard gravel under her feet, she was enabled to avoid getting lost. A sudden sense of weariness, which no doubt came from the slackening of her nervous tension, overcame her, and she was glad to sink down on the first bench she came to. This was near a gas-lamp, and in the blurred circle of light she felt safe from the attentions of any night-bird. Then a strange thing happened.

It was a sensation and nothing more: one connected with the small box she held so tightly clasped in her hand. As she gripped it, she felt—with her sixth sense, no doubt—that waves of force were radiating from its interior. Patricia's body being Celtic, was strung with extraordinarily delicate nerves, and by these she was made aware of many influences which passed by less highly organized mortals. Nine human beings out of ten would not have felt the radiating influence of whatever was contained in the box, but she did. And as wave after wave extended outward, she felt as though some invisible force was driving back invisible evil. The nervous fears she had hitherto felt—and no wonder, considering the hour and the place and the mission—vanished entirely, and she smiled to think that anything could ever have frightened her. A warm light, felt rather than seen, seemed to envelop her, and within its charmed circle no evil could come. Had a robber attacked her, had an earthquake happened, had a storm of thunder and lightning devastated the air, she would not have felt the least fear. The regular waves of this strange force passed ever outward, repelling all harm, all fear; her body thrilled to the pulsations. It was as though some unseen being was draping her in his mantle of power.

Naturally she connected these weird manifestations with the box, and that with Mrs. Pentreddle. How came it, she asked herself, that so commonplace a woman should be connected with so extraordinary an object? And then she recollected that she had not set eyes on the object, whatever it might be; yet to do so she had only to look into the box. Opening the shutter of the lantern in which the glass was set, so that she could see by the natural light and not by the red glare, she examined the box. It was a common deal case, very small and very roughly made, with the lid held down by a thin wire. In fact, it was only one of those boxes furnished by shopkeepers to customers, so that delicate goods—china, glass, and such-like—might be carried away without danger of breakage; it was not even swathed in paper or bound with string. It seemed strange that if what the box contained were valuable or dangerous more precautions had not been taken in rendering its contents safe. Then, again, the man who had delivered it in so odd a way had been overcome with fear. Patricia guessed that when she remembered his laboured breathing, the backward glance he had thrown over his shoulder, and the hurried way in which he had made off, after thrusting the box into her hand. Finally, there was no doubt that the other man, who had halted for the moment, was in pursuit. Patricia looked up when she arrived at this point of her meditations, but could see no one, although she heard some footsteps dying away and others approaching on the hard gravel. And all the time she was considering things, the waves of power still continued to radiate. As they had banished her fears, they had also stimulated her limbs, and she no longer felt weary. This being the case, she half rose to return to The Home of Art, since there was no longer any reason for delay.

But, being a woman, she was curious, and desired to see what it was that produced these queer sensations. And, indeed, a less inquisitive person would have also acted as she now did, for it is the desire of all to learn the why and the wherefore of the unknown. Almost without thinking, and certainly without consideration, Patricia untwisted the wire and peered into the depths of the box. In the vivid light of the lamp a green radiance flashed upward and outward, and she uttered an exclamation of surprise and delight.

She would scarcely have been a woman had she not done so. At the bottom of the tiny box, and as if it had been hastily thrown in, was a jewel, the like of which she had never set eyes on. With a gasp of pleasure she took it in her hand, never casting a thought to the danger of that public examination, at that dark hour, in that lonely locality. She might easily have been robbed and rendered insensible by a blow, as she sat there spell-bound, gazing at the brilliant object which just covered the palm of her gloved hand. A more lovely thing she had never seen.

The luminous green poured from the heart of a large emerald, perfectly cut and polished. It formed the centre of a flower, the petals of which were cut out of some hard, dull green stone, with exquisite art. As the girl stared, entirely fascinated by the sight, she became aware that the whole lovely jewel represented a chrysanthemum blossom, of which the emerald was the central glory. From this radiated the regular petals of the blossom, layer upon layer in perfect circles, until the outward round extended in delicate points to all quarters of the compass like the corona of the sun. And as this wonderful object lay on her open hand, Patricia felt still more strongly the waves of invisible force which radiated therefrom. It was as if some glorious power was welling up from the depths of the emerald to stream off from every carved petal. It was no wonder that she stared half hypnotized by the marvel. Suddenly even a stranger thing happened.

In a single moment, as it seemed, the force appeared to falter and weaken; the light which she felt was around her died away, and the darkness of the night closed in with uncomfortable swiftness. The radiance vanished from the jewel, and with a rush all her fears came back, as though some magic no longer kept them at bay. She felt no sensation at all; in the carved chrysanthemum, she saw no glory, no charm; it was simply a beautiful ornament and nothing more. Just as she realized this with a murmur of dismay, someone suddenly leaped lightly forward and snatched the jewel from her hand. Before she could rise to her feet, the robber disappeared into the mist, running as delicately and swiftly as a startled cat. The terrified girl was left alone in the fog with the empty box.

For a single moment she remained stunned and motionless, and then, leaving lantern and umbrella and empty box behind, she started to run wildly after the thief, vaguely guessing the direction he had taken. In a few minutes she had completely lost herself amongst the trees, and then became aware with a shock of fear that she had left the path for the grassy spaces of the Park. There was no sign of the robber, peer as she might, here, there and everywhere into the surrounding gloom, and she sank down on the wet sward under a dripping tree, to weep with shame at the failure of her mission. She had betrayed her trust; she had lost the treasure. How could she face Mrs. Pentreddle without that which she had been sent to fetch? But for her curiosity in opening the box, the valuable jewel would not have been stolen. Some thief of the night must have seen her examining its beauty by lantern light, and forthwith had secured it for his own. Or it might be—and this was a second thought—the man who had followed the other, the man who had paused to look at her, piercing the darkness with cat-like vision, was the thief. In that case, there might be a chance of recovering the jewel, as Mrs. Pentreddle might know the name of the person who desired her property. But was it Mrs. Pentreddle's property, and if it was, why should it have been delivered in so mysterious a fashion? And why should the first man have been afraid of the second man who pursued him? Finally—presuming that the pursuer had snatched the ornament from her hand—why should he have done so? Patricia's head buzzed with these questions, and she sat on the watery grass, almost weeping at her inability to answer any one of them. The position was terrible: she had lost the jewel and the five pounds also, as Mrs. Pentreddle certainly would not pay her the money.

But this was not the time for weeping, nor was Patricia Carrol a very tearful person. The only thing to be done was to return to Mrs. Pentreddle and make a clean breast of the whole occurrence. The old lady might know how to deal with the matter, seeing that there was some strange tale connected with the deal box and its contents of which Patricia was unaware. Such knowledge would probably enable Mrs. Pentreddle to take steps for the recovery of her property. The police would be called in, and—but here the girl paused. Would the police be called in, considering the mystery of the whole affair? Patricia, on swift reflection, thought not; but she thought—here her patience gave way, and she rose hastily, unable to put up further with the torment of her vexed brain. The most obvious thing to be done was to see Mrs. Pentreddle at once and explain. There was no other course open to her. But the girl's nerves quivered at the thought of the very unpleasant quarter of an hour she would probably have.

However, it was no use being a coward, and she stumbled as quickly as she could towards the broad path, anxious to reach the bench upon which she had left her umbrella, the lantern and the empty box. But the night was so gloomy and the fog so dense, that she became confused amidst the multiplicity of trees. With some violence she ran against one and falling half stunned to the ground, lay there quite unable to rise. Patricia was a clever and self-reliant girl, accustomed to act immediately and firmly in all emergencies. But this adventure had robbed her of calmness and of all will-power. She felt as though the end of the world had come, and in the cold, damp, lonely darkness she could have cried for help and comfort like a frightened child. But she retained sufficient self-command not to do so, and even exerted her will sufficiently to again stagger to her feet, and strive to find her bearings. With outstretched hands she wandered, trying to gain a glimpse of some light, but all in vain.

Then began a nightmare journey through the gloomy woods. Here was a girl in the heart of London, as wholly lost as a babe in some primeval forest. She stumbled here and groped there in an aimless fashion, until her senses became so confused that she did not know what to do. Several times she dropped, several times she rose, and for hours, as it seemed, she moved onward towards an ever-receding goal. Doubtless she was moving in a circle after the fashion of the lost, and in her vague wanderings she lost all count of time. In her heart she began to wish that the dawn would come to reveal her whereabouts, as in this darkness she certainly would never succeed in escaping from the enchantments of this urban wood. And so Patricia dragged on and the night dragged on, and the effort to get back to light and humanity became a journey in eternity towards—as it seemed to her now bewildered senses—a goal which had no actual existence.

How long she wandered she did not know, having lost count of time, but finally her instinct moved her in the right direction, and she gained the broad path. But it was not the one she had strayed from, as she speedily ascertained when she chanced upon a policeman.

"The path to Bayswater, miss," he said, turning the bull's-eye light on her face and wondering at her haggard looks and bedraggled dress. "Why, you're right on the other side of the Park, miss, near the statoo."

Patricia knew that this was so, for above her in the foggy air rose the lofty pedestal of the Achilles statue. She must have wandered deviously across the vast space of the Park, and said so. The policeman readily accepted her explanation and added one of his own:

"I dessay you've got lost in the fog, miss, and no wonder, for it's as thick as pea-soup hereabouts. Not the night for a young lady to be out, miss," he ended inquisitively, and with a note of interrogation in his voice.

"I came out on an errand," said Miss Carrol faintly, for the adventure had left her weak, "and wandered off the Bayswater path near the Serpentine."

"And it's a mercy, miss, that you didn't fall in. What will you do now, miss?"

Patricia walked with him towards the gate, near the clock. "Call me a cab," she said, for although she could ill afford it, she decided to drive, as it was quite impossible to walk. The fog forbade pedestrianism, let alone that she was much too weary to trudge all the way to Crook Street.

"What; a cab, miss? Certainly, miss, although it will be hard to find one in this fog," and the constable whistled shrilly.

"What is the time, please?" Patricia asked the same question as she had put to the other policeman.

"Half-past eleven, miss."

The girl uttered a cry of astonishment, and well she might. Having left The Home of Art at half-past eight, she must have been wandering about for at least three hours. It seemed centuries, and she hastily made for the cab which drove slowly up, looking like a spectre in the fog. What would Mrs. Pentreddle think of her being absent for so long? But this question was nothing beside the one which the old lady was bound to ask with respect to the lost emerald. "Tell the man to drive to No. III, Crook Street, Bayswater," said Patricia feverishly, and bestowed herself in the hansom; "and here!"— she handed the kindly policeman one of her precious coins, which he accepted with a salute, and gave the necessary direction to the driver. In a few minutes Patricia was on her homeward way, thankful that her strange adventure had not cost her her life, as it might have done.

But her thoughts were extremely unpleasant. She had lost her umbrella, which she could ill afford to do; also the lantern of Mrs. Pentreddle, and, worst of all, the extraordinary jewel she had been sent to fetch. How could she explain? The only answer she could find was the very obvious one, that it would be best to tell the truth. Then she began to think what words she would use, until her head became confused and she dropped into an uneasy sleep. Meanwhile the cab crawled slowly and cautiously through the fog, towards The Home of Art. Patricia was made aware that she had arrived at her destination by the sudden jerk of the vehicle, as it came to a standstill. Then, still sleep-bemused, she alighted in a stumbling manner to find herself in the arms of Mrs. Sellars.

"Oh, my dear! where have you been? It's terrible; it's terrible!" and the good lady wrung her fat hands. "Oh, what is to be done?"

"What is terrible?" asked Patricia stupidly, for her head ached.

"Mrs. Pentreddle, my own sister; poor dear Martha is dead!"

"Dead!" Patricia felt her weary legs give way with sheer terror.

"Dead!" repeated Mrs. Sellars, weeping. "Murdered! Oh, dear! oh, dear!"

"Dead! Murdered!" Patricia echoed the words faintly, then fell unconscious at the feet of the weeping, distracted old actress.

"Why did you go out? Where have you been? Martha is dead—murdered!" she babbled incoherently.

CHAPTER III

AFTERWARDS

Patricia recovered her senses to find that she was lying on her own bed, in her own room. Beside her sat fat Mrs. Sellars, with many restoratives, and with a look of anxiety on her tearful face. When Miss Carrol opened her eyes and asked vaguely where she was, Ma uttered an exclamation of pleasure and thankfulness.

"Oh, what a fright you gave me, dropping down as though you were shot," she said, producing a damp handkerchief. "I thought it was another murder, and that you had taken poison, or—"

"Wait!" Patricia with sudden vigour sat up in bed and grasped the woman's arm. "You used the word murder when I fainted."

"And I use it now, my dear," said Mrs. Sellars, with some asperity. "What other word is to be used in connection with a cut throat?"

"A cut throat!" Patricia stared at her blankly.

"Oh, don't tie me down to words," wailed Mrs. Sellars, placing her fat hands on her fat knees and rocking. "Stabbed in the throat would be better, I daresay, if there can be any better in connection with the tragic death of my own and only sister. Martha and I never got on well together, but—"

"Ah, yes," interrupted Patricia, passing her hand across her forehead with a bewildered air, as a full recollection of what had taken place came back to her suddenly. "Mrs. Pentreddle has been murdered. You said that, and I fainted at the door."

"And very naturally," lamented Mrs. Sellars dolefully. "I'm sure I'd faint myself, if it wasn't that I am needed, with doctors and policemen in the house. And after such a happy evening, too," she continued, placing her handkerchief to her red eyes. "Sammy's play was such a success. I'm sure it will go on at a West End theatre and have quite a run."

Patricia ruthlessly cut short this babble, as she was yet in the dark as to what had taken place during her absence. "Will you tell me who killed Mrs. Pentreddle?" she asked, with some sharpness.

"No, I won't, my dear, because I can't, my dear. I should rather ask you that very question, seeing that you were left in charge of her with that sprained foot of hers. Why did you go out and leave Martha all alone in this big house, and where did you go, and why are you home so late, and—?"

"I shall answer all those questions in the presence of the police-officer who has charge of the case," said Patricia firmly, and gathering her Irish wits together to face a very awkward situation. "I can exonerate myself."

"Oh, my dear! no one ever accused you."

"Someone might accuse me," said the girl dryly. "People are always prone to believe the worst of one." She scrambled off the bed. "Will you please tell me exactly what has taken place while I bathe my face and change my dress?"

"What wonderful self-command you have, my dear!" said Mrs. Sellars admiringly; "it's a thing I never have had. I'm sure when Bunson met me at the door to say that Martha was lying in the drawing-room with her jugular bleeding and all the blood out of her body—not that she ever had much, poor dear!—you might have knocked me down with a feather. I was fit for nothing, and it was Sammy who sent for the police. Fancy! how good of him, my dear, seeing that he had the success of his drama on his mind. And it *is* a very great success, I can—"

"What did Bunson say?" demanded Patricia, keeping Mrs. Sellars to the point from which, confused by trouble, she constantly strayed.

"He met me and the rest at the door, my dear, when we came back from the theatre at eleven," replied Mrs. Sellars, trying to calm herself. "His face was as white as a clown's, but it was fear and not chalk with Bunson. He and Matilda and Sarah and Eliza got back at a quarter to eleven, so that the supper might be seen to. And no one has eaten the supper," cried Mrs. Sellars, again going off at a tangent. "Such a lovely supper, too! We expected to have such a happy evening, and here is Martha lying on her bed a gory corpse, with all the bedrooms upset by the villain!"

"What villain?"

"Him who murdered poor Martha, whoever he is, the scoundrel. He first stabbed Martha in the drawing-room, and then hunted all through the bedrooms, making hay, as the boys say, in every one. Just look at your own, my dear."

Miss Carrol had already done so, but she had hitherto believed that the open drawers, with their tumbled contents, the disordered wardrobe, and the displaced furniture, had been the work of Mrs. Sellars. "I thought you had done this when you were attending to me."

"But why should I?" demanded Mrs. Sellars, somewhat tartly. "It wouldn't have done you any good to have pulled your room to pieces in this way. The police say he wanted something."

"Who wanted something?"

"The caitiff who robbed Martha of her life," retorted the ex-actress in her best theatrical manner. "He murdered the poor dear for something, and as it wasn't on her—whatever it is—he searched the house. Whether he got it or not—whatever it is—I can't say, nor can anyone else. But he went out by the front door, in spite of the drawing-room middle window being unfastened, and where he's gone no one knows."

"The middle drawing-room window could not have been unfastened," said Patricia, raising her dripping face from the basin. "Bunson locked it before he went to the theatre."

"Well, then, it must have been opened since, my dear, for the latch is undone, and it has been pushed up a little way from the bottom. Martha couldn't have done it, as her foot was so bad she couldn't have left the sofa. I daresay the villain did it."

"He could scarcely have opened the window from the outside," said Patricia.

Mrs. Sellars shook her head mournfully. "I'm not so sure of that, my dear," was her reply. "The balcony runs along the front of all three windows, and as they are old and shaky, like all the house, he could easily have slipped a knife between the upper and lower sashes and pressed back the snick."

"But in that case Mrs. Pentreddle, thinking a burglar was trying to get in, would have shrieked for assistance," argued Miss Carrol.

"Who would hear her?" asked Mrs. Sellars very pertinently. "There was no one in the house, and I daresay no one in the road, as scarcely anyone comes along so far as this; on a foggy night, too. Who would come here on a foggy night? No. The villain found poor Martha all alone and stuck her like a pig. You shouldn't have left her."

"She asked me to."

"She asked you to?" repeated Mrs. Sellars, her round eyes growing rounder with astonishment. "Asked you to what?"

"To go on an errand, and"—Patricia checked herself, as it was unnecessary to repeat her story twice, and she wished to tell it in the presence of the police-officer. "It's too long to tell you now," she said hastily, and looked in the glass to see that her hair was in order. "Come downstairs, and let me see the man in charge of the case."

"Oh!" wailed Mrs. Sellars, submitting to be led out of the room. "Oh, that I should have lived to hear Martha called a case! And Bunson called her 'the remains.' Such an insult!"

"What did Bunson say exactly?" inquired Patricia quickly.

"He said that he and Matilda and Sarah and Eliza came round by the back and entered the house by the kitchen. While Matilda made up the fire and put on the kettle, Bunson went up to the dining-room to see if the supper was all right. Nothing was disturbed, so he went to look into the drawing-room, expecting to see Martha and you. But he only found Martha lying dead and icy cold on the sofa, covered with blood from her jugular vein. She never did have much blood, poor dear!" sobbed Mrs. Sellars; "but what she had she lost, for she died from losing it, too hurriedly."

"And what else did—"

"There's nothing else," interrupted Mrs. Sellars, waving her arms in a dramatic manner. "Everyone's upset and can't eat and can't go to bed, and they're all sitting in the dining-room, because Inspector Harkness won't let them sit in the drawing-room."

"Is Inspector Harkness the man I am to see?"

"Yes. He's in the drawing-room, and told me to bring you to him as soon as you could stand. He saw the cabman who brought you, and asked him where you had entered the cab. The man said at Hyde Park Corner about half-past eleven, which may or may not be true, for I can't understand what you should be doing there at this time of night."

"It's quite true," said Miss Carrol quietly. "I lost myself in the fog."

"But why did you leave the house?"

"I shall explain that to Inspector Harkness. Dear Ma," Patricia patted the disturbed old woman's shoulder kindly, "don't cry so. I assure you I have nothing to do with the death of poor Mrs. Pentreddle."

"I never thought for one minute you had, my dear," said the poor landlady. "All the same, Martha is as dead as a door-nail. She is now with her late husband I expect, though it can't be a very pleasant place where such a rascal has gone to. Not that I want to say anything bad against them that are gone, for we may be the same to-morrow," and so poor Mrs. Sellars, quite incoherent with grief and bewilderment, maundered on aimlessly.

Patricia was invited to enter the drawing-room by a jovial-looking man, whose would-be military air did not suit his looks. He was stout, red-faced, grey-haired and bluff in his manner, resembling the typical John Bull more than anything else. He tried to be stiff, but failed in his buckram civilities when he forgot that he was Inspector Harkness and remembered that he was primarily a human being. Miss Carrol was so pretty and graceful in spite of her white face and drooping air, the result of fatigue, that the officer beamed on her approvingly. But having placed a chair for her, and one for Mrs. Sellars, who was to be present at the interview, he became aware that he had his duty to perform, and looked as stern as he possibly could.

"Now, young lady," he said, arranging some papers, and getting ready to take notes, "what do you know of this matter?"

"Nothing," said Patricia, coolly and decisively. She was now quite her own clever, ready-witted self, as the difficulties of her position had acted upon her like a tonic. In spite of Inspector Harkness's suave demeanour, she was fully aware that he would not hesitate to arrest her, if he believed she was in any way inculpated. Her curt answer rather annoyed him.

"Nothing," he repeated sharply. "That is rather a strange denial to make, in the face of the fact that you were the last person who saw this unfortunate lady alive. Do you deny that, Miss Carrol?"

"No. Why should I? I was with Mrs. Pentreddle from the time Mrs. Sellars left with the others for the Curtain Theatre—"

"Half-past six, as we thought the house would be full," interpolated Ma sadly.

—"until nearly half-past eight o'clock," finished Patricia calmly.

"And after that?" asked Harkness, noting down this fact and acknowledgment.

"I was wandering about Hyde Park, lost in the fogs until half-past eleven."

"What took you to Hyde Park on this night?"

"Mrs. Pentreddle asked me to go on an errand for her."

"What was the errand?"

"What indeed?" said Mrs. Sellars curiously. "Martha, poor dear, was always of a very secretive disposition, and never told me anything. But, as I am her own sister, she ought to have told me what she wanted."

Patricia took no notice of this remark, but addressed herself to Inspector Harkness. She wished to get the interview over, so that she could retire to bed, for she felt extremely tired, and only her will-power enabled her to sustain the examination. "Mrs. Pentreddle," she explained, and the officer took down her words, "had an appointment to-night with a man near the Serpentine Bridge on this side. Owing to her sprained ankle she could not go herself, so she promised me five pounds if I would go in place of her. At first I objected, since the conditions under which I was to meet this man were so strange; but when Mrs. Pentreddle declared that, failing me, she would ring up a messenger-boy on the telephone, I thought that there could be nothing wrong, and accepted the commission."

"For the sake of the five pounds," hinted the inspector.

Patricia threw back her head proudly. "I am not rich, and five pounds mean much to me," she said simply, but with a nervous flush. "Yes, I went for the sake of the five pounds. Though, of course," she added quietly, "I was quite willing to oblige Mrs. Pentreddle in every way. I refused the money at first, but when she insisted upon paying me, I was only too delighted to accept. Do you blame me?"

"Well, no," acknowledged the officer, after a pause. "But did you not think that five pounds was a rather large sum to pay for a simple errand?"

"And Martha was so close-fisted as a rule," put in Mr. Sellars.

"The errand was not a simple one," said Patricia quickly. "There was a very great deal of mystery about it," and she repeated the instructions which the dead woman had given her. These both impressed the inspector and startled Mrs. Sellars.

"One would think that Martha was a conspirator," she exclaimed.

"Perhaps she was and perhaps she was not," replied Miss Carrol wearily. "I have been puzzling over the question ever since the box was stolen."

"Stolen!" Harkness rose suddenly to his feet and looked at the girl's pale face with an imperious glance. "What do you mean?"

"What I say," answered Patricia, whose nerves were giving way. "A man came and snatched the jewel from my hand while I looked at it."

"The jewel!" cried Mrs. Sellars alertly. "What jewel?"

"The one which was in the deal box."

"The box which this unknown man thrust into your hand?" asked Harkness.

"Of course. I should not have opened the box, but I did so, because—" Patricia hesitated. It seemed useless to tell these two very matter-of-fact people about the weird sensations which she had felt while holding the jewel, as they would neither understand nor believe. Swiftly changing her mind, she ended her sentence differently—"because the whole circumstances were so strange that I wished to know what was in the box."

"You were afraid that Mrs. Pentreddle had sent you on a nefarious errand?"

"Yes, I was, and with good reason," said Patricia, and Harkness nodded approvingly.

Mrs. Sellars disagreed. "Why, Martha was a most religious woman, and so good as to be almost unpleasant. She would never have sent you on an errand which had to do with anything wrong, my dear."

"You can judge for yourself," said Miss Carrol, quietly. "I am telling you all that has taken place."

Harkness pondered. "You say that you left this house at half-past eight, and wandered in Hyde Park until half-past eleven. How can you prove this?"

"Very easily, Mr. Inspector. I met a policeman in Crook Street when I left the house and asked him the time. He told me that it was half-past eight. At half-past eleven I spoke to another policeman near the Achilles statue, saying I had lost myself in the fog. I asked him the time also, and told him to whistle me up a cab. He said it was half-past eleven and got me the cab. Mrs. Sellars told me in my bedroom that you had questioned the cabman, sir, so he must substantiate my story."

Harkness nodded. "Yes. He told me that a policeman had put you in the cab at Hyde Park Corner about the time you mentioned. I see that you can account for leaving the house and returning to it. But what were you doing in the meantime?"

"I have told you," said Patricia, annoyed at having her word doubted.

"Yes, you have told me; but can you prove what you say?"

"Luckily I can, unless the things are stolen."

"What things?"

"The umbrella, the lantern and the empty box, which I left on the bench in the broad Bayswater path. I was sitting there when the man robbed me."

"What was the man who robbed you like?"

"I can't say. It was foggy and he only remained for a single moment."

"And what was the man who gave you the box like?"

"I can only make you the same answer," said Patricia. "Both incidents happened so swiftly that I had no time to observe anything. But if you will send to the Park you will perhaps find the articles I left on the bench."

The inspector nodded, and rising from his chair, went out of the room. Mrs. Sellars caught the girl's hand when they were alone.

"What does it all mean, my dear?" she asked helplessly.

"I can't say," replied Patricia, shaking her head. "You know all that I know, and must form your own opinion."

"What is yours?"

"I have none. I am quite bewildered."

At this moment Inspector Harkness re-entered the room and returned to his seat. "I have sent to the Broad Walk in Hyde Park," he said bluffly; "so if your story is true, the articles will be found."

"My story is true," said Patricia, flushing with anger. "But while I was away someone may have sat on the bench and—"

"And have taken the articles," finished the officer dryly. "Well, yes; but I hope for your sake that your tale—a very strange one—will be substantiated by these proofs."

"Do you believe that I am telling you a falsehood?" asked Patricia in her most indignant manner.

"I believe nothing and I say nothing until these articles are found."

"And if they are not?"

The inspector hesitated, looked awkward, and did not reply.

Patricia stood up, trying to control her nerves, but quivering from head to foot. "Perhaps you accuse me of murdering Mrs. Pentreddle before I went out?"

"No, dear, no," cried Mrs. Sellars, catching her hand kindly. "The doctor says that poor Martha was murdered about ten o'clock, and as you can prove that you were absent by means of those policemen and the cabman, no one can accuse you of the crime. And I know," said Mrs. Sellars, bursting into tears, "that you wouldn't hurt a fly, much less Martha, who liked you in her disagreeable way."

"I am not accusing Miss Carrol, I beg to say," remarked the inspector, as soon as he secured a moment to speak; "but the whole tale is so strange that Miss Carrol cannot blame me if I desire proofs. Naturally a high-spirited young lady doesn't like to be questioned in this way, but—"

"I don't mind being questioned," interrupted Patricia, her hot Irish blood aflame. "But it is being doubted that I object to."

"Natural enough; natural enough," said Harkness soothingly; "but one cannot bring personal feelings into legal matters. I have daughters myself of your age, Miss Carrol, and I have every sympathy with your position. As a man and a father, I fully believe every word you say; but as an officer, I am obliged to disbelieve until I have proofs. If I do not demand them, the jury and the coroner will."

"When? Where?" asked Patricia, startled.

"At the inquest. You will be the most important witness, Miss Carrol."

"But I don't know who committed the crime."

"No, nor does anyone else. But you can tell the coroner and the jury what you have told me, and I hope that the articles you left on the bench will be forthcoming to prove the truth of your extraordinary story. Come, Miss Carrol, you must see that I am trying to make things as pleasant as possible for you, consistent with my official responsibility."

"Yes," said Patricia, and sat down again, for, after all, she could not deny but what her story sounded very incredible. And as yet she had not told the most incredible portion, as that had to do with her own peculiar sixth sense, which she was very certain neither the inspector nor Mrs. Sellars possessed. And as they had not got it, how useless it would be, as she fully recognized, to relate the sensations caused by the stolen jewel. Her tale was improbable enough, so there was no need to make it still more so.

"Can you describe what was stolen?" Harkness asked her.

Patricia did so, and the explanation was received with exclamations of surprise by Mrs. Sellars and with a somewhat sceptical air by the inspector. Patricia saw his doubts and grew annoyed again. "What is the use of my telling you things when you won't believe me?"

Before Harkness could answer this very natural question, a young constable entered and placed on the table the articles which had been left on the bench in the foggy Park. Miss Carrol spread out her hands triumphantly.

"Yes," said the inspector, interpreting the gesture. "I believe your story now, young lady. Here are the proofs."

"Ah, yes," groaned Mrs. Sellars, rocking. "But where is the jewel?"

CHAPTER IV

THE INQUEST

Destiny works in a most mysterious way, and frequently the evil which she brings on individuals becomes the parent of good. During the three years which had passed since the death of her father, Patricia had faced much trouble for a girl of twenty-two. She had no money, and had possessed no friends until she met with Mrs. Sellars, so her career had been a painful one of toil and penury and heart-felt despair. This last misfortune which connected her with the commission of a crime seemed to be the greatest blow which had befallen her, and she truly believed that she was now entirely ruined. For who, as she argued, would engage as a governess a girl who was mixed up in so shady a business? Even if she could prove her innocence—and she had no doubt on that score—the mere fact of her errand to the Park was so fantastic in the explanation, that many people would believe she had invented it in order to shield herself from arrest. In nine cases out of ten this might have happened; but Destiny ordained that Patricia's case should be the tenth. Through the darkness of the clouds which environed her the sun of prosperity broke unexpectedly.

Of course, next day the newspapers contained details of the murder at The Home of Art, and the mystery fascinated the public. Crook Street was never so full since it had been a thoroughfare. Motor-cars, hansom cabs, four-wheelers, taxicabs, carts, bicycles, and conveyances of every description, came to the curved *cul de sac*. Also, sight-seers on foot came to survey the house, and Number III appeared in the daily illustrated papers. When the reporters became more fully acquainted with what had taken place, the portrait of Patricia appeared also, together with an account of how the murdered woman had induced her to leave the house. It was generally considered, notwithstanding that the errand had been proved to be a genuine one, that Mrs. Pentreddle had sent the girl away in order that she might see the mysterious person who had murdered her. If this was not so, argued everybody, how came it that the man—people were certain that the criminal was a man—had gained admission into the house? An examination of the snicks to the windows had proved that they were too stiff to be pressed back from the outside, and, indeed, that the upper and lower sashes of the windows were so close together that the blade of a knife could not be slipped in between. Plainly the man could not have entered in this way, so the only assumption that was natural appeared to be that the dead woman had admitted him by the door. The fact that the middle window was unlatched and slightly open was accounted for by the presumption that the man had left in that way. But why he should have chosen this odd means of exit, when he could have more easily have left by the front door, the theorists did not pretend to explain.

However, the general opinion was that Patricia's fantastic tale was true—the finding of the articles on the bench and the evidence of the two policemen, together with the cabman's statement, proved this—and that Mrs. Pentreddle had got rid of her, as an inconvenient witness to an unpleasant interview. How unpleasant it had proved for Mrs. Pentreddle herself, could be plainly seen from the fact that she was now dead, and that a jury and a coroner were about to sit on her remains. Harkness had gathered together what evidence he could, which was not much, and the reporters were all on the *qui vive* for startling revelations to be made. The whole affair was so out of the ordinary that the journalists, anxious to fill up the columns of their respective papers during the dull season, made the most of the very excellent and unusual copy supplied to them. They added to this, they took away from that, and so distorted the truth that plain facts became even more sensational than they truly were. And this painting of the lily brought Miss Carrol into prominence as the heroine of the day.

The girl shrank from such sordid publicity, but it was useless to try and hide, as the searchlight of journalism played fiercely upon her. That she was so pretty only added to the attractiveness of the unwholesome episode, and when her portrait was published, Patricia received at least six offers of marriage. All of these she naturally refused, and was, indeed, very indignant that they should have been made. Mrs. Sellars was rather surprised at this indignation, as, having the instincts of a successful actress, she looked on such publicity as an excellent advertisement.

"My dear," she said impressively, two or three days after the murder, and when The Home of Art was the centre of attraction to all morbid people, "sorry as I am that Martha, poor darling, met with such a sad death, there is no denying that the tragedy will do the house good."

"Oh," cried Patricia, her highest instincts outraged, "how can you talk so?"

"I am a sensible woman, and must talk so," said Ma firmly; "tears and sorrow won't bring Martha back again, and perhaps she is better where she is, as she certainly never enjoyed life in a sensible way. Since this is the case, let us take good out of evil. I thought, my dear, that the Home would have been ruined, but instead of that, it has become famous. I could fill the place twice over, as so many people wish to come; but I intend to keep my present lodgers at the same prices. Never shall it be said that I made capital out of my dear sister's death. But you, my dear, need not be so particular, since you are not connected with her in a flesh-and-blood way as I am. Do you see?"

Patricia shivered. "No, Mrs. Sellars, I really don't see. I am connected with poor Mrs. Pentreddle in a blood way certainly, for if I had not gone out she would have been alive now."

"Well, my dear, you couldn't help going out, since you had to go on the errand, and no one knows better than I do how obstinate Martha was. Well, she's gone, and as soon as they've settled who killed her we must send her to Devonshire."

"To Devonshire?" echoed Patricia, surprised.

"Yes. Didn't I tell you that Squire Colpster, whose housekeeper she was, has come to London? Well, he is in town now, and called to see me to-day. He is very shocked at Martha's death, and intends to take the body back to lay in Beckleigh churchyard near that of her late husband—or, perhaps, I should say, its late husband, although I am not sure that an 'it' can have a husband. It's very kind of the Squire, but the Colpsters were always kind. He is coming to see you this afternoon before the inquest takes place."

"What about?" asked Patricia uneasily.

"He wishes to hear the story from your own lips."

"It is in all the papers; and much of what the papers say is untrue."

"All the better advertisement," said Mrs. Sellars cheerfully. "I'm quite sure, my dear, that your troubles are over. You can marry when you choose."

"I certainly shan't marry those horrid men who have had the impertinence to write to me!" declared Patricia indignantly.

"Oh, I should, if you find one of the men is nice and rich. But if you don't feel inclined to marry, you are at least sufficiently widely known to get a good situation."

Patricia shuddered again and to her soul. "Who would engage a girl connected with such a horrid crime?"

"Lots of people," said Mrs. Sellars promptly; "and the crime is not so horrid as mysterious. Who can have murdered Martha?—and why?"

"Everyone is asking that question, Mrs. Sellars."

"No one seems to obtain an answer," observed the good lady mournfully; "not even Inspector Harkness or the police. Well, my dear, I must go and see about the dinner. Remember what I said to you. You have a magnificent boom on just now, and if you take full advantage of it, you are made for life."

Miss Carrol did not know whether to laugh or to scold when Ma left her, but finally took refuge in quiet merriment, notwithstanding her disgust at finding herself the centre of such a sordid sensation. Good-natured and kind as Mrs. Sellars undoubtedly was, the idea that she could urge anyone—as she phrased it—to make capital out of her sister's death, revolted Patricia's finer feelings. Certainly, since the old actress intended to retain her children even though she could have obtained more lucrative boarders, she was behaving extraordinarily well, considering her limitations. But in spite of her own self-denial, her theatrical instincts were so very strong, that she had to induce someone to make use of the advertisement, as she could not bear to see such a chance of gaining a wide publicity wasted. It quite grieved her that Patricia should so persistently refuse, especially when she considered that the girl required money. But Miss Carrol not only declined to entertain the idea, but kept as much as she could to her own room and refused interviews to several inquisitive reporters.

"She has no business capabilities," mourned Ma to the playwright. "Why, if this had happened to me when I was on the stage, I should have doubled my salary in a week and trebled it in a month!" which statement was undoubtedly true, since the majority of people greatly enjoy the morbid.

Squire Colpster—as Patricia learned the country gentleman was always called at Beckleigh, and also by Mrs. Sellars, who was a Beckleigh woman—appeared at The Home of Art immediately before the inquest was held, and, therefore, had scanty opportunity of talking with the girl, although he managed to exchange a few words. He turned out to be a tall, lean, and rather bent man, with a dry, ivory-hued skin and gold-rimmed spectacles, perched on an aquiline nose. The term "Squire" suited the John Bull personality of Inspector Harkness better than it did this quiet student. And Patricia, although she did not learn at the moment what Mr. Colpster's particular studies were, gathered that he passed the greater part of his days in a well-furnished library. Only the tragic death of an old and valued servant, this gentleman hinted, would have brought him up to London during the very damp month of November. He spoke with considerable emotion.

"Poor Martha, how strange it is that she should have come to town to meet with this terrible doom! I was never so shocked in my life as when I read the telegram sent by Mrs. Sellars."

"Do you know why she came to London?" asked Patricia bluntly.

Mr. Colpster shook his head, which was covered with rather long, iron-grey hair, in true student fashion. "I only know that Martha wanted to go for a fortnight's jaunt to London—her own words. And I rather think, although she did not say so," added the Squire musingly, "that she expected to meet her son Harry, who is a sailor."

"Is he in town now?"

"I believe so. My nephew, Theodore Dane, told me that he had seen him over a week ago. Harry then said that he had returned from the Far East, and was going later to Amsterdam for a few days. If he has carried out his intention I expect that he is ignorant of his mother's death."

"When he hears of it will he return?"

"Immediately, I think, as Harry is greatly attached to, his mother. If anyone can find the assassin, Harry Pentreddle will, as he is smart, and very tenacious of anything he takes up. I wish I knew where he was in Amsterdam, Miss Carrol, as I could then send him a telegram."

Patricia pondered. "I wonder if he can throw any light on the motive for the commission of the crime?"

"It seems impossible, as Harry, having been on a year's voyage, has not seen his mother for twelve months. It is just possible that, as Martha was a week in town before her murder, she may have seen Harry in the interval. Of course, I understand that Martha only sprained her foot on the night previous to her death."

"She slipped on the stairs," said Patricia mechanically. "Her son certainly has not been here, or Mrs. Sellars would have told me. Have you any idea what caused the crime to be committed?"

Mr. Colpster pondered in his turn. "I rather think I will wait until the inquest is ended before answering that question," he said judicially.

"But won't you answer it at the inquest, so that the truth of the matter may be known," urged the girl, puzzled by his tone.

"I may not be asked the question at the inquest," said Mr. Colpster blandly, and declined to discuss the matter further. Indeed, there was no time, as they were summoned at this moment to the drawing-room, where the jurymen, under the control of the coroner, were waiting for the various witnesses. They had already inspected the body of the unfortunate woman, which was lying in an upstairs bedroom.

As has been before stated, Inspector Harkness had very little evidence to lay before those in authority. The criminal, whether man or woman, had disappeared in what seemed to be a magical manner. All the officer could do, and did do, was to produce various witnesses to relate baldly what had taken place; and these could say very little. Nothing could be proved save that Martha Pentreddle had been murdered, but by whom, and for what reason, it was impossible to say. The inspector gave a hurried sketch of all that had happened since he had been summoned to The Home of Art, and then called his first witness. This was Mrs. Sellars, who wept a great deal, and spoke volubly, adopting her best dramatic manner, so as to create a sensation; for she was always mindful, in spite of her genuine grief, that what she said would be printed in all the great newspapers. The chance of advertising herself as a retired star of the drama was too good to be lost.

But in spite of the good lady's volubility, she had really very little information to give. Her sister, Mrs. Pentreddle, had come to London six days previous to her death, from Devonshire, where she was housekeeper to Squire Colpster, ostensibly on the plea of shopping. She had gone out a great deal, but nearly always the witness was with her, and the deceased had not spoken to anyone in particular. She had certainly mentioned that her son Harry had returned from the Far East, and that she hoped to see him before she returned to Devonshire. But Harry had neither written nor had he called. "And I should have been so pleased to see Harry, who is a very charming nephew to have," ended Mrs. Sellars, with doubtful grammar.

"Did the deceased mention that she was expecting anyone on the night she was murdered?" asked the coroner gravely.

"Oh, dear me, no, sir. Had she done so, I should have forbidden her to receive a single person, as she was slightly feverish from a sprain caused by slipping on the stairs, and was not in a condition to see anyone. In fact, I was most unwilling to leave her, but she implored me to do so, as she knew how interested I was in the drama of Mr. Samuel Amersham. But only on the condition that someone remained to look after her did I agree to go. Miss Carrol kindly promised to remain, so I departed quite happy. Only to return," said Mrs. Sellars, with a burst of emotion, "to find that Martha had gone to that bourne whence no traveller returns."

"The deceased never hinted to you that she was in danger of her life?"

"Never! She was quite happy—that is, as happy as she could be with her religious views, which were extremely dull. She had no idea of dying, for she told me that she hoped Harry would return with her to Devonshire."

"Did you know of anything in her life which led you to believe that she had an enemy who desired her death."

"Certainly not! Martha never made an enemy in her life, although she certainly was the reverse of agreeable. She was as dull as I am bright," said Mrs. Sellars, blushing. "Comedy and Tragedy, Pa called us," and this remark ended the examination, as the witness apparently could throw no light on the darkness which environed the crime.

The doctor who had been called in to examine the body stated that the deceased had been murdered by some sharp instrument being thrust into the throat. This had pierced the jugular vein, and the miserable woman, becoming unconscious almost at once, had slowly bled to death. Her hair was in disorder, and when discovered, her body was lying half on and half off the sofa. It was the doctor's opinion that the assassin, grasping the hair, had drawn back his victim's head so that he could the more easily accomplish his deadly purpose. From the nature of the wound, it was probably inflicted by a fine and narrow blade—witness thought that a stiletto might have been used. From the condition of the body, death had undoubtedly taken place at ten o'clock, but probably, since the death was caused by hæmorrhage, deceased must have been struck down some minutes earlier. This was all the medical evidence obtainable, and although it proved clearly how Mrs. Pentreddle died, could not show who had committed the crime. But the use of the word "stiletto" gave the coroner an idea.

"Only a foreigner would use such a weapon," he remarked.

The witness disagreed. "The word suggests an Italian, because it is the name of a weapon extensively employed by the *bravi* of the Middle Ages. But a murderer of any other nation would use it just as naturally, if it came to hand.

Besides, I only assume from the nature of the wound—the smallness of the orifice—that a stiletto was used. I am sure that I am right, however!" and the coroner rather agreed, as he also was a doctor and had seen the wound himself.

"Could there have been a stiletto in the house?" he asked generally.

"Yes!" cried Mrs. Sellars unexpectedly, from her seat near the door, and became prodigiously excited.

"What's that?" asked the coroner, as the doctor stepped away from the place assigned to witnesses. "What do you say?"

Mrs. Sellars at once occupied the vacated position. "Now I remember, that only three days before poor, dear Martha met with her death, I was showing her some of my old stage dresses. There was a page's costume I wore in The Duke's Motto, and with it were the jewels and a stiletto."

"Pooh! Pooh! A stage weapon!" said the coroner contemptuously.

"Not at all; not at all! A friend of mine, who admired my acting, gave me a real Italian stiletto to wear in the part: a very dangerous weapon it was, sharp and pointed. I daresay Martha was killed with that."

"Have you missed it?"

"No. I put away the dresses and never thought of looking, but Martha could easily have taken it while my back was turned. Just wait, sir, and I'll go and see," and before the coroner could give permission, Mrs. Sellars, as active as a young girl, was out of the room.

There was a pause, as it was impossible to continue the examination of other witnesses until this important point was settled. Everyone looked at one another, but no one spoke, as it was felt that here, at least, was a tangible clue. In a very short space of time Mrs. Sellars returned, red-faced and out of breath, waving an empty sheath. "It's not here," she declared quickly and giving the gold-embroidered sheath to the coroner; "this is all that I found. Martha must have taken the stiletto."

"But why should she?" demanded the coroner, doubtfully.

"Ask me another," said Mrs. Sellars vulgarly, and with a shrug.

There was only one inference to be drawn from the absence of the weapon: Mrs. Pentreddle knew that she was in danger, and had therefore armed herself against a possible attempt being made on her life.

CHAPTER V

Until it came to the examination of Patricia, very little was learned from the depositions of the various witnesses summoned to give evidence. All that the boarders and the servants could say was that Mrs. Pentreddle, although not an extremely sociable person, had behaved herself quietly in every way. She had kept very much to herself, and had mentioned her business in coming to London to no one. And certainly she had never hinted in the slightest degree that she possessed an enemy who desired to take her life. All who dwelt beneath the hospitable roof of The Home of Art expressed themselves surprised at the death of the poor woman. There was nothing apparent on the surface of things, as one witness observed, to lead up to such a catastrophe. It was entirely unexpected and unforeseen.

Bunson, the butler, deposed that before leaving the house with his fellow-servants for the theatre, he had locked the three drawing-room windows. When the police examined the room afterwards, the middle one of these had been found unfastened and slightly open. It assuredly would not have been difficult for the assassin to have come along the iron balcony to that window and there have tapped for admittance. But Bunson swore positively that unless the deceased had opened the window, the man could not have entered. It was this witness who had found the body, and he stated that he had not touched it until it was seen by Inspector Harkness and his underlings. It was at this point, and in answer to the question of a juryman, that the inspector admitted the absence of the weapon with which the deceased had been killed. No stiletto had been found, either in the drawing-room or in any part of the house, so it was presumed that the criminal must have taken it away with him.

"I wonder that he did not place the stiletto in the hand of the dead woman, so that it might be supposed she had committed suicide," said a juryman.

"Probably he did not think that it would be proved that the deceased had taken the stiletto from her sister's room when the stage costumes were being displayed," suggested another juryman.

"We have not yet learned if the murder was committed with that weapon," was the coroner's remark. "Call George Colpster."

Then came the turn of the Squire to be examined, but he could tell nothing likely to aid in the discovery of the criminal. Mrs. Pentreddle, he declared, had been his housekeeper for over twenty years, and had rarely gone away on a holiday. She had asked him for a fortnight's leave, so that she might pay a visit to Mrs. Sellars in London, and this he had readily granted. She had never told him the reason why she wished to go to London, but he presumed at the time that she intended to see her sailor son during her stay.

When this fact, or, rather, this suggested fact, became known, the coroner recalled Mrs. Sellars, and learned again what he might have known he had learned before, had he referred to his notes, that Harry Pentreddle had never been near the house. When Mrs. Sellars stepped away again from the position allotted to the witnesses, Squire Colpster finished his evidence by swearing solemnly that his housekeeper had never hinted that she was in danger of her life.

"Yet she must have thought so," observed a juryman, "else she would not have taken the stiletto."

"We have not yet proved that the murder was committed with that weapon," snapped the coroner once more.

Of course, the real interest of the case truly began when Patricia Carrol was sworn, since she apparently knew more about the matter than did anyone else, and, moreover, had been the last person to see Mrs. Pentreddle alive. She gave her evidence quietly and clearly, relating all that had taken place from the time Mrs. Pentreddle had asked her to go on the errand to the time she returned to learn that during her absence the wretched woman had been stabbed. But on this occasion, as on the other, when Harkness had questioned her, Patricia left out any confession of her sensations when holding the stolen jewel. She judged, and very wisely too, that any statement of this kind would be put down to hysteria.

Both the coroner and the jurymen questioned and cross-questioned the witness, but in no way could they cause her to deviate from the details she originally gave. Mrs. Pentreddle had promised to explain all about the matter when the witness returned, but her unforeseen death had ended all chance of explanation in that quarter.

"But was the death unforeseen by you?" asked the coroner, catching at the word used by Patricia.

"Certainly," she replied readily. "I expected to find Mrs. Pentreddle ready to receive me when I returned."

"And expected to receive your five pounds?"

"No, sir. I had failed in the errand she had asked me to do; therefore, I did not desire to be paid."

"Can you describe the appearance of the man who placed the box in your hand and the appearance of the thief?"

"No. I told you so before. Both men came and went in a flash, and even if they had waited, it would have been impossible for me to have noticed their dress and looks, as the fog was so thick and the night was so dark."

"Did either man speak?"

"No. Each came and went in silence."

The policemen both in Crook Street and at Hyde Park Corner proved that they had met Patricia and that she had severally asked them the time. Also, the cabman deposed to driving the young lady back to The Home of Art, so, without any difficulty whatsoever, it was proved that Miss Carrol had been absent from the house when the crime had been committed. The Crook Street policeman also swore that he had seen no suspicious people haunting his beat. "And the fog was so thick," ended this witness, "that it would have been difficult to see anyone, unless someone ran into my arms as the young lady did. It was a pea-soup night, sir."

This concluded all the evidence which Harkness was able to get, and after a pause the coroner began his speech. But before he got very far, the door of the drawing-room was hastily flung open and Sammy Amersham the playwright dashed in, holding a dagger aloft.

"It's the stiletto," he cried triumphantly, and clapped it down on the table under the coroner's nose. "When you were asking questions about it, I remembered the unfastened middle window, and wondered if the assassin had opened the same to throw the weapon into the area when he had killed poor Mrs. Pentreddle. I went down and searched, and found it. He must have thrown it out, as I guessed, and then have stepped in to close the window and leave by the front door. There's blood on it, too."

"Is this your stiletto, Mrs. Sellars?" asked the coroner, passing it along.

The woman shuddered as she took it. "It's mine, sure enough," she said. "And there's blood on the handle. Ugh!" she dropped it. "Martha's blood!"

Sammy the playwright was sworn and stated again how he had found the weapon in the area below the iron balcony. "Amongst some rubbish," said Mr. Amersham.

"Is the area ever used?" asked the coroner quickly.

"No," called out Mrs. Sellars; "the tradespeople go round to the back by the side passage, and the gate in the iron railings round the area has been locked ever since I have been in this house. No one would think of looking for the stiletto there."

"The last witness did," said the coroner dryly.

"Shows that he's got the makings of a dramatist," said Mrs. Sellars proudly, although no one saw the connection between the coroner's assertion and her comment.

One thing was clear from the discovery of the weapon in the area, namely, that Mrs. Pentreddle must have been afraid of an attack, else she would never have armed herself by stealing the dagger from her sister. Also, it was certain that Sammy's shrewd explanation was feasible, and that the assassin, after killing the unfortunate woman, had opened the window to drop the stiletto into the unused area.

"The deceased must have expected a visitor on that night," said the coroner musingly, "and probably sent Miss Carrol away so that she could see him undisturbed."

"She did not tell me that she expected anyone," said Patricia quickly.

"No, she would not, seeing that she evidently desired to have a secret interview. As she was alone in the house, she assuredly must have admitted him."

"She could not leave the sofa with her sprained foot," cried Mrs. Sellars.

"Perhaps she could not have crawled to the front door," remarked the coroner; "but her will evidently enabled her to crawl to the middle window and open it."

"Why should the man have come to the middle window?"

"By appointment."

"Impossible," said Mrs. Sellars nervously. "In the first place, Martha would have told me had she intended to see anyone, and—"

"Pardon me, no, madam," interrupted the coroner sharply. "The very fact that the deceased sent away Miss Carrol showed that she desired the interview to be a secret one."

"She would not have admitted a man who intended to murder her."

"But she did. No one else could have admitted him, and the fact of the open middle window showed how he was admitted."

"He opened that to throw out the stiletto."

"Probably he did that, but undoubtedly the window was opened before. Mrs. Pentreddle could not have crawled to the front door."

"Martha had so strong a will that she would have crawled to the top of the house if she had made up her mind to. And I say again she never would have let in a man—whoever he was—to murder her, poor dear!"

"I don't believe she expected to be murdered."

"But the dagger—"

"Precisely, madam. The criminal did not bring it with him, therefore, he did not enter this house with the intention of committing a crime. The deceased was afraid of this man and thus took your stiletto so as to keep him at his distance. Probably she threatened him with it, and there was a struggle during which she was murdered. Then the assassin searched the house."

"For what?" asked Mrs. Sellars, shaking her head sadly.

"For this strange jewel, described by Miss Carrol."

"It wasn't in Martha's possession when—"

"Quite so," interrupted the coroner, dryly; "but the assassin evidently believed that Mrs. Pentreddle possessed it. He struggled with her to see if it was concealed upon her, and when she drew forth the stiletto with which she had provided herself, it was used to kill her. Then the assassin, as I said before, searched the bedrooms. One thing I would ask you, Mrs. Sellars, before we close the evidence. Did anyone know that Mrs. Pentreddle would be alone on the night of her death?"

"She wasn't alone. Miss Carrol was with her."

"Yes, I know. But did anyone know that the house would be empty?"

"I can't say. Of course, Sammy's play was talked about a lot, and everyone said they were going. I even let the servants go, and—"

"Yes, yes! But do you think anyone outside the house knew that there would be a clear field?"

"I can't say," Mrs. Sellars shook her head. "I talked a lot to everyone, both outside and in, saying that we were going. But I don't know anyone who would have murdered poor Martha?"

The coroner's speech was not very long, as really there was little to say. Whether Mrs. Pentreddle had really expected someone, and had, therefore, sent away Miss Carrol so that the interview might be private, it was quite impossible to prove in any way. That the deceased anticipated danger was more or less clearly shown by her theft of the stiletto from her sister.

Undoubtedly the assassin—as the nature of the wound and the presence of blood-stains on the handle of the weapon suggested—had turned the dead woman's means of defence against herself. Finally, the idea that the criminal desired the jewel stolen from Patricia in the Park was equally impossible of proof. "In fact!" ended the coroner wearily, for his business had been exhausting, "beyond the undoubted truth that Mrs. Pentreddle is dead, we can prove nothing in any way."

This was also the opinion of the jurymen, which was very natural, considering the scanty nature of the evidence. Without any hesitation the ordinary verdict given in doubtful cases was brought in: "Wilful murder against some person, or persons, unknown," said the jury, and all present felt that nothing more and nothing less could be said under the sad circumstances.

"And I don't believe that they'll ever learn who slaughtered poor Martha," sighed Mrs. Sellars, over a cup of tea, when everyone save the boarders had departed. "We'll just bury her in Devonshire beside her husband, and try to be cheerful again. Whatever Harry will say when he learns I don't know, for he was desperately fond of his mother. I'm sorry for that murdering villain if Harry ever lays hands on him. But he never will, bless you, my dears." And most people believed that Mrs. Sellars spoke the truth. The whole affair was mysterious; and it was confidently asserted that the murder of Mrs. Pentreddle would be relegated to the list of undiscovered crimes.

The immediate result of the inquest was an offer made by a prominent music-hall manager to Patricia, as the heroine of the Crook Street crime. It was suggested that she should appear on the stage in a pretty frock, and relate her experiences in Hyde Park at a salary of two hundred pounds a week. The magnificence of this chance almost took away Mrs. Sellars' breath, and she was greatly disappointed when Patricia refused to make a show of herself. The girl phrased it in this way, and indignantly declined.

"Oh, my dear," cried Mrs. Sellars, almost weeping; "you need money so badly."

"I would sooner need it all my life than degrade myself in this way," retorted Miss Carrol, looking prettier than ever with her cheeks flushed and her eyes sparkling. "How dare the man insult me!"

"Insult, my dear? Two hundred pounds a week an insult?"

"Take it yourself, Mrs. Sellars," replied Patricia impatiently. "After all, poor Mrs. Pentreddle was your sister, and you will be just as great an object of interest to the crowd as I would be."

"I'm not young and pretty, my dear. It's those things that tell."

Patricia shrugged her shoulders. "Well, I refuse, and I have written to the man saying that I cannot accept his offer."

"You refuse good money; you refuse to get married. Whatever are you going to do for a livelihood?" Mrs. Sellars was in despair over this obstinacy.

Patricia shrugged her shoulders once more. "Oh, I daresay I shall manage to earn my living in some decent way. Perhaps Mr. Colpster may help me."

"What makes you think so?"

"He is coming to see me this evening."

"I know he is coming," said Mrs. Sellars; "but I thought it was to see the last of poor Martha's remains. He takes them to Beckleigh to-morrow by the afternoon train. I should have gone myself to attend the funeral, but it is impossible to leave the children." She looked at Patricia curiously. "I wonder if he wants to marry you, my dear."

"I hope not," said Miss Carrol hastily. "How your thoughts do run on marriage, Mrs. Sellars!"

"Well, you are too pretty to remain single, Miss Carrol," said the old actress frankly. "Sammy would marry you if you would only encourage him. And I can tell you, Sammy Amersham has a great future."

"Then I shan't hamper him with a wife. But what makes you think that Mr. Colpster wishes to marry me. Isn't there a Mrs. Colpster?"

"There was, but she died long, long ago. He has one daughter, called by the odd name of Mara. But she will not inherit the estates, as the Squire wants a man to manage them. He has two nephews, you know, my dear: Theodore, who is the eldest, and Basil, who is an officer in the Royal Navy. I don't know which of the two Squire Colpster favours as his heir, but whosoever gets the estates will have to change his name."

"He ought to give his daughter the estates," said Patricia decidedly.

"Well, I am not so sure of that, my dear. You see, from what Martha said, it seems that Mara Colpster is queer."

"How do you mean 'queer'?"

"She is—that is, they think her,—Really," Mrs. Sellars broke off with a puzzled look, "I hardly know what to say. She's queer, that's all about it, for Martha told me very little. I rather think the Squire wants her to marry either Basil or Theodore; then justice would be done all round. But here I am talking," cried Mrs. Sellars, rising slowly to her feet, "when there is so much to be done with getting poor Martha ready for her last journey. I have to see the undertaker and his men, my dear," and Mrs. Sellars waddled away in a great hurry.

Patricia wondered what Mr. Colpster wished to see her about, and wondered also what could be the matter with the girl so oddly termed Mara. This last piece of curiosity was not gratified for some days, but she learned the first two hours later when Squire Colpster interviewed her in Mrs. Sellars' private sitting-room. What he said to her took her breath away.

"I return to Beckleigh to-morrow with the corpse of my housekeeper," said the Squire in his dry way, "and it struck me that you might be willing to come with me to Devonshire."

"Come with you, Mr. Colpster?" gasped Patricia, thunderstruck.

"Yes," he said, simply and directly. "You see, Martha is dead, and I want someone both to look after the house and to be a companion to my daughter."

"To Mara?" queried Patricia, remembering what Mrs. Sellars had said.

"Ah! you know her name." The Squire looked up quickly.

"Mrs. Sellars told me."

Mr. Colpster nodded. "I expect poor Martha has been talking," he said in a vexed tone, "and, no doubt, has been making out Mara to be weak-minded."

"Mrs. Sellars said that Miss Colpster was queer," said Patricia truthfully.

"She is not queer," declared the father, with some sharpness. "Mara is a dreamy girl who wants a brisk companion to arouse her. From what I have seen of you, Miss Carrol, you are the very person to do Mara good. So if you like to come for one hundred a year, I shall be delighted to engage you."

"Oh!" Patricia coloured, but on this occasion with joy. Of all the offers that had been made to her, this one pleased her the best of all. "I accept with the greatest pleasure. But the salary is too large."

"Not at all. We live very quietly and you will find it somewhat dull. Also, I shall want you to look after the servants now that Martha has gone. Mara is incapable of doing so. Well?"

"I accept, as I said before, Mr. Colpster," said Patricia promptly.

"In that case"—he rose to take his leave—"I shall expect you to come with me to-morrow. I hope to leave Paddington Station at four fifteen."

"I shall be there," said Miss Carrol, with sparkling eyes. "I have little to pack and no friends save Mrs. Sellars to take leave of." And when Squire Colpster went away, she thanked God that she was now provided with a home. Out of the evil of Mrs. Pentreddle's death good had come.

CHAPTER VI

A FAMILY LEGEND

Patricia packed her few belongings that same evening, and next day took leave of Ma and the children. Mrs. Sellars wept copiously, for she was sorry to lose the charming girl who made the house so bright. Also, she could not help lamenting that of all the fortunes offered to her, Miss Carrol had chosen what seemed to the old actress to be the meanest. Patricia could have married money and good looks and position, for all these had been offered to her by various letters, since her portrait had appeared in the illustrated papers. She could have been engaged at several music-halls at a lordly salary, getting twice over in one week what she had elected to receive a year. But the girl, rejecting wealth and publicity, had chosen obscurity and comparative poverty. No wonder Mrs. Sellars mourned.

"But I wish you well, my dear," she said, when the cab was waiting at the door and Patricia was shaking hands and kissing all round. "I hope you will be very happy, though from what I remember of Beckleigh, it is one of the dullest places in the world."

"I like dullness," said Miss Carrol, who was weary of argument, "and I am very thankful to get such a situation at such a good salary. Good-bye, dear Ma, and keep up your spirits. When I come to town again I shall see you."

"And write, my dear, write," screamed Mrs. Sellars, as the cab rolled away.

Patricia nodded a promise and leaned back on the cushions with a sigh of relief, as the vehicle turned the corner of the curved *cul de sac*. Her last glimpse of The Home of Art showed her Ma surrounded by her children standing at the front door, waving farewells and blowing kisses. Miss Carrol sighed. They were all good and kind and simple. All the same, she was glad to have left that dreary house, which was connected in her mind with so woeful a tragedy. The excitement was now at an end, since the verdict of the jury had been given, and it was probable that in a few days the whole affair would be forgotten, for there seemed to be no chance that interest would be

41

re-awakened by the capture of the assassin. That evil creature had stolen into the house out of the mist to kill his victim, and had then departed again into the darkness. And now Patricia herself was departing from the scene of the crime, and it seemed to her as though this horrible chapter in her life was closed for ever. "Thank God for that!" said the girl, putting her thoughts into speech.

At Paddington Station she found Squire Colpster waiting for her. The body of his late housekeeper, he informed her, had already gone on to Devonshire by the early morning train. Patricia was glad of this, as if the corpse had been in the train she was to travel in, she would have felt as though she were taking a portion of the disagreeable past with her into what she hoped would prove a very bright future. She strove to banish all the unpleasant memories of the past week, and presented a very smiling face to Mr. Colpster when he placed her in a first-class compartment. With a look of approval he commented on her cheerfulness when the train started.

"I am glad to see that your late troubles will not have a lasting effect on you," he said, placing a pile of magazines and illustrated papers beside her. "You look better than when I saw you last."

"It is because I am leaving all this unpleasantness behind," replied Patricia, with a little shiver. "And I am so thankful that you have taken me away from The Home of Art. I could not have remained there; it would have always been haunted to my fancy by the ghost of poor Mrs. Pentreddle. Yet if you had not offered me a home, Mr. Colpster, I don't know where I should have gone. In self-defence I might have had to accept the offer of that horrid music-hall manager. Beggars can't be choosers."

"You will never be a beggar again," said the Squire, with a kindly look on his clean-shaven face. "What would Colonel Carrol say if I allowed his only child to want?"

Patricia bent forward with sudden vivacity. "Did you know my father?"

"Yes. I knew him many years ago, and for this reason, amongst others, did I ask you to be my daughter's companion."

"I wondered why you made such an offer, when you knew nothing about me," said Miss Carrol thoughtfully.

"Oh, I know a great deal about you from Mrs. Sellars, who is your great admirer," said Mr. Colpster easily. "And then you have the very look of your father at times. I am asking you to Beckleigh, not so much as a companion to my daughter, as that you may become one to myself. You must look upon me as a relative, my dear girl."

"How good you are!" cried Patricia, taking his lean hand and stroking it softly. The two had the compartment to themselves, so she was able to give vent to her feelings in this way. "How can I thank you?"

"By rousing Mara from her dreamy state," said he quickly. "I want to see her more practical and take more interest in life. As it is, she always seems to be in the clouds."

"Has she ever had a companion of her own age?"

"No. All her young life she had been with older people. Certainly my nephew Theodore has been with her a great deal; but, like myself, he is inclined to study and so is much alone. Basil, who is in the Navy, is nearly always absent with his ship. Beckleigh Hall is isolated too," added Mr. Colpster thoughtfully; "so I daresay Mara's sadness and dreamy ways are due to her surroundings. All the servants are more or less old, and we live a very, very quiet life."

Patricia nodded, and quite comprehended. "I don't wonder that Mara is sad," she said bluntly. "How old is she?"

"Eighteen!"

"And you have kept her more or less surrounded by elderly people all these years," cried Patricia reproachfully. "No wonder she is sad, as I said before. I am glad I am coming to cheer her up. Has she been to school?"

"No. She has always been delicate, and I did not think it wise that she should leave home. Until last year she had a governess."

"Also elderly?"

"Yes. Miss Tibbets was nearly fifty," replied Colpster, with a smile.

"Oh, poor Mara! But does not your nephew try to brighten her life?"

The Squire's face grew dark, and his heavy grey eyebrows drew down over his keen eyes. "She does not like Theodore," he said at length, and he seemed to weigh his words. "Yet he wishes to marry her."

"He loves her?"

"So far as a cold-hearted being such as Theodore is can love, I believe he does love Mara. But he is much taken up with literary work, and studies for hours all alone in his own room. Basil is quite different, being gay and light-hearted."

"Does Mara love Mr. Basil?"

"In a sisterly way she does. The two boys and Mara have been brought up together, although Theodore and Basil are much older. I don't think Mara is earthly enough to love anyone. She always seems to live in a land of dreams, and looks more like a shadow than a flesh-and-blood girl."

Patricia nodded absently. She felt a strong desire in her heart to see this strange girl with her fancies and unearthly nature. Surrounded almost constantly by elderly people and secluded in an old country-house hidden away in a lonely corner of Devonshire, it was scarcely to be wondered at that the girl with the weird name should be unlike those of her own age.

"And Mara means 'bitter,' doesn't it?" asked Miss Carrol, following her idle thoughts.

Mr. Colpster bowed his head. "Yes. Her mother died in child-birth when Mara was born, and so I gave her the name. As the sole child of my house in the direct line, she also deserves it, for we have fallen on evil days."

"What do you mean?" asked Patricia, wondering at the strange subdued excitement of the old man, for his face was red, his eyes sparkled, and his deep voice shook with emotion.

"What I mean will take some time to tell," he said, after a pause. "It is because I had to tell you something and to question you that I engaged this compartment. We are undisturbed here, and we have some hours to ourselves before we arrive at Hendle, which is the nearest station to Beckleigh." He fixed his fiery eyes on her startled face. "Are you prepared to believe a strange story, Miss Carrol?"

"Yes," replied Patricia boldly. "I have experienced such strange things myself lately that I am prepared to believe anything."

"Good. I shall tax your credulity to the uttermost. It is strange, as you will admit, that the daughter of my old friend should be brought into my life to help the Colpster family to regain what has been lost."

Patricia echoed his words in a puzzled manner: "What has been lost?"

"The emerald snatched from you in the Park is lost, is it not?"

The girl started forward in her seat, almost too amazed to speak. That the Squire should refer to the incident on the night of the murder was the very last thing she expected. "What do you mean?" she asked again.

He replied irrelevantly, as it seemed: "Let me tell you a story, Miss Carrol. I can trace my family back to Amyas Colpster, who lived in the reign of Henry the Seventh. Who his father was, or where he came from, there is nothing to show. He was what would be nowadays called an adventurer, and in that capacity he went to the New World."

"Was the New World discovered then?" asked Patricia, wondering what all this was to lead to.

"Yes. Columbus discovered America in Henry's reign, and, indeed, the King might have fitted out the expedition had not Ferdinand and Isabella done so earlier. But I do not refer so much to Columbus as to those who followed him. It was in the early part of Henry VIII.'s reign that Cortes conquered Mexico, and it was about 1532 that Pizarro took possession of Peru."

"But what has all this to do with the emerald stolen from me in—"

"You shall hear," interrupted Mr. Colpster, rather impatiently. "Amyas, my ancestor, went to Mexico, but had no success there. Afterwards he went to Peru and there accumulated a fortune, with which he returned to England. He bought Beckleigh and a great deal of land, and so built up our family. When in Peru he saved an Inca princess from death, and out of gratitude she gave him a large emerald." Patricia uttered an exclamation. "Yes, the same emerald that was stolen from you on the night of the murder. It formerly belonged to the Temple of the Sun at Cuzco, and passed, in the way I have related, into the possession of Amyas Colpster. Being a sacred stone, it was reported to have some strange influence, which brought luck to its possessor, and Amyas believed this, as while it remained in his possession and in the possession of the son who succeeded him, everything went well. The family increased in wealth and in favour with the reigning monarch. It remained for Bevis Colpster, towards the end of Elizabeth's reign, to throw away the luck which had been bestowed on his grandfather by the Inca princess."

"Do you mean that he gave away the emerald?"

"Yes. To gain a knighthood, he presented it to the Queen. From that time the fortunes of our family have decreased gradually, and now I have only about fifty acres of land, the old Hall, and one thousand a year well invested."

"That doesn't seem to be absolute pauperism," said Patricia, with a smile.

"It is poverty compared to what our family once possessed," said the old Squire petulantly. "Once we had wide lands and much money, and great influence in worldly affairs. All these things Bevis Colpster threw away for a knighthood which did him no good, for a title which did not even descend to his children. And our fortunes have dwindled since then, until we have only what I mention. But unless the emerald is recovered, what we now possess will also leave us, and our family will die out. Even as it is," he ended bitterly, "I have no son to succeed me."

Patricia wondered at what she took to be superstition in so clever a man, but saw that he could not be argued out of his fancies. She therefore pretended to accept his beliefs as true, and asked a question. "What became of the emerald?" she inquired eagerly, for the family legend interested her.

Colpster roused himself and his sunken eyes flashed keenly. "When Will Adams went to Japan, in 1597, as a pilot of Jacques Mahay's fleet, the Queen gave him the emerald to present to some potentate in the East."

"To the Emperor of Japan?"

"No. Because the fleet which sailed from Amsterdam did not intend to go to Japan. I was wrong in saying so. It was going to the Indies. Akbar was reigning then, and the emerald was for him. But Adams was wrecked on the coast of Japan, and when he became a favourite with the Shogun Ieyasu, he presented him with the great jewel. Ieyasu gave it to the Mikado Go Yojo, and he presented it—or one of his successors did—to the Shinto Temple of Kitzuki. There it remained for hundreds of years."

"But how did it come to be in the deal box? And what had Mrs. Pentreddle to do with it? And why was it snatched from me in—"

Mr. Colpster threw up his slender hand. "One question at a time, please," he said, with a faint smile. "I can't exactly say. You can form your own conclusions from what I tell you."

He paused, as though collecting his thoughts, and Patricia did not interrupt him again. She also was thinking and recalling that strange jewel which was set in the centre of the regular circle of stiff petals. Knowing that the chrysanthemum was the royal badge of Japan, she felt certain that the whole jewel was meant to represent the same. It was at this point of her meditations that Mr. Colpster began to speak again.

"As I told you," he continued, "I was anxious that we should recover the emerald, so that our family luck should return. I therefore read many books of travel, and spoke to many Japanese about the stone. In a strange way, which I shall tell you some day, I learned that the jewel was at the Temple of Kitzuki, in the province of Izumo. It was regarded as very sacred, and how to regain it again I could not tell."

He paused once more, and then went on quietly: "As you know, I have no son of my name to carry on the line. But my only sister, whose husband was already dead, died also and left me her two sons to look after. I brought them up with my daughter. Basil went into the Navy and Theodore remained at home to look after the estate."

"Then is Mr. Theodore your heir?" asked Patricia swiftly.

"At one time I intended him to be, as I desired to marry him to Mara. He could then, as I decided, take the name of Colpster, and when I was gone, carry on the family in the female line. But while the emerald was lost I thought that the luck would not return to the Colpsters. I therefore told what I have told you to my nephews, and said that the one who brought back the Mikado Jewel—as I called it—should be my heir."

"What did they say?"

"Theodore scoffed at the idea, and said that he did not want my money. He declined to go to Japan and run any risk of getting the jewel, either by stealing or purchase."

"But surely you did not wish him to steal it?"

"Oh, no," said Mr. Colpster, so hurriedly that Patricia felt sure he had once intended to get the jewel fraudulently, if not honestly; "but I thought that the emerald might be brought back. Will Adams had no right to give it to the Shogun, as it was intended by Queen Elizabeth to cement her friendship with Akbar. We—the family, I mean—would be quite justified in taking it by force. But that was not to be thought of. I therefore gave Basil a sum of money, which I obtained by mortgaging all my property, and told him, when his ship touched at Nagasaki, to try and buy it. I am expecting his ship, H.M.S. *Walrus*, back in a fortnight."

"But the emerald is in London."

"Exactly, and it was brought to be given to Martha Pentreddle. That is what puzzles me. What do you think, Miss Carrol?"

"I hardly know what to think," said the girl, in a puzzled voice; then added, after a few moments of thought: "Perhaps it isn't the Colpster emerald after all."

"Yes, it is," asserted the Squire positively. "When I read your description of the jewel I was certain that it was the same stone. It was made into a sacred jewel by the Shinto priests of the Temple. They surrounded it with the petals of a chrysanthemum flower carved out of green jade."

"Jade!" Patricia recollected the stiff petals. "Oh, is that the kind of stone?"

"Ah!" said Colpster eagerly and with an air of triumph. "You see, you remember the Mikado Jewel. Yes, the emerald in the centre is the same which Amyas Colpster got from the Inca princess and which Bevis parted with to Elizabeth for a knighthood."

"But can you be certain?" persisted Patricia, bewildered by the strangeness of what she took to be a coincidence. "The emerald and the jade chrysanthemum may be still at Kitzuki, in the province of Izumo."

The Squire shook his head sadly. "No. Basil wrote me some time ago, saying that he had gone to Kitzuki to make an offer to buy back the emerald, but he learned that it had been stolen."

"Stolen! Who could have stolen it?"

"That is what I wish to find out. But it has been stolen, and now it appears in London, and was placed in your hands only to be taken away again by—" He paused and looked at the girl.

"I don't know who gave it into my hands, or who snatched it," she said, in a regretful tone. "You know all that I know."

"Didn't Martha tell you anything?" he asked eagerly.

"Not a word. She said that when I came back with the deal box she would explain. You know what happened before I reached home."

Colpster nodded. "She was murdered. Who could have murdered her? Unless—"

"Unless what?" asked Patricia, quickly.

"Have you read Wilkie Collins' story of *The Moonstone?*"

"Yes, many years ago."

"Well, as you know, it is about a sacred diamond taken from the eye of an idol, and is recovered after various adventures by the priests of the god."

"But what has that to do with—?"

"One moment, Miss Carrol. This emerald also has become a sacred stone; it also has been stolen. What is more likely but that some Shinto priest murdered Martha and another priest should snatch it from your hands?"

"But why should the emerald come to Mrs. Pentreddle at all?"

"That is what I wish to know," said the Squire, feverishly and clenching his hands. "And that," he added, bending forward, "is what you and I must find out. We must learn who murdered Martha and recover our family luck."

"I don't see how it is to be done," sighed Patricia.

"It must be done; it has to be done," and Colpster smote his knee hard.

"I'll try," said the girl and extended her hand. The Squire shook it warmly.

CHAPTER VII

THE GARDEN OF SLEEP

After the turmoil of London and the excitements of that last uncomfortable week at The Home of Art, the peace and beauty and rural influences of Beckleigh were extremely pleasant. Patricia arrived with unsteady nerves and an unhappy feeling of unrest, but after seven days in this somnolent corner of Devonshire, she regained her usual placidity of character. Although she was Irish, the girl, by reason of her magnificent health, escaped, to a great extent, those up-in-the-air and down-in-the-sea moods which characterize the Celt. As Arthur had been taken to the island valley of Avilion, there to be healed of his grievous wound, so Patricia felt that she had been guided to this Garden of Sleep that her irritated nerves might be soothed. And at the end of a week, she was more convinced than ever that she had chanced upon a veritable paradise of rest, which well deserved the name. "It is the Garden of Sleep," thought Patricia dreamily, "and here I shall rest until—" she paused at this point, as her future could not be foretold in any way.

The girl found Beckleigh to be a little fairy bay on the south coast of Devonshire, shut out from the world by high moorlands, over which tourists rarely came. Where the rolling downs dipped to the sea, there was a secluded nook—a dimple on the face of natural beauty, and here a quaint, rambling old house of mellowed grey stone nestled close to a mighty cliff of red sandstone. It was a quarter of a mile from the mansion to the yellow sands of the tiny beach, and the fertile acres were covered with many trees. The wood was partly wild and partly artificial, and was threaded by dozens of paths, narrow and broad. These led unexpectedly to clearings, rainbow-hued with flowers, or to sylvan glades fit for the revels of Titania and her elves. Although it was close upon Christmas, yet myriad flowers were in bloom, and stately palms, growing here and there, gave a suggestion of tropical vegetation to the miniature forest. The climate of this particular beauty-spot was truly wonderful, with almost constant warmth and sunshine. And here again it resembled Avilion, lacking snow and hail and rain, and the voice of wild, destructive winds. The ruddy cliff gathered the heat of many suns and poured it forth when the skies were clouded, while the high moors screened this favoured paradise from the cutting north winds.

"It is truly lovely," said Patricia, as she strolled with Mara through these gardens of Alcinous, day after day, and found the same bland conditions prevailing. "I would not have believed that there was such a lovely spot in this cold, grey England."

"Oh, we have bad weather sometimes," said Mara, in her soft, low voice; "the skies grow cloudy and the sea grows very rough. It rains, too, heavily at times, but I don't think we have ever had snow or hail. The cliff keeps us warm."

The two girls turned on the edge of the lawn, where the woods began, and looked upward at the mighty cliff, which towered majestically above them like the Tower of Babel. To Mara, who had dwelt beneath it for so long, it looked like a kindly guardian giant, who gave shelter and warmth to the favoured acres at its base; but Patricia thought it looked frowning and menacing.

"It looks as though one day it would fall and crush the house," she said with a shiver, for the hostility of the great mass of rock seemed certain.

Mara smiled in her slow, sad way. "It has stood there without falling since the world began, I suppose," she said wisely, "so I don't see why it should fall, now you have come."

"I suppose not. Yet," Patricia shivered again, "it makes me feel uncomfortable. Do you remember in 'Childe Roland,' how the hills, like giants at hunting, lay watching the game at bay. It looks to me like that."

But Mara had not read Browning, and could not grasp the allusion. She gazed at the vast, lowering mass with affection, for to her it was like a domestic hearth where she could warm herself. After a time she turned, and stared seaward towards the glistening sapphire waters, which flashed in the pale winter sunshine. Through the woods a broad path was cut from the lawns surrounding the house to the smooth beach, where the wavelets broke in gentle play. To right and left of the bay were tall cliffs, similar to that which guarded the mansion, and these ended in bold headlands some distance out. On one side and the other, rising gently and greenly, the vast spaces of the moorlands swept grandly away to the heights above. And in their cup was the solitary mansion muffled in its warm woods. In spite of the lateness of the season, the air was moist and heated, as if the red cliff was clasping the home of the Colpsters to its gigantic breast.

"But how do you get food here?" asked Patricia suddenly, when she saw that Mara did not speak; "are there any villages about?"

"Two on the moorlands, and one on the way to Hendle, where the railway stops."

"Ah, yes," Patricia nodded. "I remember Hendle, and how I drove here with the Squire down that winding road. But it was so dark that I could see nothing on the way, and since I have been in this place I have not explored the neighbourhood."

"We can do so whenever you like," said Mara quietly; "but it will be best to wait until Basil comes home next week. He loves this place, and knows every inch of the surrounding country."

"Doesn't Mr. Dane know it also?"

"Theodore? Oh, yes, in a way. But he is like my father, and is never so happy as when he is reading and writing. He does not go out much, and we only see him at luncheon and dinner. It is nearly luncheon now."

Patricia caught the girl's slim hand. "Let us go in now," she said. "I am hungry, Mara, but I don't believe you are. A fairy like you, lives on:—

> "'apricocks and dewberries,
> With purple grapes, green figs, and mulberries.'"

"Who said that?" asked Mara, smiling in her dreamy fashion.

"Titania said it, and Shakespeare put the words into her mouth. Mara, I must educate you in English literature. You knew nothing of Browning when I quoted him lately, and now I see that you have not read Shakespeare's plays. This is dreadful."

Mara shrugged her thin shoulders. "I don't care for reading, Patricia. It is much nicer to walk about under the open sky. I don't wish to become like Theodore and father. They stay indoors everlastingly."

"Do they never go away for a change?"

"Rarely. Both Theodore and father have been in London lately. Theodore came back first, and then father came last week with you."

"Are you sorry he brought me?" asked Patricia, slipping her arm impulsively round the girl's waist.

"No," said Mara, in so unemotional a fashion that Patricia felt chilled. "I like you, as you don't worry me. Miss Tibbets always worried me with lessons."

"But you must be educated, Mara?"

"Why? I don't see the use of learning things."

Patricia looked at her curiously, for although she had been studying the girl for several days, Mara was still an enigma to her. Mr. Colpster's only daughter and only child was undersized and slim, graceful in figure and movements, and clever enough, in spite of her dreamy ways, to look after herself in a very thorough fashion. Patricia did not at all agree with Mrs. Sellars' use of the word "weak" as applied to Mara, for that young lady made shrewd remarks at times which showed a capable character. But there was something decidedly elfish about the girl, both in looks and ways. Mara's pale golden locks and pale blue eyes and pale complexion presented her to the onlooker as a somewhat shadowy creature. Her silent movements and low voice and frequent lack of conversation gave the same impression. Patricia could not get near the shy soul clothed in this fragile, tintless body. She seemed to be scarcely human, but to be compounded of moonlight and grey mist, containing in herself all that was melancholy in Nature. The warmth and tropical luxuriance of Beckleigh did not suit her personality. She should have been placed in some sad, antique temple, isolated on a lonely plain, and under sombre skies. The Irish girl was warm, human, life-loving and affectionate, so it was difficult to make friends with this Undine, so chill and distant in her ways and looks. Patricia began to think that, after all, the salary she had thought so large was not too much, seeing that she had to warm this statue into life. But how to set about the task she did not know.

"What do you like doing?" she asked, as they walked towards the house.

"Nothing."

"Don't you get bored?"

"Not at all; I——" Mara hesitated, then turned her pale blue eyes on the flushed and lovely face of her companion—"I dream," she said quietly.

"What do you dream about?" asked Patricia curiously.

Mara passed her pale hand across her pale forehead. "I can hardly tell you," she said in her low voice, which suggested softly breathing midnight winds; "there is something wanting."

"Something wanting?"

"To bring back that which I dream about."

"But what do you dream about?" persisted Miss Carrol, more puzzled than ever, as she looked at Mara's pale, pathetic face.

"The something will tell me when it brings it back."

"Brings what back?"

"That which I dream about?"

"And that is—-?"

"I don't know."

52

The conversation was turning in a circle, and Mara was repeating her answers, as was Patricia her questions. Some invisible barrier divided the two girls, and although Patricia wished, in order to earn her salary honestly, to break it down, Mara apparently did not. Neither in look nor gesture did she make any advance, so Miss Carrol could do nothing but sigh over the difficulty of the problem which she had to solve, and renew her walk towards the house. Mara followed in silence, not sullen at being questioned and not angry. She was simply indifferent.

The Colpster homestead was two-storey and rambling, confusedly composed of various styles of architecture. The oldest portion was Tudor, and had been built by Amyas, the founder of the family, when he had first set up his tent in this solitary spot. Later Colpsters had added and taken away, so that one wing was wanting, while the other was of Jacobean style. On one side also there stood a square Georgian block of many rooms, comfortable but ugly. The effect of this mass of different orders of architecture was to make the entire dwelling look picturesque, if not strictly beautiful. Time also had mellowed the whole to lovely restful hues, and Nature had clothed many eye-sores with trailing ivy and Virginian creeper. Indeed, so thickly were the walls covered with living vegetation, that it looked as though the loosely-built, untidy dwelling was fastened to the emerald sward of the lawns. Or, as Patricia thought, halting on the doorstep for a single moment, as though the building had sprang therefrom in a single night, like a mushroom. And the house dwelt in, and fondled, and loved for many generations had about it a warm, homely feeling of intimate humanity. But over it, as the girl again observed with a shiver, ever hung the angry, red-faced cliff, menacing and sinister.

The interior of the mansion was as jumbled, so to speak, as its outside, for various additions and alterations and removals had destroyed the original plan of the dwelling, if, indeed, it ever had possessed any such design. Some rooms had doors leading into others, passages twisted and turned in a most bewildering manner, and a few ended in blank walls. A stranger would find himself stepping down into one room and up into another, as the flooring of the whole house was irregular. There were narrow doors and broad doors: many of the windows were diamond-paned casements, while others presented a large surface of modern glass. Grates were here, and vast open fireplaces there, and many rooms were as dark as others were light.

The house both pleased and irritated, as everywhere the visitor came upon unexpected corners, or was brought up short before closed entrances. It was a nightmare house, and like none that Patricia, used to extreme modernity, had ever entered.

The furniture and furnishing of the many rooms was also fantastic, and here

Patricia saw more plainly the effects of Colpster's narrow income, as everything was old-fashioned and worn. The carpets and hangings, the paper covering the walls and the paintings adorning the ceiling, were shabby and faded. The drawing-room was filled with Chippendale tables, Sheraton chairs, fender-stools of the Albert period, and Empire sofas covered with worn brocade, while the dining-room had merely a horsehair mahogany suite, aggressively slippery. The whole house looked shabby and was shabby, yet the hand of Time had so co-ordinated the furniture and decorations of various epochs that the effect of the whole was beautiful. The sombre family portraits, the tarnished silver ornaments, the subdued hues of curtains and carpets, all gave the dwelling a refined air. There was nothing modern or garish or machine-made about the place. Everything looked mellow, suitable, old-world and slightly melancholy. It was a house to dream in, as it was filled with drowsy suggestions: a mansion of meditation, as the grounds without were the Gardens of Sleep. No wonder Mara was given to vague visions. A stronger person would have succumbed to the somniferous influence of the place.

The luncheon-table, laid with snow-white linen, glittering with diamond-cut glass, and heavy, old-fashioned silver, looked very attractive in the soft light of the large room, which stole in through quaint casements. Patricia, anxious to take up her household duties, had arranged the decorations of the table, and was rapidly getting into the swing of her domestic duties. She found the servants dull and out-of-date, but very obedient; and although, with the privilege of old retainers, they grumbled at many of her innovations, they did what she asked them to do. Mr. Colpster congratulated her on her successful *début* on this very occasion.

"You are a born housekeeper, Miss Carrol," he said, when he took his place at the head of the table, looking leaner and more like a student than ever.

"I used to look after my father's house before he died," said Patricia with a sigh, "and he was very particular."

"He was, even as a boy. I remember him at Sandhurst."

"Were you at Sandhurst?" remarked the girl, looking at her host, who did not in any way resemble a military man.

Colpster laughed in his silent fashion. "Oh, yes. I had thoughts of winning the V.C., and so tormented my father to make me a soldier. But I soon grew tired of the Army, as I had not the necessary money to keep it up. I therefore retired when my father died and have vegetated here ever since. I hope you don't find our life here too dull, Miss Carrol," and he looked anxiously towards the bright face of the girl.

"I like it," replied Patricia absently; "it is such a rest after the rush and worry of London. By the way, Mr. Colpster, I wish you would not call me Miss Carrol: it sounds so stiff."

"Patricia, then," said the Squire genially, and with a bright look in his usually sad eyes which showed that he was pleased; "it is a very charming name and suits"—he made an old-world bow—"a very charming young lady."

The girl laughed and coloured and bowed in return. Then, to turn the conversation, which was becoming too complimentary, she glanced at the vacant place opposite to that of Mara's. "Where is Mr. Dane?" she asked abruptly.

"Talk of angels and you hear their wings," said the Squire, for at that moment the door opened to admit the eldest nephew.

Theodore was tall and rather stout, with a heavy face by no means attractive. His skin was pale, and he possessed very bright blue eyes, and reddish hair, worn—as was his uncle's—rather long. His jaw was of the bull-dog order, and with this, and his bulky figure, to say nothing of the piercing look in his eyes, he appeared to be rather a formidable personage. But he was so good-natured and conversational that Patricia liked him, and thought—which was probably true—that his bark was much worse than his bite. He dressed much more carefully than did Mr. Colpster, and one noticeable point about him were his delicate white hands, which he was rather fond of using to emphasize his conversation. Patricia guessed that the man was proud of those hands, as one of his rare good points, and liked to draw attention to their perfection.

"I am sorry that I am late, Miss Carrol," said Theodore, sitting down with an alacrity surprising in so heavy a man. "I was taken up with a new manuscript which I acquired when I was in London."

"What is it about?" asked Patricia politely.

"Occult matters. You would not understand even if I explained." Theodore stopped; then looked into her face and added: "Yet you are Irish."

"What has that got to do with your remark, Mr. Dane?"

"Only this: that the Celt is usually more in touch with the Unseen than is the Saxon. I come of the latter race, and have no psychic powers; but I think you have, Miss Carrol."

"What do you mean exactly by psychic powers?"

"You can see things and feel things, which is more than many people can do by reason of their limitations. Ah!" he looked at her sharply, as he saw her face change. "You have felt something, or you have seen something."

"Well, yes," answered Patricia, and regretted the admission. At the moment, she was thinking of the Mikado Jewel and her sensations when holding it. Fearful of being ridiculed, she had not said anything even to Mr. Colpster about this, and did not wish to speak even to Theodore, although she guessed from his talk that he was less sceptical about such things than the ordinary man. "I may tell you about my experience some day," she added, quickly, seeing from his face that he was about to press his questions. "Not now."

Theodore nodded. "I shall keep you to your promise," he said alertly, "and we might try some experiments. Mara won't let me experiment with her."

"I don't like your experiments, Theodore," said Mara quietly, and looking up with a nervous look on her pale face, "they are dangerous."

"There is always danger, my dear girl, when one is exploring a new country, and the Realms of the Unseen are new to us. Your dreams—"

Mara flushed. "Never mind about my dreams," she said frowning, and with a sudden glance at Patricia.

"And never mind continuing this unwholesome conversation," said Mr. Colpster, who had been opening letters, "it is not good for Mara. By the way, Basil is coming home in three days. His ship is at Falmouth."

"Oh, I am so glad!" cried Mara delightedly. "I love Basil. He's a dear!"

"Let us hope that Miss Carrol will love him also," said Theodore grimly.

"I love everybody who is nice to me," said Patricia, laughing, although she wondered why Mr. Dane made such a remark.

"Oh, Basil will be nice! He's a universal lover," scoffed the man shrugging.

Patricia looked at him sharply and noticed the acrid tone. It seemed to her that Theodore was not fond of his brother. "I wonder why?" she asked herself, but naturally could obtain no reply to such an intimate question.

CHAPTER VIII

THEODORE

Life went so softly and gently at Beckleigh that it was like dwelling in an enchanted land, in a fabled heaven of drowsy ease. Patricia compared the place to the island of the Lotus-eaters, and after the storms of her early experiences, she enjoyed to the full its calm seclusion. Never was there so solitary a place. The Colpsters were a county family of respectable antiquity, and it was to be presumed that in the ordinary course of things they knew many people of their own rank. But either their friends and acquaintances lived too far away or were not invited to the house, for no stranger ever came near the place. Not even the inevitable tourist chanced upon this charmed spot. Beckleigh might have been situated in the moon, for all connection it had with the outside world.

The dwellers in this quiet haven did not seem to mind being left alone in this odd way. The servants, mostly old and staid, were contented with the house and grounds, and occasionally ventured on the quiet waters of the fairy bay in rowing-boats. Once a week the elderly butler drove to Hendle and to the adjacent villages, to bring back groceries and such things as were needful to support life. The postman came on a bicycle, once a day, with news from the outside world, and Patricia found that the library was well supplied with magazines and newspapers. There was no complaint to be made on that score, as the inhabitants of Beckleigh always knew what was going on both at home and abroad. They might be secluded, but they were not ignorant, and although not rolling stones, they gathered no moss. This warm, forgotten nook was an ideal home for a student.

And both Theodore and his uncle were students, as Patricia gradually learned. Mr. Colpster was writing a history of his family, and had been engaged for many years in doing so. From Amyas downward the Squire traced the history of his forebears, showing how they had risen to wealth and rank until the middle part of Elizabeth's reign, and how, from that period, by the selfish conduct of Bevis Colpster in parting with the emerald, his sons and grandsons had lost the greater part of their possessions. Also, he related various romantic stories dealing with the attempts of Georgian Colpsters to redeem the family fortunes. And, finally, when he reached the conclusion of the book, as he told Patricia, he intended to relate how the emerald had been recovered, and how again it had worked its spell of good fortune.

"But if you don't recover the emerald?" asked Miss Carrol very sensibly.

"I must recover it," said the Squire vehemently. "If I do not, the family will die out. When the Mikado Jewel is again in our possession, she can inherit the estates on condition that she marries Theodore or Basil."

"Are you speaking of Mara?" questioned Patricia, noting the vague way in which her companion talked.

"Of course; of course," he answered testily. "She must marry one of her cousins, and her husband can take the family name. Then the emerald will draw plenty of money to us, and we will again buy back our lost lands."

"How can the emerald draw back money?" asked Patricia, again thinking, as she very often did, of her sensations when holding the stone.

"I don't know; I can't say. I am only using a figure of speech, as it were, my dear girl. But in some way this emerald means good fortune to us, as was amply proved by the success of Amyas, his son and grandson. They owned all the land as far as Hendle; but when the emerald was lost the acres and their villages were lost also." Mr. Colpster rose and began to walk to and fro excitedly. "I must find that emerald; I must; I must!"

"How are you going to set about it?" asked the girl, doubtfully.

"I cannot say." He resumed his seat at his desk with a heavy sigh. "There is no clue to follow. If we could learn who murdered Martha we might discover the assassin and regain the jewel."

"But how can the assassin have it, Mr. Colpster? Assuming that he murdered poor Mrs. Pentreddle in order to steal the emerald, you know that it was not in her possession."

"No. That is quite true. While the assassin was searching the house, the emerald was being stolen from you in the Park. But undoubtedly the emerald was meant to be given to Martha since you went to receive it. How did she manage to get it? I want an answer to that question."

"Why not ask it of Harry Pentreddle?" suggested Patricia quietly.

Colpster raised his head and stared. "Why? What could Harry possibly know about the matter?"

"I am only putting two and two together," continued the girl, thoughtfully looking out of the window. "You told me that the emerald was taken to Japan, and also that Harry Pentreddle had returned from the Far East. He—"

"What?" Colpster rose excitedly to his feet. "You think that Harry brought it with him; that he stole it from the Temple of Kitzuki?"

"Why not?" demanded Patricia swiftly. "Japan is in the Far East, and Harry Pentreddle came from there. Also, his mother came up to London to meet him and receive the emerald. I feel sure of it."

"But Harry never came near the house," expostulated the Squire. "That was clearly proved at the inquest."

"Quite so. But do you remember what you told me about the emerald being a sacred stone, and how you mentioned Wilkie Collins' novel of 'The Moonstone'? Perhaps some priests were on Harry Pentreddle's track, and so he did not dare to go openly to his mother. He must have arranged the signal of the red light in the Park, so that he could give his mother the emerald secretly. She could not keep the appointment by reason of her sprained foot, and so sent me. I now believe, on these assumptions," declared Patricia firmly, "that it was Harry Pentreddle who gave me the deal box."

Colpster grew very excited. "It sounds a feasible theory," he muttered. "Of course, Martha knew all about my desire to get back the emerald. But why should she get her son to steal it? I can understand the secrecy of the meeting in the Park, as undoubtedly the priests of the Kitzuki Temple would make every effort to regain the stone. Harry had to give the emerald to his mother secretly, and probably for the same reason he is now in hiding at Amsterdam. It all fits in. But"—Mr. Colpster paused and looked straightly at the girl —"why did Martha want the emerald?"

"Perhaps to give it to you."

"In that case, she would have told me of her plans."

"I think not," said Patricia, after a pause. "She might fancy you would not approve of the jewel being stolen. However, it is all theory, and the only way in which you can get at the truth is by questioning Harry Pentreddle."

"The question is how to find him," murmured the Squire musingly. "If he thinks the priests are after him, he will remain in hiding."

"If he has seen the report of his mother's death and of the inquest," said Patricia coolly, "he will see that there is no longer any reason for him to dread the priests of Kitzuki."

"Why not?"

"Because I believe that Harry was followed by one on that night, and that the second man who stole the jewel from me was one of the priests."

"If that is so, why was Martha murdered?"

"I can't say. Of course, like the Moonstone guardians, there may have been three priests. One followed Harry and one went to The Home of Art."

"And the third?"

"The third may have directed the other two. It is all fancy, perhaps," said Patricia, hesitating; "but I think that my theory is correct."

"I am positive that it is," said the Squire, with decision. "Where a man argues to reach a point, a woman jumps in the dark intuitively. Gradually I might have arrived at the same conclusion you suggest by reasoning; but I feel certain that you have given me the truth by using that subconscious mind which is more active in woman than man. Yes, yes!" Mr. Colpster opened and shut his hands excitedly; "you have given me the clue. Harry was told by his mother to steal the emerald; she did not tell me, as she knew that I would not approve. Harry secured the emerald and was followed by those who guarded it. Being in danger of death, he made the secret appointment with his mother which you kept, and passed along the jewel. The Japanese who was following saw that what he wanted had changed hands, and leaving Harry, came after you. When you looked at the jewel he snatched it. Meanwhile, in some way, these priests knew that the jewel was to go to Martha, and so one must have gone to get it from her. She refused to say anything and was killed by the man, who afterwards searched the house for the emerald. It is all clear, perfectly clear."

"What will you do now?" asked Patricia, catching fire from his enthusiasm.

"Do?" almost shouted the old man, straightening his bent frame. "I shall try and find Harry Pentreddle and see if he will endorse your story."

"My theory," corrected the girl quickly.

"Well, theory, if you like. But Harry must be found. No doubt, thinking he was in danger of his life, he went abroad and is in hiding."

"How can you find him, then?"

"I shall ask Isa Lee. She lives at Hendle, and is the girl to whom he is engaged. He must have written to her, and—and—"

"And why not ask Mara," broke in a quiet voice.

Patricia looked up with a start, so unexpected was the observation. From behind a screen which was placed in front of the door came Theodore Dane. For so huge a man—and in Patricia's eyes he looked more gigantic than ever at the moment—he moved as quietly as a cat. Mr. Colpster seemed rather annoyed by this stealthy entrance.

"I wish you would make more noise," he said irritably.

"I thought you did not like noise, uncle," said Theodore calmly, and allowed himself to drop into a saddle-back chair.

"No more I do. All the same, I don't care about being surprised in this way. You should have knocked at the door, or have rattled the handle, or—"

"I did knock, I did rattle the handle," said Dane carelessly, and thrust one white hand through his leonine masses of reddish hair; "but you were so interested in your conversation with Miss Carrol that you did not hear me."

"And you listened?" continued the Squire irritably.

"I ask pardon for doing so. But the conversation was about the Mikado Jewel, which always fascinates me, and I could scarcely help overhearing a few words. But if the conversation is private—" He heaved up his big frame as if to go away.

"It's not private," snapped Colpster, sitting down at his desk; "only your unexpected appearance startled me. I would have reported the conversation to you later, as I know that you are as anxious as I am to recover the palladium of the family."

"I should certainly like to recover it personally," said Theodore with point, "as I know the succession to the estate depends upon its being given to you. If I get it, I inherit; if Basil is the lucky finder, he obtains all the property. You know what you arranged."

"Yes, and I hold to that arrangement. But as neither Basil nor you have secured the Mikado Jewel—"

"Neither one of us inherits?" finished Dane quietly.

"The one who marries Mara gets it," said Colpster decisively. "She is my only daughter and must benefit under my will. Marry her, Theodore, and be my heir. Mara is a nice girl; you can't object."

"Mara will. She likes Basil better than she does me."

"In that case, she must marry Basil, and he can become master here, when I pass over," said Mr. Colpster, with a shrug.

Theodore's white face flushed and his blue eyes glittered even more brightly than usual. Patricia, who was watchful of his every movement—for the latent strength of the man impressed her—guessed that he was furiously angry, but was reining in his passion with an iron hand. "If Basil inherits he will turn me out of doors," he said heavily.

"Oh, you can make your own arrangements with Basil," said the Squire. "You and he never get on well together, so—"

"Because I am the ugly duckling," burst out Theodore, his eyes flaming like sapphires. "Basil is the popular one; he has all the looks and all the—" He checked himself suddenly and smiled in a wry manner. "But these family arrangements cannot interest Miss Carrol. Let us leave marriages and any arrangement that may come after your death, uncle, alone for the moment. We have to find the emerald."

"In what way?" asked the Squire directly, and rather sourly. There did not seem to be much love lost between him and his burly nephew.

"We must find out where Harry Pentreddle is and question him. Isa Lee may know, but in order not to lose time, I suggest that we question Mara."

"No," said Colpster sharply. "Last time you put her in a trance she was ill for days. I won't have her constitution tampered with."

"Mara's spirit got beyond my control," said Theodore quickly, "and remained away longer than was wise. It would not obey!"

"The child might have died," growled the Squire, who did not seem surprised at this strange speech of his nephew's. "Leave her alone. Isa Lee will certainly be able to tell us where Harry is. Mara is useless."

"She was not useless when she told you where the emerald was to be found," said Theodore calmly, and lounging in his deep chair.

Mr. Colpster looked at Patricia, who was privately amazed at this extraordinary conversation, which dealt in a matter-of-fact way with super-physical things, and laughed at the expression on her face. "I promised to explain one day how I came to learn where the emerald was," he remarked.

Patricia nodded. "Yes, you did, Mr. Colpster. In the train."

"I remember. Well, then, Theodore here put Mara asleep, and told her to look for the jewel. She went unerringly to Japan and saw that it was in the Temple of Kitzuki in the province of Izumo. At the time I did not believe this, but it proved to be true, and the shrine which held it, as Basil wrote home to me, was precisely described by Mara when in her trance."

"But I don't believe in these things," burst out Patricia, staring aghast at what she regarded as gross superstition.

"And the Inquisition did not believe that the earth went round the sun," said Theodore coolly. "But although they forced Galileo to deny that truth, the earth continued to circle the sun and took the disbelieving Inquisitors along with it. Do not measure everything by your own brain, Miss Carrol, for there are more things in heaven and earth than are dreamed of in your—"

"Oh, I have heard that quotation so often," cried Patricia impetuously; "but nothing can be proved."

"Not to those who only possess physical brains. But those who have eyes can see and those who have ears can hear. To those people Christ appealed."

Patricia laid her delicate hands on her lap despairingly. "I don't know what you are talking about," she observed, with a shrug.

"Well, never mind," Theodore hastened to say, seeing that she was rather annoyed. "Some day you will understand. Just now all you need know is that Mara told us that the emerald was to be found in the Temple of Kitzuki in Japan. That proved to be true, although it was learned in what appears to you to be a nonsensical way. I believe," he fixed her gaze with his keen blue eyes strongly, "I believe that you are psychic yourself."

Mr. Colpster jumped up a trifle nervously. "I won't have it, Theodore. Leave Patricia alone. I am quite sure your experiments with Mara have done her a great deal of harm, and have made her more dreamy and unpractical than ever. I won't have Patricia caught in these evil nets."

"There is no evil in searching for the Unseen," protested Theodore warmly. "In that case—if it was regarded as evil, I mean—men would cease to inquire and there would be no inventions."

"If the searching you mention was regarded as evil," said the Squire grimly, "men would certainly search more willingly than if the powers were regarded as good. However, I put my foot down. I am not an unbeliever, as you know, but I don't think it is right to pry into what God wishes to be concealed. 'Thus far shalt thou go and no further!'"

"That was said of the ocean," retorted Theodore. "And yet we have reclaimed lands from the sea and prevented the waves from going as far as they used to. Everything is good if rightly used, and—"

"I won't hear; I won't hear;" Mr. Colpster walked abruptly to the window. "You are always arguing. Leave Patricia alone."

"What does Miss Carrol say herself?" asked Dane, turning to the girl.

"I agree with Mr. Colpster," she rejoined promptly. "I don't like such things, and think they are evil."

"Very good. We will talk no more of the matter," said Theodore quietly. "Only one thing I will ask you, since I believe you to be a sensitive. Have you not experienced strange sensations yourself?"

"In connection with the emerald I have," replied Patricia, who was anxious to have her curiosity in this respect gratified. And Dane certainly seemed a man who could do so.

On hearing her reply, Mr. Colpster turned away from the window and walked back to plant himself before her. "What do you mean?" he asked abruptly.

"I mean that while I held the emerald I felt the strangest sensations. It was because I felt these that I opened the box."

Theodore leaned forward with his hands on the arms of his chair. "I knew you were psychic," he said triumphantly. "All Irish people are, more or less, as they come along the Chaldean-Egyptian-Carthagenian line."

"What do you mean?" asked Patricia, completely puzzled.

"Oh, never mind; never mind," broke in the Squire impatiently. "Theodore can explain himself later. Meanwhile tell me what sensations you felt?"

Patricia stared straight before her, striving to recall what she had experienced on that terrible night. "Both when the jewel was in the box and in my hand," she said slowly, "I felt a sensation as though it held some great force which was ever pushing outward."

"Pushing outward!" muttered Theodore, pinching his nether lip. "How?"

"I can scarcely explain. Wave after wave of this invisible force seemed to radiate from the petals of the flower."

"What flower?" asked Colpster, greatly interested.

"The chrysanthemum blossom which was formed of the carved jade petals, with the emerald in its centre. The radiating force seemed to push back all darkness and all evil, so that I did not feel afraid. It seemed as though I were in the middle of a circle of light, and thus was safe from any harm."

Theodore muttered again and bent forward eagerly. "Was there any sign carved on the emerald?" he demanded breathlessly.

"What sign?" she asked, greatly puzzled.

"A triangle; a circle; a—a—oh, any sign?"

"I did not observe," replied Patricia simply. "The jewel was so lovely, and my sensations were so strange, that I kept staring at it in silence, feeling happy and safe. When it became cold and dark I then was afraid."

Theodore held up his hand to prevent his uncle from speaking. "When did the jewel become cold and dark, as you phrase it?" he asked sharply.

"Just before the man snatched it. The radiance seemed to die away, and the power appeared to falter. When I felt that I was holding a mere ornament, dull and dead and cold, the thief snatched it away from me."

Dane rose slowly, and nodded towards his uncle. "It certainly was a priest who stole the jewel," he observed. "Probably it is now on its way back to Japan. You will never get it, uncle, as now it will be guarded more carefully."

"Why do you think the thief is a priest?" questioned the Squire abruptly.

"Well, you thought so yourself," said Theodore lightly. "And it seems natural to suppose that the priests of Kitzuki would be more anxious than other people to get back their sacred talisman."

"Talisman!" echoed Patricia.

Theodore turned heavily towards her. "Yes," he said emphatically. "The emerald in some way has been impregnated with the radiating power you mention, for some purpose which I cannot say. Perhaps, as you suggest, to keep off evil and darkness. At all events, the man who stole it had some way of neutralizing the power, which he did when he saw you staring at the jewel. It might be that he could not take it from you until he had destroyed the barrier of light which you felt. But in any case, seeing that he was able to take away the force, he must have been a priest of the Temple, who knew all about the Mikado Jewel. You understand."

"No," faltered Patricia. "I don't understand at all."

"Neither do I," growled the Squire; "but I intend to recover the jewel some day and in some way. It is mine, and I shall regain it."

Theodore shook his head. "You will never regain it," he said firmly. "It is now on its way back to the shrine whence it was taken by Pentreddle."

CHAPTER IX

BASIL

The odd conversation with the Squire and Theodore Dane strangely affected Patricia, and in rather an unhealthy way. She was an ordinary commonsense Irish girl, whose father had been a matter-of-fact military man, and in her conventional life there had been no place for the supernatural. And when, with Colonel Carrol's death, came his daughter's subsequent poverty, Patricia had been far too much taken up with battling for existence to think of the

Unseen. To be over-inquisitive about the next world seemed to her sensible mind unnecessary, since there was so much to be done on earth. She knew very well that she was sensitive to things which other people did not perceive, but she put this down to having highly-strung nerves, and thought very little about the matter. Now, apparently, the time had come for her to consciously use organs hitherto unguessed at.

Patricia could scarcely help feeling that the atmosphere of Beckleigh Hall was unusual. The isolation, the dreamy nature of Mara, the uncanny conversation of Theodore, which his uncle appeared to accept as quite ordinary—all these things had an effect on her mind. She began to be vaguely afraid of the darkness, and her sleep was greatly disturbed by vivid dreams. In vain she assured herself that all this was owing to her imagination, and that she was losing her nerve in a most ridiculous manner, for the spell of the place was laid upon her, and she felt that she was being caught in those nets of the Unseen of which Mr. Colpster had spoken. To a healthy-minded girl, such as Miss Carrol undoubtedly was, the feeling was highly unpleasant, and she resented the influence which seemed bent upon controlling her, even against her will. Yet to this influence which she vaguely felt, but could not describe, she could not even put a name. The only thing she could tell herself was that some powerful Influence was setting itself to capture her mind and will and body and soul—all that there was of herself that she knew.

Later, she became aware that the Influence seemed to be centred in Theodore, for when in his presence she felt more than ever the desire to peer behind the veil. He had always been polite to her, since the night she arrived, but had looked upon her, she felt certain, as merely a pretty, commonplace girl, content with earthly things. And this was surely true, or had been, until the Influence came to draw her away from the concrete to the abstract. But since she had confessed to experiencing the weird sensation of the Jewel, Theodore had haunted her steps persistently. He talked to her during meals; he strolled with her in the gardens; he exerted himself to please her in every way, and finally asked her to visit his special set of rooms, which were at the back of the house. With a sense that some danger to the soul lurked within them, she at first refused, but finally, over-borne by his insistency, she consented to enter along with Mara. The girl was absentminded and indifferent; still she would form a convenient third, and would prevent Theodore from performing any of the experiments she hated. And, as a matter of fact, Mara mentioned that she objected to these.

"You need not be afraid, my dear cousin," said Dane dryly, as he led the way along the corridor. "I only wish to show Miss Carrol my books and have a chat with her about psychic matters."

"I don't think it's healthy," murmured Patricia, feeling distressed and uneasy. "I wish you would talk of something else."

"There is nothing else which interests me in the world," retorted Theodore, throwing open a door. "This is my study, Miss Carrol, and through that door is my bedroom, so you see I have this part of the house all to myself."

The room was large and broad, with a low ceiling, and a wide casement looking towards the east. The walls were plastered with some darkly-red material, smooth and glistening, and a frieze of vividly-coloured Egyptian hieroglyphics ran round them directly under the broad expanse of the ceiling, which was painted with zodiacal signs. The floor was of polished white wood, with a square of grimly red carpet in the centre. There was scarcely any furniture, so that the vast room looked almost empty. The casement was draped with purple hangings, and before it stood a large mahogany table, covered with papers and writing materials. There was also a sofa, two deep arm-chairs, besides the one placed before the table, and one wall half-way up was lined with books. A purple curtain also hung before the door which led into the bedroom. The apartment looked bare and somewhat bleak, and an atmosphere of incense pervaded it generally, so that when Patricia sat down in one of the arm-chairs, she involuntarily thought of a church. Yet there seemed to be something evil hanging about the place which was foreign to a place of worship.

Mara felt this even more than did her companion, for she walked to the casement and threw it wide open, so as to let in the salt breath of the sea. It was growing dusk, and the room was filled with shadows which added to its eerie appearance and accentuated the eerie feeling of Miss Carrol. Yet Theodore did not offer to light the lamp which stood on a tall brass pedestal near an alcove, masked with purple curtains, which was at the end of the room opposite the casement. Patricia noted that there was no fire-place.

"Don't you feel cold here at times?" she asked, more because she wished to break the silence than because she desired to know.

Theodore smiled. "I am never cold," he said smoothly; "cold and heat and pain and pleasure exist only in thought, and I can control my thoughts in every way. Why did you open the window, Mara?"

"I don't like your stuffy atmosphere," said the girl bluntly; then her nostrils dilated, and she sniffed the air like a wild animal. "Pah! What bad things you have in this room, Theodore!"

"What kind of things?" asked Patricia, looking round uneasily.

"Things that dwell in darkness and dare not face the light," chanted Mara in soft tones. "This room reeks with selfishness."

"So does the whole world," retorted her cousin with a sneer.

"Yes; but the effect is not so great as you make it."

"What do you mean?"

"You have transferred the selfish energies to a higher and more fluid plane."

"Mara!" Theodore came close to the girl and peered curiously into her pale face with vivid curiosity. "Who told you that?"

"It came to me."

"You don't know what you are talking about," he said roughly.

"Perhaps not," she replied dreamily; "but what I mean is plain to you. I can see your soul shivering with shame at being forced to obey the animal."

Theodore shrugged his great shoulders and looked at Patricia. "I sometimes think that Mara is mad," he remarked impolitely; "do you understand?"

"No," answered Patricia truthfully; "what does she mean?"

Mara slipped off the writing-table whereon she had perched herself, and pointed one lean finger at Theodore. "I mean that he is an utterly selfish man, who strives to sweep aside all who stand in his path. By egotism he isolates himself from the Great Whole, and wishes to dwell apart in self-conscious power." She faced Dane, and in the twilight looked like a wavering shadow. "There is nothing you would not do to obtain power, and for that reason your punishment will be greater than that of others."

"Why?" asked Theodore tartly, "seeing that all desire power?"

"You have more Light. You know, others do not." Mara paused as though she was listening. "It is a warning," she finished solemnly, "a last chance which is given to you, who are so strong in evil might."

"But, Mara—"

"I have said all that I am told to say, and now I say no more," said the pale girl enigmatically, and returned to seat herself on the table and gaze into the rapidly gathering night.

"What does it all mean?" asked Patricia, under her breath.

"Simply that Mara doesn't like me," said Dane coolly, but Miss Carrol noticed that he wiped the perspiration from his high forehead as he spoke; "her standard is too lofty for us ever to become husband and wife. I can see plainly that Basil will marry her and inherit the property." He looked round the room with a savage expression. "To lose all this is terrible!"

"But your brother will let you stay here," said Patricia consolingly.

"No, he won't. Basil doesn't care for my occult studies, and he doesn't care for me. You would never think we were brothers, so different he is to me. We are Cain and Abel, Esau and Jacob, Polynices and Eteocles, and have never been friends since birth. I hate him, and he hates me."

"Oh, no, no, Mr. Dane," said Patricia, quite distressed and shocked, "you must not talk in that way. It is wrong."

"It is human," retorted Theodore bitterly. "All his life Basil has been the petted darling. Uncle George always loved him and ignored me. Basil is good-looking; I am not. Basil is popular; I am not. Basil will marry Mara and inherit Beckleigh, while I am forced to wander homeless and friendless. And if—"

His cousin, who had been listening quietly, interrupted at this moment. "I shall not marry Basil," she said very decidedly. "We are good friends, but nothing more."

"If you don't marry him, Mara, you will lose the property."

"I don't care," she answered indifferently. "I can always live somewhere."

"If you would marry me," said Theodore eagerly, "you could go away and live where you liked. I only want to inherit Beckleigh."

"Oh!" cried Patricia, revolted by this selfish sentiment.

Theodore wheeled to face her. "It is a brutal thing for a man to say to a woman, is it not?" he asked derisively; "and if Mara loved me, I would not say what I have said. But she hates me, as you can see."

"I don't hate you!" put in Mara. "I am merely indifferent to you! Besides, as you said just now, you only want the property."

"Yes, I do," declared Dane boldly; "and I only put into words what other people think. I wish to have this house all to myself."

"Why this house particularly?" asked Patricia, after a pause.

"Because it is so secluded, and so safe for my purpose."

"What is your purpose?"

"I wish to continue my occult studies. I wish to get others to join me so that we may form a school. If I teach what I have learned to others, we can create a power which will be able to dominate the world. Here," he grew excited and seemed to swell with arrogance, "in this hidden spot, and by the exercise of certain powers, it is possible to sway the minds of men at a distance. The Wisdom of Solomon is no fable, Miss Carrol."

"And for that reason," said Mara, in her cold, unemotional voice, "you will not be permitted to acquire it."

"I know much," retorted Dane, still bulking hugely in the shadows, "and as time goes on I shall know more."

"The time is very short now," whispered Mara.

Patricia, peering through the soft twilight, saw the big man's face suddenly grow white. He moved, soft-footed as a cat, to the girl's side. "Mara," he breathed, and his voice was sick with terror, "do you see danger?"

"Great danger, and very near."

"What is it? Where is it? Look and see!" He raised his hands and made a pass before her face. Mara slipped from between him and the table like an eel.

"I won't submit to your experiments," she said angrily. "Father told you that you were not to worry me."

"But the danger?" faltered Theodore, who seemed to be quite unnerved.

"I can sense it, but I cannot see it," said Mara, wearily; "and all this talk makes me tired." She walked across to the other arm-chair and sank down into its depths gladly. "I am glad that Basil will soon be here."

"When do you expect him?" asked Patricia, anxious to turn the conversation, which had taken a mystical turn of which she did not approve.

"He may be here at any minute. Father said that he received a letter by the mid-day post. I like Basil; I love Basil, and I am glad he is coming."

"Let us ask Mr. Colpster when he will arrive," said Patricia, rising.

She moved two steps towards the door, but before she could reach it, Theodore had placed himself before her. "Don't go, Miss Carrol," he entreated, "just wait for a few minutes. Perhaps you don't like the darkness, so I shall light the lamp." He walked towards the tall brass pedestal.

"You need not be in a hurry, Patricia," said the voice of Mara out of the gloom, "it will be an hour before Basil appears."

Patricia sat down again, although her instinct told her to fly from this room and the evil influences with which it was impregnated. "I shall wait for a few minutes," she said, determined not to be cowardly; "but do let us talk of more healthy things, Mr. Dane."

The lamp was lighted by this time, and its radiance spread gradually through the room, as the wick was turned up. Patricia felt more comfortable in the flood of cheerful light, although the shadows still lurked in the corners. Silent and pale, in her deep chair sat Mara, but her cousin moved about the room actively and brightly: with an effort, however, as it seemed from the glimpse she caught of his eyes. These were filled with a vague terror, and he frequently moistened his dry lips. Nevertheless, he began to talk lightly and discursively about this, that, and the other thing, evidently anxious to keep his guests. He described the neighbourhood to Patricia, and the people who dwelt therein. He advised her to make excursions round about with Mara, and examine old rocking-stones and the remains of British villages and Phoenician towers. He extolled the healthiness of the place, and the beauty of its landscapes, and finally promised to take the two girls out in a sailing-boat. "Oh, we can give you much pleasure here, in spite of our isolation, Miss Carrol," he declared, with laboured gaiety, "and in spite of this danger which Mara says that I stand in. Who is going to hurt me, Mara?" he asked with assumed lightness, but real eagerness.

"No one," she replied quietly; "but"—she drew her hand across her face and said peevishly, "I wish you wouldn't ask me silly questions."

"You have told me such silly things," retorted Theodore snappishly. "You mustn't mind what Mara says, Miss Carrol: she does nothing but dream."

"We must rouse her out of such dreaming, Mr. Dane."

"Of course; of course! She ought to have a season in London; that would do her endless good. There is too much lotus-eating about this place. It suits me, but it would not suit all. That is why Basil entered the Navy: he loves to travel about the world, and only comes to see us once in a blue moon. By the way, Miss Carrol, you must not take what I said about him too seriously, for Basil is really a good fellow. We have different ideas of life, that is all; and fire and water won't mix you know."

In this way he rattled on, and then produced a chafing-dish of bronze on which a charcoal fire smouldered, with thin wisps of smoke curling up. "I find the atmosphere of this room too chilly, Miss Carrol. Would you mind my throwing some incense on this fire?"

"Not at all," said Patricia innocently; but Mara moved with uneasiness.

"Don't you try any experiments, Theodore. Remember what father said."

"My dear child," said the man impatiently, and planting the smoking dish of charcoal at Patricia's elbow, "when I make a promise I always keep it. This is no experiment. By the way, Miss Carrol," he added, while he went to a cupboard and brought back a metal box, "when your eyes are closed at night, do you see colours?"

"Oh, frequently."

"I thought so," muttered Dane, opening the box. "And pictures?"

"Sometimes."

"Have you ever wished to be in any picture you saw?"

"No—that is—I don't exactly follow you, Mr. Dane."

"No matter. I quite understand. If you did wish to find yourself in the picture," he went on with emphasis, "you would find yourself there. I knew you were psychic, and all you tell me makes me more certain than ever."

Patricia shuddered. "Don't talk about these uncanny things. I don't like them: they make me uncomfortable."

Theodore laughed in a constrained manner, and with a spoon threw some powder on the charcoal. At once a thick bluish smoke arose like a column, and a strong perfume spread through the chill atmosphere of the room. "A pleasant scent, is it not, Miss Carrol?" said Dane, restoring the box to its cupboard and fixing his eyes on the girl's face. "It is made after a recipe of Moses. 'Sweet spices, stacte, and onycha and galbanum; these sweet spices with pure frankincense: of each shall there be a like weight.' You will find those words in Exodus. Result of mingling such things a sacred incense, as this is. Smell it; breathe it; the perfume is beautiful."

It was assuredly a wonderful smell, but too overpoweringly sweet. Patricia drew in a deep breath through her nostrils, and the fragrance seemed to impregnate her whole being. She began to feel languid and singularly content, and unwilling to move. And all the time Dane's vividly blue eyes were fixed on her face. They seemed to be sapphire flames. But as she breathed the perfume and looked into his deep eyes, she heard a movement and removed her own eyes—with an effort, as it appeared to her now confused senses. She then saw that Mara was on her feet, moving towards the door. But not as an ordinary human being would walk. She rather appeared to be dancing in a rhythmic way, swaying from side to side, and waving her arms gracefully. With clasped hands she seemed to be shaking some invisible instrument. Theodore put out his hand to stay her, but she waved him aside and danced— if it could be called dancing—through the door. As she disappeared, Patricia tried vainly to rise.

"I must go to her! she is ill!" murmured Patricia, and then fell back in the chair again, enveloped—as it seemed to her—in a dense cloud of perfumed smoke. Her eyes closed, her breath seemed to leave her, and then she appeared to go away to a league-long goal.

Where she went, or how she went, she could not say. Her inward perceptions were only conscious of a vividly brilliant atmosphere through which she passed as swiftly as a swallow. And far away she heard a thin voice, like one speaking through a telephone, bidding her search for the danger. It was the voice of Theodore.

But as Patricia, in her dream or trance, or whatever was her state of being, passed swiftly on, soaring to some unknown end, she became aware that her flight was being stopped. She faltered, paused, then turned, and came swiftly back with the speed of light. Her senses returned to feel water being poured on her forehead, and to feel also the cool night air. She was out of doors, and in the arms of a man, who bathed her face.

"Don't move; don't move," said the man anxiously; "you have fainted."

"Who are you?" asked Patricia, gazing upward at the handsome face.

"I am Basil," said the man, "and my brother has been trying his devilries on you."

CHAPTER X

THE NEW-COMER

Patricia was not a particularly imaginative girl, considering that she was of Irish descent and blood. But there was something in the clean-shaven face of the young naval officer which appealed to her. The clasp of his arms thrilled her, and although, on recovering her senses, she extricated herself from them hurriedly, yet for days she seemed to feel them round her. Basil was so strong and kind-hearted and virile, that all Patricia's femininity went out to him, and he became her ideal of what a man should be. Tall and slim, well-made and wiry, young Dane was as handsome and clean-limbed a man as anyone could meet in a day's march. His hair was brown, his skin was tanned by sea and wind and sun, and his eyes were hazel in colour. He had a firm chin and a well-cut mouth, which Patricia could well imagine could be set firmly at times. And, indeed, when she opened her eyes to find herself in his arms, the mouth was stern enough. It was evident that Basil did not at all approve of his brother's experiments.

Theodore protested that he had intended no experiment. "I simply burnt the incense to dispel the chilly feeling in the atmosphere of the room," he declared, "and the scent was too much for Miss Carrol."

"If that was all," questioned Basil dryly, "why did Mara come out to say that you had put Miss Carrol into a trance?"

"Oh, Mara!" Theodore looked disdainful. "You know what crazy things Mara says when she wakes up to ordinary life."

"Don't talk like that, Theodore."

"Well, then, don't quarrel with me the moment you arrive home," retorted Theodore, and Patricia, drying her wet face with her handkerchief, saw the latent animosity between these two ill-matched brothers leap to life. To throw oil on the troubled waters of fraternal strife, she began to laugh—somewhat artificially, it is true, but still sufficiently naturally to show that she was now entirely herself and not hysterical. "It was silly of me to faint," she said in a matter-of-fact way. "Don't trouble about me, Mr. Dane"—she spoke to Basil. "I am all right. It was my fault, not Mr. Theodore's, that I lost my senses. He was trying no experiments."

"There, you see," said Theodore, with a triumphant glance at his brother.

"You shouldn't burn these strong perfumes," said Basil angrily, and walked away without looking at Patricia. He evidently was annoyed that the girl should champion Theodore's doings in this pronounced way.

"One moment, Miss Carrol," said Theodore, when Patricia was about to depart also, for it was close upon the dinner-hour and she had to dress. "You called my brother Mr. Dane. That is wrong. I am the eldest, and *my* name is Mr. Dane, whereas he is called simply Mr. Basil."

Patricia heard the venomous tone of his voice and saw the angry look he darted at Basil, as that young gentleman stepped into the house. Her first inclination was to make an angry retort, but when she considered swiftly how wrong it would be to increase the enmity between these brethren, she curbed her temper, and replied deliberately: "You must excuse my mistake. I shall not make it again. When did Mr. Basil arrive?"

"He rushed into the room just when you fainted. Mara told him and he took you up in his arms and carried you out here into the fresh air."

"I did not faint," said Patricia, looking at him searchingly. "And although I defended you to smooth things over, you really did try and experiment on me. Is that not so?"

"You are such a sensible girl that I can admit as much," said Theodore, with an ironical bow. "Yes, I did use the perfume to put you into a trance. I wished you to—to—" He hesitated.

"To look for the danger which Mara said threatened you," she finished.

"Yes. How do you know?"

"Because when I was miles and miles away, bathed in a flood of light, I heard your voice very clearly, telling me to search."

Theodore gazed at her eagerly. "So you can bring back consciously what you see on the other plane. Did you learn what this danger was?"

"No. Some force drew me back."

"Basil." Theodore clenched his hand and his face grew black. "If he had not interfered, you might have found out."

"I doubt it; and, moreover, if I had found out, I should not have told you."

"Why not?" he asked, astonished.

"Because I don't like these experiments."

"But you ought to. Many people's souls depart and see things and can explain them when in a trance. But few like yourself can bring back consciously what they see. Tell me what you—"

"I shall tell you nothing, because I have nothing to tell. But I ask you to explain one thing to me?"

"What is that?"

"Why did Mara dance towards the door. I saw her as I became insensible."

Dane looked worried. "I don't know. When she smells that perfume she always acts like that. It isn't a dance exactly, but it is certainly a measured movement. I don't understand Mara," he confessed candidly. "She has powers which are not under her own control. I could control them, but she will not allow me to."

"She is quite right," said Miss Carrol emphatically, "and never again will I allow you to put me in a trance. It is dangerous," and with a nod she also went into the house.

Theodore Dane, with a lowering face and a savage gleam in his blue eyes, stood where he was, with bowed head, considering what the coming of Basil had cost him. He was greatly attracted to Patricia, not by love for her beauty or sweet nature, but because she possessed certain psychic powers which he wished to control. She could, as he now knew, go and return consciously, and that capability showed an advanced state of spiritual evolution. With such a messenger to send into the Unseen, since he could not go himself and Mara refused to obey him, he could accomplish great things. Had he been left alone with the girl, for a certain period, he might have managed to sap her will power and render her his slave. But the coming of Basil changed all that. Basil was young and handsome and ardent, and with a sailor's keen sense of beauty, would be certain to admire, and perhaps love, Patricia. If this was so, Basil certainly would prevent any more experiments being made, and Theodore's evil heart was filled with black rage at the unexpected thwarting of his aims.

"Curse him!" he muttered, alluding to his brother. "He always crosses my path and puts me wrong." And as he spoke he raised his head to survey the goodly heritage which assuredly Basil would gain in the end. "I shall not be driven from here," raged Theodore furiously. "I shall marry the girl and gain the property by getting Basil out of the way. But how is it to be done with safety to myself? I must think."

This meant that Theodore intended to draw to him certain evil counsellors, who, being supernatural, could guide him in the selfish way which he wished to take. And these powers, being evil, would be only too glad to minister to his wicked passions, since by doing so they secured more control of him, and could use him for their own accursed ends, to sow discord on the earth-plane. But Theodore, not being possessed of psychic powers, could not come directly into contact with these beings so malignant and strong. He was obliged to find a medium, and since Mara would not act in that capacity, and since Patricia was lost to him, or would be, through the influence of Basil, the man's thoughts turned to old Brenda Lee, the grandmother of Isa, to whom Harry Pentreddle was engaged. She was accredited with being a witch, and possessed powers which Theodore knew only too well to be real. He had made use of her before, for there was an evil bond between them, and he now intended to make use of her again. Pending a near visit to her and a consultation of those creatures he intended to summon to his assistance, Theodore smoothed his face to smiles and went in to dinner.

It was a very pleasant meal on this especial evening. Squire Colpster appeared to grow young in the cheery atmosphere of Basil's strong and virile youth. The sailor of twenty-five was so gay and bright, and talked in so interesting a manner of what he had seen and where he had been, that even the dreamy Mara was aroused to unexpected vivacity. And Theodore, with rage in his heart and smiles on his face, behaved so amiably and in such a truly brotherly fashion, that Basil and he were quite hand in glove before the time came to retire to rest. The younger brother, straight, honest-natured and kind-hearted, did not credit Theodore with crooked ways, although he knew that his relative was not so straight as he might be. But Basil, calling him internally a crank, set down his deviation from the normal to his secluded life and uncanny studies.

"You ought to go about the world more, Theo," he said at dinner. "It would do you a lot of good."

"Perhaps I may travel some day," said Mr. Dane, in a would-be genial manner. "Just now I have so much interesting work in hand that I don't want to move."

"Some of your cloudy schemes?"

"They are not so very cloudy, although you may think them to be so," said the elder brother significantly, and there was a look in his blue eyes which made Patricia move uneasily. The girl's instinct, let alone what she had seen when she recovered from her trance, showed her clearly how deadly was the enmity between these brothers. But it is only just to say that the dividing feeling was rather on the part of Theodore than on the part of Basil. The latter only mistrusted his brother as a slippery and unscrupulous man, who was to be avoided, but he did not seek to do him any injury. On the other hand, Theodore hated Basil with cold, calculating malignancy, and was on the watch—as Patricia by her sixth sense perceived—to hurt him in every possible way. But nothing of this was apparent to the eyes of Mr. Colpster as he sat at the head of the table, smiling at his newly-returned nephew.

"Tell me," said Mr. Colpster, when Mara and Patricia had retired to the drawing-room, and the three men were smoking comfortably over their coffee, "tell me exactly what happened about the emerald?"

"I can tell you nothing more than what I set forth in my letter," replied Basil, his frank face clouding over. "I went from Nagasaki to Kitzuki, when I arrived in Japan, and offered to buy the emerald. The priests laughed at me for daring to make such an offer, and then told me that the emerald had been stolen."

"Whom by?"

"They could not say. And yet," added Basil reflectively, "I believe they knew something, although they declined to speak. Indeed, because of my offer for the jewel, they believed that I had something to do with the theft."

"What nonsense!" said Theodore lightly. "The very fact that you offered to buy the jewel openly, showed that you did not take it."

"The priests thought that I did that to throw them off the scent. I was waylaid one night and searched. It might have gone hard with me, as I had a nasty knock on the head. But Akira came along and saved me."

"Akira?"

"I should rather say Count Akira," explained the young sailor. "He is in the Japanese Diplomatic Service, so he told me, and is of high rank. His father was a famous daimio over thirty years ago, when Japan was mediæval, and Akira would be a daimio also, if things hadn't changed. As it is, he is high in favour with the Mikado and is very clever. He certainly saved my life, for my assailants would have killed me had he not come along. However, you will hear all about it from his own lips."

The Squire sat up alertly. "Is he coming down here?"

"With your permission, sir. I told him I should ask if you would allow him to come. If you agree, I can write to him; he is at the Japanese Embassy in London, and can come at once."

"Write to him by all means," said Mr. Colpster excitedly. "He may be able to tell me about the emerald."

"I don't think he knows anything about it, save that it was one of the treasures of the Kitzuki Temple, and had been given to the then high-priest centuries ago by Mikado Go Yojo. Akira is too modern to bother about such things. But as a loyal Japanese, he certainly mourned that the emerald should have been lost. I wonder if it will ever be found?"

"It has been found," said Theodore quickly, "and is now on its way to Japan."

Basil let the cigarette fall from his well-cut lips. "What do you say?"

"Oh, that is Theodore's idea, although I don't entirely agree with it," said the Squire impatiently. "It's a long story and has to do with the murder."

"Ah, poor Martha!" said Basil regretfully. "I am so sorry to hear of her terrible death. I was so very fond of her and she of me. I read a lot about the tragedy in the newspapers, but there is still much that I should like to hear. Particularly how Miss Carrol, who was one of the witnesses at the inquest, comes to be here as Mara's companion."

"I met her when I went up to the inquest," said Colpster quietly. "And as I had known her father, Colonel Carrol, at Sandhurst, I invited her to come to Beckleigh as housekeeper and Mara's companion. The poor girl had no money and no friends, so my offer was a godsend to her."

"I am glad you made it, sir," said Basil, heartily. "She is one of the very prettiest and most charming girls I have ever seen."

"Don't fall in love with her, Basil," said his brother, with a disagreeable laugh, "as uncle here wants you to marry Mara and inherit the property."

"Oh, I don't think Mara would marry me," said Basil lightly. "And, in any case, I disbelieve in the marriages of first cousins. Besides, it would be better for you, Theo, to get the property, as I am always away."

"The one who marries Mara, or who recovers the emerald, shall have the estate," said the Squire decidedly. "You both have known that for a long time. But we can talk of that later. Meantime, you ask about the emerald. Well, it was stolen from Patricia on the night Martha was murdered."

"The deuce! What has Miss Carrol to do with it?" Basil sat up quickly, and his hazel eyes brightened. Theodore observed with a thrill of annoyance that any reference to Patricia seemed to stir up his brother, and augured ill from the interest displayed by the sailor.

"Listen," said the Squire in slightly pompous tone, and related all that he knew from the time Patricia had left Mrs. Pentreddle in the drawing-room of The Home of Art, to the time she had returned without the jewel and found the old woman a corpse. Basil, ceasing to smoke, listened in breathless silence, and drew a long breath when the interesting story was ended.

"What a perfectly ripping girl!" he ejaculated, talking of Patricia the moment Mr. Colpster ceased; "so brave and cool-headed."

"Not very cool-headed, seeing she lost the emerald," said Theodore dryly.

Basil nodded absently. "It was a pity she took it out of the box. Of course, that talk of a drawing-power is nonsense."

"Perfect nonsense from your material point of view," said the elder brother with a sneer. "But in my opinion some priest who followed snatched the jewel —stole it, in fact, and now has taken it back to Japan."

Basil shook his head. "I never heard either at Kitzuki or Kamakura that anyone was suspected. And I don't approve of the word stolen. If, indeed, a priest of the Kitzuki Temple followed the thief and recovered the emerald in the way you state, he had a perfect right to do so."

"The emerald is ours," said the Squire, fuming.

"Pardon me, uncle, but you know that I have never agreed with you on that point," said Basil significantly. "Amyas Colpster gave the jewel to Queen Elizabeth for a knighthood, so our family has no right to get the emerald back again. Unless, indeed," added the sailor, with an afterthought, "the jewel is freely given; and I don't think, seeing that store is set by it at Kitzuki, that such a gift will be made. But who could have stolen the emerald?"

"Miss Carrol suspects Harry Pentreddle," said Theodore, lighting a cigar.

"Ah! it might be so. I heard that his ship was touching at Japan. Martha wrote to Hong Kong and told me. But why should he steal it?"

"And why should he wish to give it secretly to his mother?" questioned the Squire. "We wish to learn both those things, Basil, my boy."

"Ask Harry, then?"

"We don't know where he is. He went to Amsterdam, I fancy, when he was last heard of. He can't know that his mother has been murdered, or he would have certainly returned long ago."

"He's sure to turn up sooner or later," said Basil easily, and rising to his feet. "Poor Martha! she was a good friend to me. Where is she buried?"

"In the churchyard on the moors, beside her husband," said Colpster, also getting on his feet. "I am sorry myself, as Martha was such a good housekeeper. But Patricia is succeeding very well."

"And, moreover, is more agreeable to look at," sneered Theodore.

"What beastly things you say!" observed his brother sharply. "I haven't seen you for a year, Theodore, but your manners have not improved."

"I paid Miss Carrol a compliment."

"I think that she can dispense with your compliments," retorted the fiery sailor; "and, in any case, you spoke slightly of the dead. Martha was very dear to me, and should be to you also. When our mother died, Martha stood in her place. Remember that, if you please."

"Boys! boys! Don't quarrel the moment you meet," said the Squire.

"It's Basil's fault."

"It is the fault of your bitter tongue, Theo," said the younger Dane, trying to curb the anger with which his brother always inspired him. "However, I don't wish any ill-feeling. Let us go to the drawing-room and ask Miss Carrol to give us some music."

"Always Miss Carrol," murmured Theodore resentfully, and felt that he hated his brother more than ever. All the same, he threw down his half-smoked cigar and moved with the other two men towards the door.

The Squire placed his hands over the shoulders of his nephews and walked between them proudly. "There are only three of us to represent the family," he said affectionately, "since Mara, being a girl, doesn't count so much as a man. We must stick together and recover the emerald, so that our good fortune may return. And heaven only knows how badly I need good luck! There's that lawsuit over the Hendle water-rights, and a bad hay-season with the continuous rain—not here, but miles away—and—and—"

"If your luck depends upon the emerald," said Theodore crossly, "it will never return. It is on its way to Japan, I tell you."

"Well, we have one piece of good luck," cried Basil gaily. "Miss Carrol is in the house."

"Damn you!" thought the elder brother amiably. "I'd like to wring your neck, you self-satisfied beast."

CHAPTER XI

HARRY'S SWEETHEART

With the arrival of Basil Dane, life became much brighter and more lively at Beckleigh. The young sailor was active-minded and light-hearted, so that he was always glad to provide amusement for himself and others. He took Patricia and Mara out sailing in the fairy bay, and walked with them across the windy spaces of the moors to view various centres of interest. In the evenings, having a sweet tenor voice, he sang to them, while Miss Carrol played his accompaniments, and, of course, he had much to tell them about foreign parts. No one could possibly be dull while Basil was in the house, and even the Squire left his beloved history of the Colpster family to enjoy the breezy humours of his favourite nephew. The old house awoke, as it were, from sleep, to enjoy a brief holiday of innocent amusement.

But although Basil was attentive to Mara, since he greatly wished to arouse her from those dreams which set her apart from others, he gave Patricia most of his company. From the moment he had set eyes on her, he had been attracted by the beauty of her face. Now that he knew her better, and found that she had a heart of gold, he frankly fell in love with such perfections. And very wisely, for Patricia was a rare specimen of her sex. She was not, on her part, averse to his wooing, as, of all the men she had ever met, Basil appeared to be the most trustworthy and fascinating. It was the old story of love at first sight, that miracle at which material-minded people scoff, but which is a veritable truth in spite of such scepticism.

Theodore, needless to say, was not pleased to see the fulfilment of his prophecy. He had known, the moment Basil arrived, that something of this silly sort—so he phrased it—would happen. Knowing nothing of love himself, for his selfishness swallowed up all other qualities in his somewhat narrow nature, he had scanty patience with this folly. He wished to get Patricia entirely to himself, because of her rare psychic qualities, and to do so was even willing to marry her. Of course, by such an act, he would cut himself off from all chance of acquiring the property, since it was very evident that the Mikado Jewel would never be found. Theodore was certain that it had gone back to Japan, and there would be no chance of its being stolen a second time. This being the case, only by marrying his cousin could he secure Beckleigh and carry out his design of forming a school of Occultism. But this ambition—as has before been stated—he was willing to surrender, provided that he could dominate Patricia and her mediumistic powers. With those at his disposal, he felt that he could do much to forward his selfish desires. Moreover—and this was a factor also in his decision— Mara disliked him so intensely that she certainly would never marry him.

But none of Theodore's feelings appeared in his looks and manners. To reach his ends he had to play a comedy, and did so with the skill of a clever actor. His face was all smiles, his behaviour most deferential, and he carefully avoided any possible quarrel with his brother. Also, he did not speak of his occult studies, since a discussion of such things was not welcome to others. Theodore, in fact, appeared in quite a social *rôle*, and seconded his brother in promoting a brighter and more active state of things in the old mansion. He was clever at conjuring, and gave exhibitions in the drawing-room when the girls grew weary of music and conversation. And always he was polite and genial. So much did he impose upon Basil and Mara and the Squire that they believed Theodore had—as the saying is—turned over a new leaf. But Patricia did not credit as genuine this too suave demeanour. She knew, if no one else did, that the leopard could not change his spots, and what is more, that this particular leopard did not wish to.

Beckleigh was certainly the Vale of Avilion, for in spite of the bad weather prevailing in almost every other county in England, this favoured spot preserved, more or less, a serene calm. Of course, it rained at times, but not very long and not very hard. As the Squire had said, his hay-crops at Hendle were completely ruined by the wet, and he anticipated a great loss, which he could ill afford in his straitened circumstances. But the flower gardens round his family seat bloomed in almost constant sunshine. Also, when snows fell— it was now close upon Christmas, and the hard frosts were coming—they spread a mantle of white on the moors above, but did not descend upon Beckleigh. It is true that, owing to the season, many of the trees in the demesne were leafless, but a goodly number, being foreign, were evergreen, and still clothed themselves in leaves. Throughout the winter, when severe conditions prevailed on the high lands, the climate of this little nook by the sea maintained a mildness and warmth little short of miraculous. The place might have been situated on the Riviera.

Patricia thought that these extraordinary circumstances—for an English winter—were due to the great red cliff which sheltered the vale. During the day it drew in much heat into its breast, and breathed it forth at night when the airs grew chilly. It was like being warmed by a good-humoured volcano, she thought, for Patricia, after the manner of Browning, always humanized the forces of Nature. But undoubtedly she was right in her surmise, for the solar fire constantly drawn to the cliff and radiated from the cliff, created an artificial summer, which endured throughout the year. Beckleigh was like the Garden of Eden for climate and fruitfulness and beauty, and Theodore was the intruding snake. But as yet, even to herself, she did not dare to confess that she was a modern Eve to Basil's Adam. Or, if a passing thought of this nature did cross her mind, she blushed and did not dwell on it. If she had, she would never, in her maidenly confusion, have been able to meet the eye of her lover. Yes, it had come that far: he was her lover.

Of course, Theodore, always on the watch, saw that the pair were falling deeper in love daily, and savagely felt that he could do nothing to prevent a happy ending to the romance. The Squire might want Basil to marry his cousin, but Mara merely loved the young man in a sisterly fashion, and did not dream of any closer tie. Colpster was not the man to force his daughter's affections even for the sake of the family. So it was probable that, if Mara refused Basil, which she assuredly would do if he offered himself, and if Patricia accepted the young sailor, Mr. Colpster would settle the Beckleigh property on his daughter, and give up his fancy of re-establishing the family. Moreover, he was now strangely fond of Patricia, and would be glad to have her for his niece by marriage. Look what way he could and would, Theodore saw that his chances of gaining either Beckleigh or Miss Carrol were very small indeed.

It was then that he determined to seek out Brenda Lee and see what the future had in store for him. After Mara's warning, he had always been haunted by a sense of ever-nearing danger, although he could not tell from which quarter it would come. Granny Lee would know, however, as she was a clairvoyant and could look into the seeds of Time as did Macbeth's weird women. Of course, in this material age, most people contemptuously dismiss such things as hanky-panky, but that did not matter to Theodore. Sceptics might refuse to shape their course by such a vague chart, but he knew positively from experience that, under certain circumstances, the devil could speak truly. And if Granny Lee, with her malignant disposition and greedy venom, was not the devil, who was? Granny Lee, therefore, was the one to solve riddles, and to Granny Lee Theodore went a few days before Christmas. Yet, so as to impress upon his uncle that he was going on a harmless and friendly errand, the young man sought him out in the seclusion of his library.

"I am going to see Isa Lee, and ask if she has heard anything about Harry since his return to England," said Theodore abruptly.

"You are going to Hendle?"

"No. Isa, so I have been told, is stopping for Christmas with her grandmother in that miserable hut on the moors. I can go and return in three hours."

"I should like to come with you," said the Squire alertly. "I am most anxious to know the whereabouts of Harry Pentreddle. We must question him about the emerald. I wonder if he really knows anything?"

"I am perfectly certain that he does," rejoined Theodore, positively; "if he did not, he would not have stayed away from Isa. But I do not advise you to come with me, Uncle George, as there is deep snow on the moors, and you are not so young as you were. Besides, I can ask all necessary questions."

"Well, do so. If you can recover the emerald, you know what your reward will be," said the Squire, and turned again to decipher an old document, which dealt with the adventures of Amyas Colpster in Peru.

Theodore shrugged his big shoulders and departed with a grimace. Much as he would have liked to secure the emerald, if only to inherit Beckleigh, which was a kind of Naboth's vineyard in his greedy eyes, he felt quite sure that Harry Pentreddle could tell him little that would be helpful. Harry undoubtedly had stolen the Jewel, and had given it to Patricia as his mother's emissary; but having departed for Amsterdam almost immediately, he would know nothing of its unexpected loss. Apparently he did not even know that his mother had been so barbarously murdered. If he did know, he assuredly would have returned to avenge her, in spite of any danger there might be to him from the guardians of the great gem. And that danger was now, as Theodore fully believed, a thing of the past. The emerald had been recovered, so it was only natural to suppose that the priests of the Kitzuki Temple would leave well alone. With these thoughts in his scheming mind, Theodore, well wrapped up in furs, mounted the winding road which led to the moors.

The vast grassy spaces were covered more or less deeply with snow, but Dane, accustomed to the country since his boyhood, and possessing great strength, made light of the drifts. Far away on the dazzling expanse, brilliantly and blindingly bright in the sunshine, he saw the many dark dots, which marked the village, near the cromlech, where Mrs. Lee had her home. A glance backward over the cliff showed him the verdant acres of Beckleigh, and a flash of colour where late flowers still bloomed. There was no snow below, but only emerald swards and green woods running to the verge of the sapphire bay, where the wavelets lipped the curved streak of the yellow sands. The contrast between the summer he was leaving and the winter he was going into struck Theodore forcibly.

"I wish I could get it all to myself," he groaned. "Basil is out of it if he marries Patricia Carrol, and Mara hasn't the sense to look after it. I may secure it, after all. But Patricia," he scowled; "I don't want her to become Basil's wife!" a speech which showed that Theodore both wished to have his cake and eat it, since he wanted both the girl and the property.

However, it was useless to moralize over possibilities, so Dane resolutely struck across the moors, and ploughed manfully through the drifts. After a mile or so, he came to the high road up which tourists came to view the rocking stone and the cromlech. This was comparatively clear, and he had no further difficulty in gaining his goal. Swiftly walking—and in spite of his great bulk Theodore could walk swiftly when he chose—he soon arrived at the handful of houses, sheltered immediately under the brow of the gently swelling hill, or boss, which marked the highest point of the moors. It was a most unlikely place for a village, as there seemed to be no chance of its inhabitants gaining food. But they acted as guides to tourists, drove them in vehicles from and to Hendle, shepherded droves of Exmoor ponies, and flocks of hardy sheep, and, if rumour was true, employed much of their spare time in poaching. The village—Boatwain was its name—had not a good reputation in general, and amongst its inhabitants Granny Lee, in particular, had the worst name.

Theodore soon found the tumbledown house in which she lived, and at the door came upon Isa Lee, just stepping—so she said—to post a letter. Dane saw his opportunity and took it immediately.

"You are writing to Harry," he observed, looking at the tall, robust, deep-bosomed woman, who always reminded him of Wagnerian heroines, with her fair, flaxen hair and Brunehild aspect.

Isa evidently saw no reason to deny the truth. "Yes, sir," she replied, in a deep contralto voice which boomed like a bell.

"Is Harry still abroad?"

"Yes, sir. He is stopping at Amsterdam, hoping to get a ship."

"Does he know of his mother's death?"

"Yes," answered Isa. "I told him, and sent him the papers."

"What does he say?"

"He intends to return here and pray by her grave."

Theodore shrugged his shoulders cynically. "He had much better avenge her death," was his remark.

"He wants to," said Isa stolidly; "but he says that he can't guess who killed her, and does not know how to begin. He is very sorrowful over the death, Mr. Dane, as he loved his mother."

"He doesn't seem to be so very sorry," snapped Theodore sharply, "or he would return and learn who murdered her."

"I am writing to him to advise him to do so," said the woman quickly. "Oh, don't think that Harry is hard, sir! He is—he is—afraid!"

"Of what?"

"I don't know: he refuses to tell me, sir."

Dane knew very well when she said this that Patricia's suggestion was a true one. Pentreddle had evidently stolen the jewel and now feared lest he should be assassinated. But with the recovery of the jewel by one of the priests—and he believed that there was more than one on the hunt—all danger had passed. "Isa," he said, impressively, "go back and add a postscript to your letter, telling Harry that there is now no danger, and that the Squire, my uncle, wishes to see him."

"What about, sir?" asked Isa suddenly, and with an anxious look.

"He wants to talk to him about Mrs. Pentreddle's death. She was our housekeeper, you know."

"Yes, sir, and a grand funeral the Squire gave her," said the woman, with a flush, for, like all the lower orders, she attached great weight to postmortem ceremonies. "He *has* been kind."

"Well, he wants to be kinder," said Theodore, not hesitating to tell a lie in order to gain his ends. "He has some idea of who killed Martha, and wishes to talk about it to Harry, who should avenge his mother's death. Will you go back and add that to your letter?"

"Yes, sir; oh, yes, sir!" said the girl eagerly; "and very glad Harry will be to hear it, as he has been fretting dreadfully over his mother's death. But he did not return because of this danger, whatever it is. Do you know, sir?"

"I can guess," answered Theodore significantly, "so you can tell Harry that he can come quite safely to England. Now go and write your letter, and say that he is to come back at once. The Squire wishes to see him at Beckleigh, as he has news for him. Meanwhile, I shall speak with your grandmother."

Isa nodded, and stepped aside to allow her grand visitor to enter the house, although it was scarcely worthy of the name. It was rather a hovel, and possessed only three rooms—a large one, used for all living purposes, and two tiny bedrooms. The old hag—she was nothing else—sat beside a small fire, smoking a short-stemmed clay pipe, and only vouchsafed Dane a grunt when he greeted her. She was about eighty-six years of age, but looked even older with her wrinkled, copper-coloured face and scanty white hair streaming from under a thrum cap. Her eyes were small, black and piercing, and full of vivid life. For the rest, she was hunched up in a basket-chair, stroking a large black cat, and looked a typical witch of James's time. Perhaps she dressed for the part and lived up to it, black cat and all, for she made much money in summer by telling fortunes to tourists. But undoubtedly her appearance was so old and wicked, that she would have tasted of the tar-barrel in Stuart days, almost without the formality of a trial. Granny Lee was a witch in grain, if ever there was a witch.

"Good-day," said Theodore, sitting down on a chair with no back, while Isa went into an adjoining bedroom to add the postscript to her letter. "How do you find yourself this weather, Granny?"

"Mrs. Lee, if you please," snarled the old woman, glaring at him in a malignant way and removing the pipe from her almost toothless gums.

"Mrs. Lee then be it; Mrs. Brenda Lee, if you like," said Dane, who had his reasons for keeping her in a good temper. "How are you?"

"How should I be in this damned weather? I'm all aches and pains and they dratted rheumatics."

"You shouldn't attend so many Sabbaths," chuckled Theodore, loosening his fur coat. "Riding a broom-stick with no clothes on is dangerous at your age."

"Leave my age alone, drat ye!" growled the amiable old lady, beginning to cut a fresh fill of tobacco with a clasp-knife. "As to Sabbaths, I don't believe in 'em, or I'd ha' gone long ago. There ain't any now, and I don't believe as there ever was. I don't go to Them, but They come to me."

Theodore cast a bold look round the miserable room. "Are They here now?"

Granny Lee chuckled in her turn. "Mine don't need to show when you're here, Mr. Dane. You've brought your lot along with you, and the biggest of them is looking over your shoulder at this blessed moment."

The big man turned his head, but, of course, not being gifted with mediumistic powers, could see nothing. "I wish I could have a look at him," he said regretfully. "What is he?"

"Just your thought grown big."

Theodore nodded quite comprehendingly. "Of course, thoughts create beings on the astral plane out of the essence. What special thoughts—?"

"There's lots of 'em, and none of 'em pleasant," interrupted Mrs. Lee, pointing with her pipe-stem. "Yon's Greed of what belongs to other folk, an' he's not a small one. Then there's Selfishness,—quite a giant—and Hatred, and Lust, and Ambition, and Murder—"

"Why murder? I haven't murdered any one," said Dane quickly and coolly.

"It's in your mind. That brother of yours—"

Theodore ground his teeth. "I'd like to strangle him," he growled, "only I might be caught. Yes, I daresay the murder thought is there."

Knowing what he did about occult matters, he had not the least doubt but what Mrs. Lee saw his thoughts made visible, since she possessed the astral vision—what the Celt calls "second sight" and could behold the Unseen. Ordinary matter-of-fact people would laugh at Mrs. Lee's pretensions, but Dane knew that they were only too truthful, and that she actually saw the hideous offspring of his brain with which his evil passions had surrounded him. However, he put the delight of conversing generally with this mistress of Black Magic aside for the moment, since at any moment Isa might finish writing her postscript and come out. It was time to get to business, and he did so without delay.

"I feel there is some danger near me," he said abruptly, "and I want you to see what it is."

Granny laid aside her pipe and stretched forth a skinny hand. "Give me the ring you are wearing. I must get your condition to see," she said.

Dane pulled off his signet ring and passed it along, as he knew that otherwise she could not come into contact with his magnetism. Mrs. Lee put it to her wrinkled forehead and closed her beady eyes. After a few moments she began to speak slowly, listening at times as if some of the viewless Things around her were speaking.

"It's danger from above," she muttered.

"What danger?"

"I can't tell. That shell of yours which holds your wicked soul is stretched out as flat as a pancake."

"How does that happen?"

"I can't tell, drat ye! But it won't happen if you don't let It come into the house."

"What is It?"

Granny listened for a moment. "A voice says that you're not to know."

"But how can I guard myself, if I'm not to know," protested Theodore in a vexed tone. "What is the use of warning me, unless the remedy's suggested?"

Granny shook her weird old head. "There's innocence against you, and Them as works for you can't get over."

"Get over what?"

"The barrier of innocence. Don't ask me more questions for the mist is hiding all." She handed back his ring. "What I get plainly is: Don't let It come into the house."

"But hang it!" raged Theodore, "what is It?"

"I can't tell, drat ye!" said Granny again, and resumed her pipe.

Theodore gave her a shilling and left the hut more doubtful than ever. His Oracle, as an Oracle should be, was too mystical for every-day comprehension.

CHAPTER XII

A JAPANESE DIPLOMATIST

If Count Akira was indeed anxious to visit Beckleigh, he certainly did not betray much alacrity in accepting the Squire's cordial invitation. He did write to the effect that he would be delighted to come, but postponed his arrival until the second week in January. Official business, he stated, would keep him employed during the next few weeks, and he would be unable to leave his chief. Consequently there was only a family party present at the Christmas festivities. Mr. Colpster, being of a conservative nature, always kept these up in an old-fashioned, hospitable style. Indeed, he invited several friends to join on this occasion, as his nephew was at home, but the friends, having their own families and own festivities, declined to put in an appearance. The Squire was not sorry, as he disliked the trouble of entertaining visitors.

As it was, he gave the servants a dinner, and bestowed coals and blankets and hampers of wholesome food on the inhabitants of Hendle, Boatwain, and the other hamlets, all of which had at one time belonged to dead and gone Colpsters. For this reason did the Squire act so generously, and he hoped when the emerald was recovered—for he refused to believe that it had gone back to its shrine in Japan—that the future good fortune which would come with it would enable him to buy back the lost lands. Meanwhile, by acting as the lord of a lost manor, he retained the feudal allegiance of the villagers. There was something pathetic in the way in which the old man persistently looked forward to the rehabilitation of his family. He made sure that the Mikado Jewel would come back; he felt certain that the land would be recovered, and was convinced that when he passed away, the husband of Mara would start a new dynasty of Colpsters, through the female branch, whose glories would outshine the ancient line. But who Mara was to marry did not seem quite clear.

He spoke to the girl on the subject and suggested that she should become the wife of Theodore or Basil. Mara shuddered when he mentioned the first name, and her father noted the repugnance the shudder revealed.

"I don't approve much of Theodore myself," he said apologetically, "as he is extremely selfish. But he has no bad qualities which would lead him to waste money, and, moreover, he loves this place. You might do worse, dear."

"If Theodore was the only man on earth and offered me a kingdom, I would not marry him," said Mara, speaking decisively and in a firm way, which contrasted strongly with her usual indifference, "He is a bad man."

"My dear child, he has no vices. He neither drinks, nor gambles, nor—"

"If he had all the vices of which a human being is capable," interrupted Mara loudly, "I would not mind. But his bad qualities are inhuman. He is selfish and dangerous, and all his time is given to Black Magic."

The Squire laughed incredulously. "I know that Theodore dabbles in such things," he said disbelievingly; "but it is all imagination, Mara. There is no such a thing as any power to be obtained in that way."

"Yes there is. I know," said Mara, looking at her father significantly.

"Can you prove what you say, my dear?"

"No. And I don't want to talk any more about the matter. I won't marry my cousin Theodore, even if you leave the property away from me."

"I don't want to do that. You are my heiress, and my idea was for you to marry your cousin. Then he could take your name, and—"

"I shan't marry Theodore," cried Mara for the third time, and stamped.

"Basil, then. You can have no fault to find with Basil."

"I haven't, father, but"—Mara stopped, and a strange smile spread over her small, pale face—"I shall ask Basil to marry me, if you like," she said in an abrupt way. "He can but say no."

"He won't say no, my dear. Basil loves me too well to thwart my wishes. But it is his part to woo and yours to listen. Let him ask."

"I should have to wait a long time before he did that," said Mara dryly. "I wish to know the best or worst at once," and she left the room, still smiling strangely. Mr. Colpster could not understand why she smiled. But, then, neither he nor anyone else understood the girl, who seemed to hang between two worlds, the Seen and the Unseen, without making use of either, so indifferent was her attitude towards all things.

As it happened, Patricia was busy attending to the servants, as it was her housekeeping hour. Mara was thus enabled to find Basil alone, for when Miss Carrol was available he constantly followed at her heels like a faithful and adoring dog. But Patricia would not appear for some time, so the sailor read the daily paper in the smoking-room and solaced himself for the absence of the eternal feminine with his pipe. Mara knew where to find him, and entered in her light, noiseless way, to perch on the arm of his chair like a golden butterfly. Without any preamble she plunged into the reason for her intrusion into bachelor quarters.

"Basil, will you marry me?" she asked, coldly and calmly and unexpectedly.

Looking on his cousin as a child, the young man thought that she was joking, and laughed when he answered: "Of course. Will we start now for the church on the moors where all the Colpsters have been married?"

"I am in earnest, Basil," she said seriously.

"So am I," he rejoined lightly, "only it will be the marriage of Bottom and Titania with you, my airy elf," and he slipped his arm round her waist, looking at her with a smile on his handsome face.

Mara, who disliked being touched, even by Patricia, much more by this confident male thing—as she called Basil in her mind—slipped off the arm of the chair and floated like thistledown into the centre of the room.

"Don't be silly, Basil. I have just come from my father. He wants me to marry you or Theodore. I hate Theodore, and would sooner die than become his wife, but I told father that I would ask you to become my husband."

Basil saw that she really meant what she said, and, moreover, knew of his uncle's strong desire to unite the two branches of the dwindling Colpster family. Laying aside his pipe, he grew red to the roots of his closely-cropped hair. "I—I—don't want to," he stuttered ungallantly, and feeling very much confused. "I—I hope you don't mind."

A wintry smile gleamed on the girl's white face. "I should have minded a great deal had you really wished to marry me."

"Then why ask me?" demanded Basil, much relieved, but still confused.

"To set my father's mind at rest," replied Mara quietly, and as self-possessed as her cousin was disturbed. "Now that you have declined, I can tell him!" and she flitted towards the door.

"But, Mara!" Basil rose and ran across the room to catch her arm. "How can you be certain that I mean what I say?"

She turned on him with an amazed look. "You think that I am a child, Basil, but I am not. I have eyes and ears and common-sense. You will marry Patricia, will you not?"

Young Dane grew redder than ever. "I—I—have said nothing to her," he stammered nervously. "She—she doesn't know that I—that I—"

Mara's scornful laughter stopped his further speech, and she became quite friendly for so bloodless a person. "You silly boy!" she cried, ruffling what hair the barber had left him. "Patricia knows."

"But how can she?"

"Because she is a woman," said Mara impatiently. "Women are not like men, and don't require everything to be put into words. I saw from the moment you met Patricia that you loved her. I'm glad; I'm glad," she ended, with conviction, "as I don't want to marry you or anyone else."

Basil, with lover-like selfishness, did not pay attention to the end of her speech, but to the earlier part. "If you saw, then Miss Carrol must have seen."

"Miss Carrol!" mocked Mara, with dancing eyes. "Why not Patricia?"

"Oh!" the shy sailor blushed. "I shouldn't care to call her that."

His cousin took him by the coat-lapels and shook him with frail strength.

"Silly creature! If you have not the courage to take what you can get, Patricia will have nothing to do with you. Women like a bold lover."

"I don't believe she will ever return my love," sighed Basil dolefully.

"Oh, as to that, she returns it already."

"Mara!" he flushed again, this time with sheer delight, "do you think—"

"I don't think. I know, and I'm very glad, for Patricia is a darling. I hope that father, who is as fond of her as I am, will give her Beckleigh on condition that she marries you, who can't say 'Bo' to a goose."

Basil looked serious and sighed again. "I'm sorry to upset Uncle George's plans, for he has always been kind to me. But not even for the estate could I give up Miss—that is, Patricia."

"No one wants you to give up either," said Mara impatiently. "Father will no doubt give you Beckleigh."

"No, dear. That would not be right. You are the heiress."

"And what would I do with it? Keep a boarding-house, or start a convent of nuns? I would much rather have a small income and be able to move round as I please."

"You will marry some day, Mara. Mr. Right will come along."

"Mr. Right will never come along," cried Mara, and coloured crimson, which was unusual, "unless he comes from the other world."

"What do you mean?" asked the sailor, greatly puzzled by this weird speech.

"Oh, never mind," retorted Mara, pitying his lack of comprehension. "Sit down and dream of your Patricia. I am going to tell father that my heart is broken." And shooting a whimsical glance at the amazed and startled Basil she slipped out of the room.

Five minutes later Miss Carrol arrived, with her household work completed for the day. In spite of what Mara had told him, Basil would not follow the path she had pointed out. He was rather more attentive than usual to Patricia, and gave her to understand that he would wreck continents for her sake. But the modesty of a man, which is greater than that of a woman, kept his tongue quiet and his eyes unintelligent. Patricia did not entirely approve of this restrained attitude, as she knew that he loved her, and wished to be told so in plain English. She could not understand why he did not speak. But Basil himself understood very well. He waited for Patricia to give him a sufficiently strong hint that she adored him, and then he could lay himself at her feet. It did not seem right, so Basil thought, to act on what he had learned from Mara, as that would be taking advantage of illicit intelligence. But for the sailor's rigorous views of honour, the situation could have been adjusted then and there. All the same, it was not, because she could not speak and he would not.

As for Mara, she returned to her father and demonstrated to him very plainly that her cousin wished to marry Miss Carrol, and that when the time came he would do so. Colpster felt annoyed. Mara could not marry Basil, and would not many Theodore, so his plans for the future well-being of the family were all disarranged.

"What would you say if I gave Beckleigh to Basil?" he asked pointedly. "He could marry Patricia, you know, and take my name."

"I should be very glad," replied Mara quietly.

"Well, then, I won't," said her father, greatly annoyed. "You are the last of the direct line and should have the property."

"I wouldn't know what to do with it."

"You could live here when I am gone."

Mara raised her faint eyebrows. "All alone?" she questioned. "You know I would not allow Theodore to stay, and that Patricia would go with Basil, who is always moving round the world. Oh, I couldn't."

"What's to be done, then?" asked the Squire helplessly.

Mara threw her arms round his neck, a rare demonstration of affection from so usually a self-controlled girl. "Wait," she whispered, "wait and see what is about to happen."

"What is about to happen?"

"I don't know. But something is coming along to change all our lives."

"How do you know?"

"I can't tell you. I only feel that there is something in the air to—"

"Oh!" Colpster grew angry; "more of your occult rubbish. I wish you were an ordinary girl, Mara, and not a dreaming visionary. I shall wait until the emerald comes back, and then you must make up your mind to marry

Theodore, since Basil's affections are engaged."

Mara reflected and thought how very certain Theodore was that the emerald had gone back to Japan never to return. The recollection gave her a chance of pacifying her father, and of securing her freedom. "Very well, then," she said quietly. "When you get the emerald, father, I shall marry him," and in this way the affair was settled for the time being. But think as she might, Mara could not guess how her father expected the Mikado Jewel to return to the Colpster family. And even if it did, she could not understand how its possession would affect things in any way.

Meanwhile the days and weeks passed by and the time drew near for the visit of Count Akira. Mara, although she said nothing, was looking forward to his arrival. Why, she did not know, for, as a rule, she was quite indifferent to those who came to Beckleigh Hall. In her heart, however, she felt that he was coming into her life, either for good or ill, and it was this feeling which made her say to her father that a change was about to take place. But she could not have put her feeling into words, and did not attempt to do so. With the fatalism which was inherent in her character, she waited passively, certain that what was meant to be would certainly become when the hour struck. There was nothing more to be said.

Theodore had duly told his uncle of the interview with Isa Lee, although for obvious reasons he said nothing about the *séance* with the grandmother. The Squire was, therefore, anxiously awaiting the arrival of Harry Pentreddle, as he then hoped to learn how and why the young man had stolen the emerald. Also, he might be able to guess who had snatched it from the hand of Patricia, and, if so, could then tell in whose possession it now was. A great deal depended upon what Pentreddle had to say, and Colpster watched daily for his coming. But Count Akira was the first to arrive, and in attending to a new and fascinating guest, the Squire almost forgot his anxiety to hear the evidence of young Pentreddle.

The Japanese came late in the evening, having arrived at Hendle by the express, to be driven to Beckleigh by Basil. The young man went to meet his friend, and brought him to the Hall in time to dress for dinner. It was not until the meal was in progress that Mara set eyes on him, and then she was so excited by his presence, although she did not show her feelings, that she could scarcely eat. What she had expected—vague as it was—had come true. This man from the Far East was the man who would change her life. Into what he would change it, and down what new path he would lead her, she could not say. All she knew was that with the hour had come the man.

Count Akira was a small, neat person, with a bronze-coloured skin, a clean-shaven face, black hair and black eyes, and a very dignified manner. At the first sight he did not look particularly impressive, as the European evening-dress did not entirely suit his aggressively Oriental appearance. But when those gathered in the drawing-room came to notice his keen, dark eyes, so observant and piercing, to listen to his carefully-worded speech, and to look at his nobly-formed head, they became aware that he was no ordinary man. Race was apparent in his gestures and glances and dominating manner, so quiet yet imperious. He came of a noble line accustomed to rule, and his personality made itself felt more and more as something strong and dangerous, while the hours passed. He was the past, the present, the future of the island empire, the epitome of Japan, the representative of the highest type of the Yellow Race, filled with far-reaching ambitions.

"Is it true that you worship the sun in Japan?" asked Theodore tactlessly.

Akira turned his shrewd eyes on the speaker, and smilingly displayed a set of snowy teeth. "Some do and some don't," he replied evasively; "but I assure you, Mr. Dane, that if you ever saw the sun in England you would worship him also, and with very good reason."

"Oh, we get the sun here," said the Squire patriotically.

"You get a name, but not the real central planet," said Akira, with a shrug. "Clouds and mist obscure his rays. Only in the East does the true sun exist. Is that not so, Dane?" he spoke to Basil, whom he always addressed in this way, although he was more ceremonious with Theodore.

"It is," assented the sailor, with a laugh. "And yet, Akira, when under your painfully blue skies and in your blazing sunshine, I have often longed for the cooling mists of England you so despise."

"That is quite poetical," smiled Patricia.

"Sailors are always poetical, although they don't show that side to landsmen. The solitary spaces of sea and sky, when one is driven back on one's self to think out high things, is enough to make any man poetical."

"Well," said Mara shrewdly, "if sailors don't show that side to landsmen, they probably show it to landswomen. Is that not so, Basil?" and she mischievously glanced from him to Patricia and back again.

"To some women," replied Basil briefly, and colouring through his tan.

"What! When a sailor has a wife in every port!" sneered Theodore; then aware that he had said more than he ought to in the presence of ladies, he quickly turned to Akira. "Perhaps, Count, you will tell us about Japan."

The little man blinked his keen eyes and politely assented. He made himself comfortable, and in many coloured words placed fairy-land before their eyes.

With great charm of manner, he told of cool Buddhist temples, wherein weird ceremonies take place; he related the delightful legend of Jizo-Sama, that kindly god who protects dead children; he pictured the vivid life of toy cities, all colour and movement, and drew the attention of his fascinated hearers to the charm of Japanese and Chinese lettering, which lend themselves to fantastic and odd decoration. After a time he gave a description of a pilgrimage he had made to Fuji, that sacred mountain, which appears in a thousand and one pictures of Dai Nippon. "My country with Fuji-Yama left out is like *Hamlet* without the Prince," he said, smiling. "That mountain is the guardian genius of the land."

Then he told about the rice-fields, with their delicate springing green, of the cherry-orchards in blossom, of the pine forest where fox-women lurked, and sketched out many charming legends. His talk was like a page of Lafcadio Hearn, and Mara hung breathlessly on his words. As he proceeded, her breath became quick and short and her eyes grew larger. She looked at the narrator, through him, past him, as though all he described were passing before her like a panorama of byegone centuries. Suddenly she clapped her hands.

"I remember; I remember," she cried, rising unsteadily to her feet. "Your land is my land. I remember at last," and stopping suddenly, she sank unconscious at the feet of the astonished Japanese.

CHAPTER XIII

THE UNEXPECTED

Next day Mara was quite her old indifferent self. With feminine craft, she denied what she had said, even though five witnesses were ready to repeat the words. "I didn't know what I was saying," said Mara impatiently. "Of course, the heat was too much for me."

"The heat?" repeated her father; "in January?"

"Beckleigh isn't England. My nerves are out of order.—Count Akira had some funny Japanese scent on his handkerchief.—Theodore was looking at me, and that always upsets me." And in this way she made idle excuses, none of which would hold water. "I wish you would leave me alone," she ended, angrily.

As there was nothing else for it, she was left alone, and the queer episode was passed over. Mara was polite to the Japanese and nothing more; but her eyes were constantly following him about, and she came upon him by design in unexpected places. Akira was too shrewd not to notice that he was an object of interest to this pale, golden-haired English maid, and inwardly was puzzled to think why she should pursue him in this secretive fashion. Mara everlastingly inquired about Japan, and about its people. She wished to know the manners and customs of the inhabitants, and entreated the Count to draw word-pictures of Far-Eastern landscapes. But he observed that she never asked him questions when anyone else was present. With a delicate sense of chivalry, he kept silent about this secret understanding which her odd conduct had brought about between them. For there was an understanding without doubt. Akira found himself wondering at times if she was really English, for towards him, at all events, she did not display the world-wide reserve for which the island race of the West is famous.

Of course, Squire Colpster seized the first opportunity to question his guest about the emerald. But Akira professed that he knew little more than the facts that there was such a stone and that it had been stolen some months before from the temple. "I have been to Kitzuki," said the Count, "as my religion is Shinto, and in Izumo is the oldest of our shrines. A very wonderful building it is, and was built in legendary ages by order of the Sun-goddess."

"But the same temple surely does not exist now?"

"Oh, no. It has been rebuilt twenty-eight times, and—"

The Squire interrupted him with an exclamation. "I remember! Lafcadio Hearn says that in one of his books."

"He was a very clever man, and loved our people," replied Akira quietly.

"Yes! yes!" Colpster nodded absently. "It is strange that he did not say anything about the Mikado Jewel."

"It is not generally shown to strangers," explained the Japanese. "I have seen it myself, of course."

"What is it like?"

"Like a chrysanthemum blossom of green jade with an emerald in the centre, Mr. Colpster. I believe it was given to the shrine by one of our Emperors, called Go Yojo."

"It was; and he received it from Shogun Ieyasu."

Akira fixed his sharp black eyes on the tired face of his host. "You seem—

pardon me—to know a great deal about this jewel," he observed inquiringly.

"I ought to. The emerald belonged to our family centuries ago."

"You astonish me."

"I thought I would!" cried the Squire triumphantly. "Yes; an ancestor of mine gave the emerald to Queen Elizabeth, and she sent it, through an English pilot called Will Adams, to Akbar, the Emperor of India. Adams, however, was wrecked on your coasts, Count, and presented the jewel to Ieyasu."

"How very interesting," said Akira, his usually passive Oriental face betraying his wonder. "Thank you for telling me all this, Mr. Colpster. I must relate it to the priests of the Kitzuki Temple, when I return to my own land. I do so in a month or two," he added courteously.

"But the Jewel is now lost!"

"So I understand. I read the report of the death of your housekeeper."

Colpster gazed in astonishment at the little man. "Did that interest you?"

"Naturally," rejoined Akira, unmoved, "seeing that her death was connected with the Mikado Jewel."

"Are you sure that it is the same?" asked Colpster breathlessly.

"Assuredly, from the description. I expect the thief, whosoever he was, brought the emerald to London."

"But who stole it from Miss Carrol?"

Akira shrugged his shoulders and spread out his small hands. "Alas! I do not know. But you should, Mr. Colpster, seeing that the thief proposed to transfer it to your housekeeper through Miss Carrol?" He looked very directly at his host as he spoke.

The Squire reflected for a few minutes. "I will be frank with you, Count," he observed earnestly. "That emerald brought good luck to our family, and since it has left our possession, we have had misfortunes and losses. I wished to get back the jewel and gave Basil a sum of money to—"

"To offer to buy it back," interrupted Akira, nodding. "Yes, I know. You sent him on a dangerous errand, Mr. Colpster. But for me he would have been murdered, as perhaps you know."

"Basil told me the story," said Colpster, drawing himself up stiffly; "but I cannot really agree with you as to the danger. I merely offered to buy back what belonged to an ancestor of mine."

"Your ancestor parted with it," said Akira, readily and rather dryly, "so, as the stone has become a sacred one, it was impossible for the priests to take money for it. I know Dane had nothing to do with its disappearance."

"Ah!" the Squire became cautious. "I don't know who had anything to do with the theft. I wish I did."

"What then?"

"I would seek out the thief and regain the jewel."

"By your own showing the thief parted with the emerald to Miss Carrol," was Akira's quiet remark. "That it was taken from her is strange."

"Oh, I don't think so, Count. Some thief saw Miss Carrol looking at it—you remember, of course, the details given at the inquest—and snatched it."

Akira was silent for a few moments. "Mr. Colpster," he said earnestly, "if you are wise, you will make no attempt to regain this stone. It brought your family good luck centuries ago, but if it comes into your possession again, it will bring bad luck."

"How do you, know?"

"I don't know for certain; I don't even know why it was snatched from Miss Carrol, or where it is now," said Akira coldly, "but I do know," he added with great emphasis, "that since the emerald has been adapted to certain uses in the Shinto Temple at Kitzuki, the powers it possesses must be entirely changed."

"Oh, I don't believe it has such powers," said the Squire roughly.

"Yet you believe that it will bring you good luck," said Akira with a dry little cough. "Isn't that rather illogical, sir?"

Mr. Colpster could find no rejoinder to this very leading question, and dropped the subject. It was very plain that Akira knew very little about the matter, and also it was dangerous to speak to him on the subject. If, indeed, the jewel was in the possession of a London thief, it might be recovered sooner or later. And if Akira knew that it had again passed into the possession of the Colpster family, he might get his ambassador to claim it for Japan. The Squire rather regretted that he had spoken of the matter at all, since his explanation might arouse his guest's curiosity. But as the days passed away, and Akira did not again refer to the abruptly terminated conversation, Colpster thought that he was mistaken. The Japanese really was indifferent to the loss of the Jewel, and no doubt had never given the subject a second thought. But the Squire determined, should he learn anything from Harry Pentreddle, to keep his knowledge to himself.

"Akira doesn't care," he meditated; "but one never knows. If I can get the emerald by some miracle, he may want it for Kitzuki again. I shall hold my tongue for the future. I was a fool to speak of the matter."

Having decided to act in this manner, he warned Theodore and Basil and Mara not to refer in any way to the Mikado Jewel. Yet, strangely enough, he did not warn the person who knew most to hold her tongue. It therefore came about that one day, while Patricia was showing the gardens to Akira, he abruptly mentioned the subject of the inquest and incidentally touched on her adventure in Hyde Park.

"Were you not afraid, Miss Carrol?"

"Yes and no. I was not afraid until the emerald was taken from me," said Patricia frankly.

"Why?" asked the Count politely, and with seeming indifference.

She hesitated. "I fear you will think me silly." Then in reply to his wave of a hand that such an idea would never enter his head, she added hastily: "When I held the emerald I felt a power radiating out from it."

"Ah!" the Japanese started in spite of his usual self-command. "Then you have occult powers and sight and feeling and hearing?"

"I have not," replied Patricia, vexed with herself that she had spoken so freely. "I am a very commonplace person indeed, Count. I felt that feeling because I was worried and hungry."

"Naturally!" muttered Akira to himself; "you get in touch with it when the physical body is weak."

"Get in touch with what?" asked Patricia crossly, for she began to think that this beady-eyed little man was making game of her.

"With what you felt; with what you saw."

"I shan't say anything more about the matter." Patricia turned away with great dignity. "I'm sorry I spoke at all."

"Your secret is safe with me, Miss Carrol."

"It isn't a secret. Mr. Colpster and his two nephews know."

"I don't suppose they understand."

"Mr. Theodore Dane does!" snapped Miss Carrol fractiously, for the persistence of the man was getting on her nerves.

"Yes," said Akira with a ghostly smile; "in a way; but he doesn't know enough. Pity for him that he doesn't."

"What are you talking about, Count?"

"Nonsense!" he replied promptly; "after all, Miss Carrol, I am here to play."

"I wonder you came here at all to such a quiet place."

"Oh, I don't care for orgies, Miss Carrol. But if you ask me, I wonder also why I am here."

Patricia felt that he was speaking truthfully and turned on him with a look of amazement. From all she had seen of the small Japanese, she judged that he was a man who knew his own mind. As she looked, by some telepathic process he guessed what was in hers. "Sometimes I do," he answered; "but on this occasion I don't—exactly"—and he drawled the last word slowly.

Patricia almost jumped. "You are a very uncomfortable man," she remarked.

"The East and the West, dear lady—they never meet without misunderstandings."

This cryptic remark closed the conversation, and they went in to afternoon tea. Akira said no more, nor did he explain his puzzling conversation in the least. However, he still remembered it, for every time he looked at Patricia he smiled so enigmatically that the mother which is in every woman made her wish to slap him and send him to bed without any supper.

That same evening in the drawing-room a strange thing took place, which made Patricia wonder more than ever. Theodore had been performing some conjuring tricks with cards at which Akira smiled politely. Basil had sung, and she had played a sonata of Beethoven. Feeling tired, no doubt, of Shakespeare and the musical glasses, Mr. Colpster had stolen to his study to look at his beloved family tree. The young people had the drawing-room to themselves. As all save Mara—who invariably declined to contribute to the gaiety of any evening—had done his or her part, it was the turn of the Japanese.

"Amuse us in some way, Count," commanded Patricia, crossing to a sofa, and throwing herself luxuriously on the silken cushions.

"Alas! I am so foolish, I know not how to amuse. I have told you so much of my own country that you must be tired."

"No! No! No!" cried Mara, with shining eyes and an alert manner. "I never grow weary of hearing about Japan."

"Why?" asked the Count, half-closing his eyes.

Mara's face became strange and cold. "I don't know," she said, in a hesitating manner. "I seem to know Japan."

"But, Mara," cried Basil, staring, "you have never been there!"

"All the same I know it, and especially I know the Temple of Kitzuki."

"Ah! but you *were* there!" put in Theodore, glancing at the Count, whose eyes were curiously intent upon the girl's pale face.

"How? When?" he asked suddenly.

"She went in her astral body in search for the Mikado Jewel, and—"

"Don't talk of these things," interrupted Mara, in an angry tone. "The Count doesn't want to hear such rubbish."

"Of course; it is all rubbish," said Akira promptly; but Patricia, mindful of his afternoon conversation, did not believe that he spoke as he felt.

"Ah!" sneered Theodore quietly, "you are one of the scoffers. Yet I thought that the East believed in such things."

"We believe in much we never talk about," replied Akira calmly. Then there was a pause, until he suddenly produced from his pocket a bamboo flute. "I can play this," he said, with his eyes on Mara, as though he addressed himself to her; "it is a simple Japanese instrument. Have you a drum?"

Basil, who was addressed, laughed. "I don't think so. There's the dinner-gong."

"That will do," said Akira serenely. "Would you mind getting it and beating it rhythmically like a tom-tom—softly, of course, so as not to drown the notes of my flute. And a hand-bell," he added, casting his looks round the room.

"You are arranging an orchestra," laughed Basil, going out to fetch the gong.

"Here is a bell!" cried Mara, taking a small silver hand-bell from a table covered with nicknacks.

"Hold it, please."

"But what am I to do with it?" asked the girl, bewildered.

"The music I play will tell you," said Akira, somewhat grimly, and then Patricia began to see that there was some meaning in all this preparation. More, that the same was in some hidden way connected with Mara. However, she said nothing, but waited events.

Presently Basil, tall and slim, returned, carrying the brazen gong and sat down to flourish the stick. "Punch and Judy," said Basil; "now for it."

Akira said nothing. He looked at Patricia and Theodore, who were staring at him with astonishment, and at Basil laughing over the gong, and finally at Mara, who held the hand-bell and appeared puzzled. Suddenly the Japanese rose from his seat, and, crossing to the fire, threw something into it.

Immediately a thick white smoke poured into the room, and a strong perfume came to Patricia's nostrils, which seemed to be familiar.

"The incense of Moses," she heard Theodore mutter; "hang it, the fellow does know something of these things!"

Mara also smelt the perfumed smoke. Her eyes grew fixed, her nostrils dilated and—as Patricia had seen in Theodore's room—she began to make a shaking motion with both hands. And, as formerly, she closed them together, holding the silver bell, mouth downward. As the fragrant smoke was wafted through the room, the shrill piping of the flute was heard, and Basil, according to his instructions, began to beat a low, muffled, monotonous accompaniment on the gong. The music sounded weird and Eastern, and was unlike anything Patricia had ever heard before. The stupefying incense and the smoke and the sobbing flute, wailing above the throbbing of the gong, made her head swim.

Suddenly Mara, as if she was moving in her sleep, rose slowly and walked into the centre of the room. There she began to move with swaying motion in a circle, shaking the silver bell with closed hands. Her feet scarcely made any figures, as she only walked rapidly round and round, but the upper part of her body swung from side to side, and bent backward and forward. It was like an Indian nautch, weird and uncanny. Basil seemed to think so, for he stopped his measured beating, but the smoke still wreathed itself through the room in serpentine coils, the flute shrilled loud and piercing, and Mara danced as in a dream. All at once she reeled and the bell crashed on the floor. Basil flung down the gong and sprang forward.

"She is fainting," he cried angrily, catching Mara in his arms. "Akira, what the devil does this mean? She is ill!"

"No! No!" said Mara, as the flute stopped and the scent of the incense grew faint. "I am not ill, I am—I am—what have I been doing?" and she looked vacantly round the room.

Akira laid aside his flute and spoke with suppressed excitement. "You have been performing the Miko dance," he said, trying to control himself.

"Miko! The dance of the Miko!" cried Mara, stretching out her hand; "I know, I remember. The Dance of the Divineress! At last. At—"

"Mara, you are ill!" cried Basil roughly, and catching her by the arm he hurried her, still protesting, out of the room.

"What does it mean?" asked Patricia, who had risen.

"Don't *you* know?" asked Akira, looking at Theodore.

"No," said Dane, puzzled and a trifle awed. "When Mara smells that scent, she always dances in that queer fashion. But I never saw her keep it up for so long as she has done to-night. Where did you get that incense!"

"It is an old Japanese incense," said Akira carelessly; then he turned to Patricia. "I now know why I have been brought here," he said.

"I don't understand," stammered the girl nervously.

"I shall explain. I did not intend to come to Beckleigh, but I was compelled to come. You, with your sixth sense, should know what I mean, Miss Carrol. I wondered why I was brought to this out-of-the-way place. *Now* I know. It was to meet a former Miko of the Temple of Kitzuki. Oh, yes, I am sure. I now know why Miss Colpster declared that she remembered my country and loved to hear me talk about it. She is a reincarnation of the dancing priestess who lived ages since in the province of Izumo."

"Do you believe that?" asked Patricia scornfully.

Akira nodded. "All Japanese believe in reincarnation," he said, in a decisive tone; "it is the foundation of their belief. You believe also?"

Theodore, to whom he spoke, nodded. "Yes. And I wish—I wish—" he turned pale.

Akira looked at him imperiously. "Wish nothing," he said; "she is not for you; she is not for the West; she is for Dai Nippon."

CHAPTER XIV

THE JEWEL

It was judged best by all concerned to keep the episode of the Miko dance from Mr. Colpster, since he undoubtedly would have been very angry had he known of the strain to which Mara's nervous system had been subjected. Not that the girl suffered any ill-effects, but she was extremely tired, and remained in bed for the greater part of the next day. Patricia attended to her tenderly, but could learn little from her as to why she had acted in so strange a way under the influence of the incense and the music. But she intimated vaguely that the dance had re-awakened her recollections of a previous life, when she was not Mara Colpster, but quite another person. Miss Carrol was quite distressed by what she regarded as an hallucination, and privately consulted Basil the next morning after breakfast.

"I am greatly annoyed myself," said Dane, frowning. "Akira should not have acted in the way he did without consulting me."

"You would not have given your consent to the experiment," said Patricia.

"Certainly not. Mara is too highly strung to be subjected to these things, and might easily lose her reason. It is just as well that we have decided not to tell my uncle. He would be furious, and then there would be trouble with Akira, who has not the best of tempers under his cool exterior. But why do you call it an experiment?"

"Can't you see?"

"No! I merely think that Akira wished to give us a specimen of Japanese music, and it influenced Mara, as you saw. Perhaps we have been too hard on Akira, and he did not know what she would do."

"If he did not intend something to happen, why did he throw that incense on the fire?" asked Patricia meaningly.

"I can't say, unless it was to heighten the dramatic effect of his silly nonsense," retorted Basil, whose temper was still hot.

"It was to revive Mara's memory."

"About what?"

"About her past life in Japan."

Basil stared at her. "Surely, Miss Carrol, you don't believe in what Akira said last night?" he observed, with some displeasure and stiffly.

"Don't you?" Patricia looked at him keenly, and the young sailor grew red.

"Well," he said, at length, "there is no doubt that much common-sense is to be found in the belief of reincarnation. I have been so long in the East that I don't scoff at it so much as Western people do. All the same, I do not go so far as to say that I entirely believe in it. But you—you who have never been east of Suez—you can't possibly credit the fact that Mara some hundreds of years ago was a priestess in Japan?"

Patricia looked straight out of the window at the azure sea, and the bright line of the distant horizon. "I dislike these weird things," she said, after a pause. "They are uncomfortable to believe, and since I have known your brother Theodore I dislike them more than ever, as he makes bad use of what he knows. I am certain of that."

"Does he really know anything?" asked Basil, sceptically.

"Yes," said Patricia decidedly. "I really believe he has certain powers, although they are not so much on the surface as mine. Everyone—according to him—has these powers latent, but they require to be developed. I don't want mine to be brought to the surface, as my own idea is to live a quiet and ordinary life."

Basil's eyes had a look in them which asked if she wished to live her ordinary life alone. All he said, however, was: "I quite agree with you."

Patricia nodded absently, being too much taken up with her own thoughts to observe his expression. "As I therefore have a belief in such things," she continued, "and a belief which has been more or less proved to my mind, by the strange feelings I experienced while holding the Mikado Jewel, I see no reason to doubt the doctrine of reincarnation. That seems to me better than anything else to answer the riddle of life. Mara is certainly, as you must admit, a strange girl."

"Very strange indeed," assented Basil readily; "unlike other girls."

"She has always—so she told me," went on Patricia steadily, "been trying to remember her dreams, by which, I think, she means her previous lives. She could never grasp them until last night. Then the music and the incense brought back her memories. They opened the doors, in fact, which, to most people—you and I, for instance—are closed."

"Then you really believe she lived in Japan centuries ago?" asked Basil, in rather an awed tone.

"Yes, I do," replied Miss Carrol firmly; "although I know that many people would laugh if I said so. This morning Mara is staying in bed and will not speak much. But I gather that the past has all returned to her. Remember how she loved to hear Count Akira's stories, and how she followed him about. He noticed that, and so acted as he did last night."

"But why did he think of the Miko dance in connection with Mara?"

"Theodore confessed to me—oh"—Patricia blushed—"I should not call him by his Christian name."

The young man suppressed a pang of jealousy. "I dare say you do so because you hear us all calling one another by our Christian names. I often wonder," he added cautiously, "that you do not call me Basil."

Patricia blushed still deeper, and waived the question. "I have to tell you what your brother said," she remarked stiffly. "He related to Count Akira how Mara danced in that weird manner when she smelt certain incense. That gave the

Count a hint, and he acted upon it, as you saw." She paused, then turned to face Basil. "What is to be done now?"

The sailor had already made up his mind. "In the first place, my uncle must not be told, as he would make trouble. In the second, I shall take Akira to Hendle to-day sightseeing, so that he may not meet Mara. In the third, I shall hint that it would be as well, seeing the effect his presence has on Mara, that he should terminate his visit. Do you approve?"

"Yes," said Patricia, nodding. "You are taking the most practical way out of the difficulty. There is one thing I am afraid of, however?"

"What is that?"

"Mara may fall in love with Count Akira, if, indeed, she is not in love with him already."

"What! with that Japanese?" cried Basil furiously, and his racial hatred became pronounced at once. "That would never do. She must not see him again."

"He is bound to return here, so she must see him."

"Can't you keep her in her room until Akira goes?"

Patricia shook her head. "Mara is difficult to manage. However, although she may love the Count, he may not care for her. Let us hope so. All we can do is to act as you suggest. Now I must go and see after the dinner."

Basil would have liked to detain her, to talk on more absorbing topics. But the question of Mara and her oddities was so very prominent, that he decided against chatting about more personal matters. With a sigh he watched her disappear, and then went away to seek out Akira and take him out of the house for a few hours.

The Japanese, with all his astuteness, did not fathom the reason why he was asked to drive round the country, and willingly assented. He asked a few careless questions about Mara, but did not refer to the scene of the previous night. Basil, on his side, was acute enough to let sleeping dogs lie, so the pair started off about noon for their jaunt in a friendly fashion. They talked of this thing and that, and all round the shop—as the saying is—but neither one referred to the scene of the previous night. Yet a vivid memory of that was uppermost in Basil's mind, and—as he very shrewdly suspected—was present also in the thoughts of Akira. But judging from the man's composure and conversation he had quite forgotten what had taken place. Basil was pleased with this reticence, as it saved him the unpleasantness of explaining himself too forcibly.

Meanwhile, Patricia drew a long breath of relief when Basil drove away with the Japanese diplomatist, and she went at once to see if Mara was all right. The girl, feeling drowsy, was disinclined to chatter, but lay back with a smile of ecstasy on her pale face. Her lips were moving, although she did not open her eyes, and Patricia bent to hear if she required anything. But all that Mara was saying amounted to a reiteration that she had recalled the past. Doubtless, since the door was now wide open, she was in fancy dwelling again in her Oriental home. However, she was quite happy, so Miss Carrol, seeing that her presence was not necessary to the girl's comfort, stole on tip-toe out of the room.

It was when she came downstairs that she chanced upon Theodore in the entrance hall. The big man looked both startled and surprised, and spoke to her in an excited tone.

"Come into my uncle's library at once, Miss Carrol," he said, touching her arm. "It has come."

"What has come?" naturally asked Miss Carrol, puzzled by his tone and look.

"It came by post," went on Theodore breathlessly, "and was not even registered. There is not a line with it to show who sent it."

"I don't know what you are talking about, Mr. Dane."

"Uncle wants you to hold it again in your hand and see if you can feel the drawing-power you spoke of. Come! Come quickly!"

At last Patricia knew what he meant and her face grew white. "Have you the Mikado Jewel?" she asked, leaning against the wall, faint and sick.

For answer Theodore unceremoniously led her into the library, and she saw Mr. Colpster standing near the window, gloating over something which he held in his hand. As he moved to face the girl, a vivid green ray shot through the subdued light of the large room.

"Look! Look!" cried the Squire, stuttering in his excitement, and he held up the jade chrysanthemum with the emerald flashing in its centre, as the sunlight caught its many facets.

"The Mikado Jewel!" gasped Patricia, and her legs refused to sustain her any longer. She sank into a chair. "How—how did you get it?"

"It came by post—by the mid-day post," explained the Squire, repeating what his nephew had said earlier. "Just carelessly wrapped up in brown paper and directed to me. Not even registered, and packed in a small tin box tied round with string. The postmark is London, so it must have been sent through the General Post Office. No district name is stamped on the covering. Oh, wonderful! wonderful! The luck of the Colpsters has returned."

"But who sent it?" asked Patricia, looking with ill-concealed repugnance at the sinister gem, which had indirectly brought about the death of Mrs. Pentreddle. "The man who committed the crime?"

"No, no!" struck in Theodore impatiently; "that's impossible. The assassin of poor Martha never had it in his possession, although, as we know, he hunted the house to find it. The thief who snatched it from you in the Park, Miss Carrol, must have repented and sent it to its rightful owner."

"And I am its rightful owner," said the Squire, drawing up his spare form to its full height. "This gem belonged to my ancestor, and it is only fair that I should possess it."

Patricia could not approve of this speech, as she knew from Colpster's own lips that Sir Bevis had given it to Queen Elizabeth in exchange for his knighthood. But she knew, also, that it was useless to argue with the Squire, as he appeared to be obsessed by the Jewel, to which he ascribed such fantastical powers. Nothing, she was convinced, would ever make him give it up, and she was confirmed in this opinion by his next words.

"Say nothing to Basil, or Akira, about the arrival of the emerald," he said hurriedly to his companions. "I don't trust that Japanese. He thinks that the Jewel belongs to the Temple of Kitzuki."

"So it does," remarked Patricia quickly.

Colpster snarled, and his face became quite ugly and animal in its anger, when he turned on her sharply. "It belongs to me! to me! to me!" he cried vehemently, and pressed the Jewel close to his breast. "I shall never give it up; never, never, never. Tell Akira at your peril."

"I don't intend to say a word to the Count," said Patricia, retreating a step before his malignant expression. "It is none of my business. But if you are wise you will throw it away."

"Why? Why? Why?" chattered Colpster, still angry at her opposition, and perhaps pricked in his conscience by her words.

"I think it will bring evil upon you. You shouldn't let it come into the house," she panted, and felt that what she said was true.

Theodore started and grew pale. Granny Lee had used almost the same words when he had asked her about the possible danger. The old woman had refused to say what the danger was, or perhaps—as she stated—she could not put a name to it. But after hearing Patricia's remark, Theodore felt that perhaps the Mikado Jewel had been referred to as "It." Granny Lee had said plainly: "Don't let It come into the house!" And now this girl, who also possessed certain powers, declared that it should not be allowed to remain under the roof lest it should bring evil in its train.

"You are talking rubbish," said Theodore roughly, and trying to conceal his dismay. "How can that jewel hurt anyone?"

"I don't know; I can't say; but it should not be allowed to remain here."

Squire Colpster laughed and laid the lovely thing down on his desk, where it flashed gloriously in a ray of sunshine. "It shall remain here always and bring good fortune to the family," he said vaingloriously.

Patricia, impelled by some outside power, rose and went up to lay a warning hand on the old man's arm. "There is something wrong," she urged. "Consider, Mr. Colpster! How could the thief have sent the jewel to you unless he knew more about the matter than we think? If an ordinary tramp stole it, he would have pawned it; if a priest of the temple took it, he would have carried it, as Mr. Theodore suggested, back to Japan. Why is it sent to you?"

"I don't know. That is what puzzles me," said Colpster, and his mouth grew more obstinate than ever. "But I'm going to keep it, anyhow."

"What do you say?" Miss Carrol turned to Theodore.

The big man winced and grew a shade whiter, for the warning of Granny Lee still haunted his mind. But the sight of the Jewel, and the knowledge that he might one day possess it, awoke all his covetous nature, and he could not make up his mind to suggest that it should be sent away. And, after all, the "It" to which Brenda Lee referred might not be this gem. "I say keep it," he remarked, drawing a deep breath. "The luck of the family is bound up in it, I am certain."

"The bad luck of the family," said Patricia bitterly.

"Oh, you have been listening to Akira," said the Squire crossly. "He declared that probably the power had been changed. How he could know when he never set eyes on the jewel I can't imagine. I admit that it is very strange that it should have been sent to me, and I can't conceive how the thief either obtained my address, or how he knew that I wanted his plunder."

"He might read in the papers—" began Theodore, only to be stopped by his uncle, who looked at him sharply.

"You talk rubbish, my boy. I said nothing at the inquest about my interest in the jewel, and no one outside our own family knew that I desired it."

"I shouldn't wonder if Akira knew," said Theodore quickly.

"Impossible. You have heard all he had to tell. All the same, it will be as well to say nothing about our recovery of the gem while he is in the house. I have your promise, Miss Carrol?"

"Yes. I shall say nothing."

"And you, Theodore? Good. Don't even tell Mara or Basil, else they may let out something to that infernal Japanese. I shall lock the jewel in my safe yonder," and he pointed to a green-painted safe, standing in an alcove of the room. "Now we shall see the luck returning! I shall win that lawsuit; I shall sell that ruined hay to advantage; I shall—"

Patricia stopped him. "I believe everything will go wrong with you."

"How dare you say that, girl!" exclaimed Colpster furiously.

"Because I feel that I must. That jewel has been sent to you for no good purpose, I am convinced."

"Your sixth sense again, I suppose," scoffed the Squire angrily.

"Perhaps," said Patricia simply. Privately she believed that the Jewel was already beginning to do harm, since the old man behaved so rudely. As a rule he had always treated her with politeness, but now he revealed a side to his character which she had not seen. His eyes shone with greed, and he showed all the instincts of a miser. Looking at her and then glancing at his nephew, he continued to speak to her.

"Hold this in your hand and see if you still feel the drawing-power you spoke of."

In silence Patricia took the cold jade blossom, and it lay outstretched on her pink palm. She did not speak, but a bewildered expression gradually took possession of her face. The two men, who were watching her closely, both spoke together, moved by a single impulse.

"What do you feel?"

Patricia did not reply directly. "This is not the Mikado Jewel," she said in breathless tones. "I am sure it is not."

The Squire became pale and Theodore looked amazed. "What makes you think that?" demanded the latter, who was first able to command his voice.

"The drawing-power is reversed in this jewel," said Patricia. "Yes! oh, yes! I feel it quite plainly. Instead of the power radiating and keeping away evil, it is drawing danger towards itself."

"Danger?" gasped the Squire, and his nephew, mindful of Granny Lee's warning, winced visibly. "Danger and darkness. Wave after wave of fear is coming towards me, while I hold the stone, and the darkness is swallowing me up. Oh!" Patricia shivered and deliberately dropped the jewel on the floor. "Take it away! I don't like it at all."

Colpster picked up the gem. "Are you sure?"

"I wouldn't have let the emerald fall otherwise," said Patricia, who was now trembling as if with cold. "When I last held it waves of light went out, and I felt absolutely safe. Now tides of darkness press in on me on every side, and there is a sense of danger everywhere."

"What sort of danger?" asked Theodore nervously.

"I can't say; I can't put my feelings into words. It looks like the Mikado Jewel, but it can't be, when it feels so different."

"I am certain that it is the Mikado Jewel!" cried Colpster angrily.

"Whether it is or not I can't say," retorted Patricia, backing towards the library door, "but it is dangerous. Get rid of it, or suffer." And she went quickly out of the room, leaving the two men staring at one another.

CHAPTER XV

PENTREDDLE'S STORY

Squire Colpster locked the recovered emerald in his safe and again repeated his orders that Theodore was to say nothing about it. Notwithstanding Patricia's doubts—founded upon the different sensations felt by her when holding the stone—the master of Beckleigh Hall really believed that he possessed the Mikado Jewel. But he could not comprehend why it had been forwarded to him, or how the thief had obtained his address, or why the thief should think that he wanted it. Had the Squire been less obsessed by the ornament, he might have taken Patricia's advice with regard to getting rid of it. And in this, perhaps, he would have been supported by Theodore, who was feeling uncomfortable, since Granny Lee's statement was always in his mind. But, as it was, he said nothing to urge his uncle to take such an extreme course, and the Squire certainly never suggested that the gem should be sent away. So there it lay in the safe, with its influence, either for good or bad, ready to become apparent.

Patricia, on her side, put the matter of the emerald out of her mind, as she did not like to think about occult matters, and, moreover, had to attend to her duties as housekeeper. A visit to Mara's room in the afternoon showed that the girl was up and dressed, and apparently quite her old indifferent self. She said nothing about the Miko dance in which she had figured, so Patricia did not remind her of it in any way. Once or twice she asked where Akira was, but on learning that he had gone sightseeing with Basil, she appeared to be satisfied.

The two gentlemen returned in time for dinner, tired and rather damp from the moisture of mists they had encountered on the moors. Akira expressed himself as pleased with the English country, although he shivered when he mentioned the absence of the sun. Yet, as Basil reminded him, Japan did not possess a particularly tropical climate. The conversation took place when the soup arrived, and, as usual, when any mention was made of the East, Mara grew a delicate rose-pink, and fixed her eyes eagerly on the diplomatist. Akira gave her an indifferent glance and answered the sailor's speech.

"In the north of Japan we have very cold weather, but it is sufficiently warm in the south. But in any case, there is nothing depressing in my country, such as a foreigner finds in England."

"It is the English climate, to a great extent, which has made us what we are, Count," observed Colpster seriously.

"I can say the same of Japan. Hardy climates make hardy men, sir. Do not think that I don't admire your country, for I do; but oh, these swathing mists and damp fields!" He shivered smilingly.

"At least, we have no earthquakes," put in Patricia with a nod.

"Ah, there you have the advantage of us," answered Akira, wiping his mouth; "but in some places we can keep earthquakes away."

"What do you mean?" asked Theodore, scenting something occult.

"Yes." Akira guessed what he vaguely felt. "There are laws which control earth waves."

"Scientific laws?" said Basil quickly.

"You might not call them so," said Akira quietly; "but in the East, you know, we are aware of natural laws which the West has not yet learned."

"Well, then, tell us how to control earthquakes," said the Squire, with a sceptical look on his face.

"Curious you should ask me that, sir. You should ask Miss Carrol."

"Ask me?" Patricia looked amazed.

"You held the Mikado Jewel in your hand," said Akira coolly.

Theodore, Colpster and Patricia exchanged looks, and wondered if the Japanese was aware that the gem reposed in the library safe. It was impossible, of course, since he had been absent all day with Basil. Yet it was strange that he should refer to an object which was uppermost in their minds. "I don't understand," said Patricia doubtfully.

"I can explain, Miss Carrol. Had you examined the emerald you would have seen the sign of the Earth-Spirit graven thereon. That sign shows that a power to control earth-forces lies in the stone."

"Oh, I can't believe that, Count."

"Yet you felt—so you told me—the radiating rays, which keep back all earth tremors—steady them, as it were."

Colpster looked up suddenly. "I thought you knew nothing about the Mikado Jewel, Count," he said sarcastically.

"I know very little, and told you what I did know," replied Akira quietly; "but this conversation about climates revived a memory of what one of the Kitzuki priests told me. The emerald has had certain ceremonies said over it, and has been set on the radiating petals of a jade chrysanthemum. Thus it possesses a repelling power, and was kept in the temple to repel earthquakes from shaking the ground upon which the temple stands."

Theodore stole a glance at Patricia, who looked sceptical. "If," he suggested in a low voice, "if the power, instead of radiating, was drawn to the emerald you speak of, Count, what would happen?"

Patricia was not quite sure, but she fancied that she saw a subtle smile on the bronzed face of her neighbour. But it might have been her fancy or the tricky light of the candles glimmering through their rosy-coloured shades. However, he replied courteously enough: "In that case, Mr. Dane—according to occult law, about which I confess I know little—the earthquake danger, instead of being repelled, would be drawn to the place where the jewel lay."

"Oh, we never have earthquakes here," said Mara, with a gay laugh.

"If the Mikado Jewel were here, and the power was reversed, as is suggested by Mr. Dane, you would soon feel an earthquake, or else this mighty cliff at the back of the house would fall and overwhelm the place."

Theodore shivered. Granny Lee had mentioned that she had seen him crushed as flat as a pancake, and he wondered if what Akira so idly said could really be true. It seemed so, for should the jewel have the in-drawing power—and that it assuredly had, if Patricia was to be believed—there was a great chance that Mrs. Lee's prophecy might be fulfilled. For was not the fatal gem in the house at this moment? Yes, Theodore shivered again, as he became more certain of belief. The Mikado Jewel was the "It" which the sibyl had warned him should never be allowed to enter Beckleigh Hall.

"Oh, it's all rubbish," said the Squire, who, not knowing anything about the occult, refused to believe what Patricia had told him, and what Akira had so strangely affirmed. "And even if such is the case—which I don't believe—the jewel is not here."

Akira laughed and nodded. "Now you can understand why I warned you not to seek for your family emerald again," he said.

"I'm afraid I'll never see it," said Colpster, lying with great ease. "From what Theodore thinks, it must be now on its way back to Japan."

"Let us hope so," said Akira politely. "As a native of that country, and because my religion is Shinto, I regret very much that the gem should have been stolen. In the hands of ignorant persons it may well bring about deaths. You understand," he looked at Patricia.

"Not at all," she confessed, and really in her heart she scouted the idea that the emerald should be endowed with such malignant powers. "Please do not talk any more about these horrid things. I hate them!"

"So do I," said Basil, who was growing restless at the way in which his brother eyed Patricia. "Let us change the subject," which was accordingly done.

After dinner the Squire went into the drawing-room with his family, but scarcely had he seated himself, to digest his meal, when the butler entered with the whispered information that a man wished to see him particularly.

"Who is it, Sims?" asked the old man, impatiently.

"Harry Pentreddle, sir," said Sims, who was an old retainer, and knew as much about members of the family as they did themselves.

116

Colpster bounded to his feet, and Theodore, who was standing before the fire, came hastily forward. Basil and Patricia also looked startled, as they knew the suggested connection between Pentreddle and the giving of the jewel. Only Akira and Mara, who were talking quietly in a corner, appeared unmoved, and continued their conversation. "I'll go at once," said the Squire, eagerly advancing towards the door.

"Let me come too, uncle," asked Theodore, following.

"No; I shall hear his story—if he has any to tell—myself, and then can repeat it to you. Stay where you are, Basil, and you, Patricia. I shall see Harry alone." And he went out hastily, while those left behind, with the exception of the Japanese and Mara, looked greatly disappointed.

Mr. Colpster walked quickly into the library, and found seated there before the fire a thick-set young man, blue-eyed and fair-haired, with the unmistakable look of a seaman. He rose as the Squire entered the room, and twisting his cap in his strong brown hands, looked bashful. In fact, he was a trifle nervous of his reception, and had every reason to be, for Mr. Colpster, who had known him from babyhood, fell on him tooth and nail.

"So here you are at last, Harry," he said, with a frown. "You have given me a lot of trouble to hunt you out. What do you mean? Just tell me that. I didn't expect this behaviour from you, Harry. Your mother, my old servant, has been murdered in a most abominable manner, and instead of coming to assist me in hunting down the scoundrel who did it, you go away and hide. Are you not ashamed of yourself?"

Colpster thundered out the words largely, but they did not seem to produce much effect on the young man. Harry Pentreddle stood where he was, still twisting his cap, and stared at the Squire with steady blue eyes. This composure seemed to be not quite natural, nor did the silence. "Can you not sit down and speak?" demanded Colpster, throwing himself into his usual arm-chair and getting ready to ask questions.

Harry sat down quietly, and still continued to stare steadily. "I am not ashamed of myself, sir, because I can explain my conduct fully."

"Then do so," snapped the Squire. "Your mother and father were both my servants, and you were born at Beckleigh. As your parents are dead, I have a right to look after you."

"Do you think that I need looking after, sir?" asked Pentreddle, with a faint smile and a glance at his stalwart figure in the near mirror.

"You know what I mean, Harry. I wish to see you married to Isa and commanding a ship of your own. I intend to help you to get one."

"It is very good of you, sir."

"Not at all. You were born on the estate. And now that your future is settled, suppose you tell me why you didn't come back before?"

"If I tell you, sir, will you promise to keep what I say secret?"

"Yes—that is, in a way. I may tell my nephew Theodore, perhaps my other nephew—I can't say."

"I don't mind anyone in Beckleigh knowing," said Harry hastily, "but I do not wish the whole world to know."

"I am not acquainted with the whole world," said Colpster dryly, "so there is no chance of what you say being told to the entire inhabitants of this planet. Are you satisfied?"

"Quite. Well, then, sir, I went to Amsterdam to wait for a ship which I know is going to Japan. She is coming from Callao and is late."

"How do you mean late?"

"She is a tramp steamer, and I know her captain. She comes to Amsterdam to discharge a cargo, and then proceeds to Japan. I can get an engagement as second mate when she arrives. She is expected every day. I heard from Isa that you wished to see me, and so I came over. But I shall go back in two days, as I can't afford to lose the chance of getting to the Far East."

"Why do you want to go there?"

Harry looked down. "I can't exactly say," he observed in a low voice.

The Squire looked at him keenly, then leaned forward. "Do you go to Japan to punish the priest who murdered your mother."

The young man dropped his cap and half rose from his chair, only to fall into it again. He seemed utterly taken by surprise. "What priest?" he faltered.

"You heard me," said Colpster impatiently. "The one who murdered your mother—a priest of the Temple of Kitzuki."

"How did you know, sir?" Pentreddle stared open-mouthed.

"By putting two and two together. Martha—your mother, that is—sent Miss Carrol to get the emerald, and she could only have got it from you, who had—as you told Theodore—just returned from Japan. By the way, do you know all about the death?"

"Yes," said Pentreddle, stooping to pick up his cap and thus hide his emotion, for his lips were trembling. "I read everything in the papers, and I did not come over because I wished to return to Japan and to kill the priest who, I believe, is the assassin."

"Are you sure that a priest of Kitzuki killed her?"

"Yes, I feel sure."

"And to obtain possession of the emerald?"

"Yes. I am certain that was the motive for the crime."

"You stole the emerald?"

"Yes," said Pentreddle boldly. "I did." He laughed softly. "It is very clever of you to guess, unless my poor mother told you."

"She told me nothing," snapped the Squire, with a glare. "All she did was to ask me for a London holiday. She got it and went to her death. It was Miss Carrol—you must have read about her in the papers—who suggested that possibly you might have passed her the emerald."

"I did, although at the time in the fog and darkness I believed it was my mother. Only when reading about her death did I know that she had been kept at home with a sprained ankle. She—"

"Wait a bit," said Colpster, throwing up his hand; "you are confusing me. I want to hear all from the beginning." He paused, and seeing that Pentreddle looked nervous and was beginning to twist his cap again, swiftly made up his mind to a course of action to suggest confidence. "Wait a bit," said Colpster again, and went to the safe. When he returned to the table he placed the Mikado Jewel under the lamp.

Harry rose and bent over it quite speechless with astonishment. "I thought it was snatched from Miss Carrol in the Park," he gasped.

"So it was. But someone—the thief, I presume—sent it to me. It arrived here without details. You are sure that it is the Jewel?" he asked quickly.

"Yes, it's the Jewel right enough," answered Pentreddle, returning to his seat. "But how did the thief know you wanted it?"

"I can't say, and I am not even aware if the thief sent it. All I know is that there lies the Luck of the Colpsters, and that I have shown it to you, so that you may see I repose confidence in you. And in return, Harry," the Squire leaned forward and touched the young man's knee, "I wish to hear all about the theft of the emerald from the Kitzuki Temple."

Pentreddle thought for a few moments, while he looked at the winking green ornament under the lamplight. Then he glanced at his watch and nodded. "I must get away soon," he said briskly. "I am staying at Hendle and a friend of mine is waiting on the Moor Road with a trap. It won't take me long to tell you everything, sir."

Colpster leaned back and placed the tips of his fingers together. "I am ready to hear you," he said quietly and bending his head.

Harry began his story in a hurry. "My mother, as you know, sir, nursed your nephews. Mr. Basil was always her favourite, but she never could abide Mr. Theodore. She learned from you, sir, that you intended to leave the estates to the nephew who got back the emerald, which is the family luck."

"Yes. Such was my intention. Well?"

"My mother," went on the sailor, twirling his cap, "was determined that Mr. Theodore would never inherit, so, as she knew that I was going to Japan, she asked me to steal the emerald."

"You had no right to steal it. I would have forbidden Martha suggesting such a thing," said the Squire angrily.

Pentreddle nodded. "I know. For that reason my mother kept the affair a secret. I readily agreed to do what she wanted, as Mr. Basil has always been kind to me, whereas Mr. Theodore—" he halted.

"Oh, go on," said Colpster, with a cynical smile. "I know that Mr. Theodore is not a favourite with anyone."

"How can he be, sir, when he behaves so badly? He insulted me and—but that is neither here nor there, sir, and I have no time to talk of that matter. I told my mother that I would get the emerald somehow, and when I landed at Nagasaki, I set about looking for it."

"But in what way?"

"Well, you see, sir, my mother learned from you all about the giving of the emerald to that Shogun chap, and then she told me how Miss Mara, in some funny way, knew that it was at the Temple of Kitzuki. I went there on the chance, and a man who kept a tea-shop told me all about the jewel. He said that it had been given to the temple by a Mikado. I thought it was a Shogun."

"The Shogun, who got it from Will Adams, gave it to the Mikado, and he presented it to the temple," explained Colpster. "Go on."

"Oh, that's it, is it, sir? Well, then," he went on, twirling his cap, "I got a sight of the Jewel in the temple and stole it."

"But how, when it was so carefully guarded?"

"I don't think it was guarded over-much," said Pentreddle thoughtfully. "You see, sir, the tea-shop man told me that the emerald was under the spell of the Earth Spirit—he called him some queer name I can't remember—to keep away earthquakes. No Japanese would dare to touch the jewel, and it lay—as I saw—on a small altar near the shrine. I managed to stop inside the temple after dark, and stole it."

"How did you get away?" said the Squire, wondering at this daring.

"I'll tell you that another day, sir, as it is getting late. I did manage to get away and stow the Jewel on board my ship; but I was followed."

"Followed? By whom?"

"Japanese. I suppose they were priests. I was nearly knifed at Nagasaki and once I was drugged. But I had hidden the emerald away, and they could not find it. When I got to the Port of London I thought that I was safe; but I soon found that I was dogged there also."

"By whom?" asked Colpster once more.

"Japanese," said Pentreddle again. "Wherever I went I met Japanese. They swarmed all round me. I had written to my mother saying that I would give her the emerald if she came to London. She did, and wrote asking me to go to The Home of Art. But I knew better than to do that, sir. I felt certain that if I gave the jewel to my mother she would run a chance of being killed. There was one big chap with a scar across his cheek. I believe he killed my poor mother."

"What makes you think that, Harry?" asked Colpster eagerly.

"Because I was loafing round The Home of Art one evening trying to catch a glimpse of my mother, when I saw the beast watching me and the house."

"Was the man with the scar a priest?"

"He just was," said the sailor vigorously; "a Shinto priest. I saw him in the temple at Kitzuki. Then I was certain that I was being followed by the priests, and wrote and told my mother that I could only give her the emerald secretly. She replied, saying that the whole household at The Home of Art had an appointment to see some play—"

"I know all that," said the Squire impatiently. "Skip that."

"Well, then, sir, my mother said, that being alone she could leave the house at night without suspicion being aroused. She told me to meet her at nine o'clock at the right-hand corner of the Bayswater side of the Serpentine Bridge, and to look for a red light. But, of course, as I learned later, she was kept in by her sprained foot, and sent Miss Carrol."

"Why did you not speak to Miss Carrol?"

"I hadn't a chance," said Harry simply. "I guessed that I was being followed."

"By the priest with the scar?"

"No. By a smaller and slighter-built chap. He dodged at my heels in the fog, so I had just time to shove the box into Miss Carrol's hand—into my mother's hands, as I thought—and then run off in the hope the little beast would follow me."

"He did, didn't he?"

"For a time. Then I fancy his suspicions must have been aroused by the red light, and by my stopping for a moment. I lost him, or he lost me in the fog, and then, instead of returning to my lodgings in Pimlico, I made for Limehouse Docks. I heard next morning of the death."

"Why didn't you then come to The Home of Art?"

"What was the good, sir," remonstrated Pentreddle. "I should only have been knifed by those Japanese, and there would have been two murders instead of one. No, sir; I wasn't such a fool, as my going to The Home of Art wouldn't have brought my mother back to life. I bunked over to Amsterdam and lay low. Then I read in the papers how Miss Carrol had been robbed of the gem."

Colpster nodded. "You should have returned then."

"It was of no use, sir," said the sailor gloomily. "I knew that the emerald must have got back into the hands of the priests, and that they would return to Kitzuki, in Japan. I was certain, and I am now, that the big man with the scar on his cheek stabbed my mother, so I waited for the ship I told you about to go back to Japan and kill him. Then Isa wrote me and said if you saw me you could help me. But," Pentreddle looked at the emerald, "it seems to me that things are more muddled up than ever. Here is the Mikado Jewel, but where are the priests?"

Colpster pinched his nether lip and looked perplexed. "I can't say. By the way, Theodore met you in London?"

"Yes, sir. By chance in Pimlico."

"Why didn't you give him the emerald?"

"Why?" Harry looked astonished. "Because it was to prevent Mr. Theodore becoming your heir that my mother took all this trouble, and so met with her death." He rose to his feet. "I'll go now, sir."

The Squire rose also, "Yes, unless you prefer to stay here for the night."

"No, sir. I want to get back to Hendle. I'll come and see you again if you want to hear more."

"I think it will be as well. I should like you to repeat this story in the presence of my nephews. Meanwhile, good-night," and the Squire, having shaken hands with the sailor, sent him away. He wished to be alone to think over things, and while doing so he put away the Mikado Jewel in the safe.

Ten minutes later he returned to the drawing-room. "Where is Count Akira?"

"Akira was tired and went early to bed," said Basil. "I'm off too, uncle."

CHAPTER XVI

LOVERS

Next morning, it occurred to the Squire that he had dismissed Pentreddle too abruptly, or, rather—since the man wished to go—had given him leave too easily. A thousand and one questions came into his mind, which he desired to ask, and which he should have put to the sailor during their hurried interview. But a recollection that Harry was stopping at Hendle, and was holding himself at the disposal of his feudal chief—modern style—reconciled him to the oversight, and he decided that the second examination would be a longer one. "I shall drive over to Hendle to-day and cross-examine him," thought the Squire; and completing his toilette he descended to breakfast with an excellent appetite.

At the meal he heard news, for Akira stated that he would have to return that day to London, as his Chief wanted him. "But I am coming down again in a few days," said the Japanese, stealing a glance at Mara, who sat opposite to him, rosy-faced and interested, "in my yacht."

"I didn't know you had a yacht, Akira," said Basil, with the keen interest of a sailor in his craft.

"Oh, yes," replied the Count, composedly; "a very good yacht, my friend. I have much money, you know, and have taken to your English ways so far as to buy a steam yacht. Later, I propose returning to my own country in her."

Colpster was frankly relieved that Akira intended to leave. He did not for one moment connect him with those who were hunting, or who had been hunting for the Mikado Jewel; but while that curious object was in the house he preferred the Count's absence to his presence. There was no doubt that if the little man did learn how the gem had returned to its original possessors, that he would clamour for its restoration to Kitzuki. And that was not to be thought of for one moment. The Squire had not yet solved the problem as to why the jewel had been sent to him, or how the sender had known that its presence was desired at Beckleigh Hall by its master. He would have liked to question Akira, for if a priest, according to Pentreddle, had snatched the emerald from Patricia, Akira, as a Japanese, would best be able to explain that same priest's reasons for sending it to Devonshire. But it was obviously impossible to ask such a question, so Colpster contented himself with expressing regret that the Count had been compelled to cut short his stay at the Hall. "I trust when you return in your yacht you will at least complete your interrupted visit by sleeping under my roof," said Colpster.

"Thank you, no, sir," replied the Japanese politely. "I shall remain on my boat for the few days I stay here. And I hope," he added, with a comprehensive bow to all present, "that you will allow me to return your great hospitality, Mr. Colpster, by giving an entertainment on board."

"An entertainment!" cried Mara, and her eyes sparkled.

"Yes! A Japanese entertainment, with Japanese food and drinks and amusements, Miss Colpster. It will be a change for you, and no doubt will give you a great deal of pleasure."

"It will give us all pleasure," said Patricia, smiling, for the black eyes of the little man were fixed on her face.

"Then I ask you all to my entertainment. Even your servants must come, Mr. Colpster. They never see anything unusual down here, so it will amuse them to see how we Japanese live. I presume," added Akira, with an attempt at humour, "that you can allow this house to be empty for one night?"

"Oh, yes," said Theodore, laughing; "there are no robbers about here."

"In that case, I hope my invitation will be accepted."

"Certainly, Count, and thank you for the invitation," observed the Squire in a hearty manner. "On behalf of myself, my family and my household, I accept."

Akira bowed. "That is good, sir, for, as I depart for my own country, after I leave this place in my yacht, I will not see you again for many a long year. I have to remain at Tokio for official business. But I have had a delightful stay here"—he looked round pleasantly—"and you will see, all of you, how I can return your kindness."

"But won't you be tired travelling to London to-day?" said Theodore, quickly.

The Count's piercing eyes seemed to look the questioner through and through as if inquiring why he asked this particular question. "I retired early last night, as you know, Mr. Dane," he said quietly, "and so I am not at all weary. Dane," he turned sideways to Basil, "you will drive me to Hendle?"

"You must allow me to do that, Count," put in the Squire. "I have to go to Hendle on business to-day."

"Thank you, sir. You show true hospitality."

Basil felt uneasy as he did not know if the guest spoke ironically or not, and resolved to test the matter. "I can come also, Akira."

"Ah, but no, it is not necessary." Akira held up a protesting hand. "I shall enjoy the drive with your uncle. Stay here, and we shall meet again on board the *Miko*."

Mara started. "The *Miko!*" she cried eagerly, and with shining eyes.

"The name of my yacht, Miss Colpster. I named her after the Divine Dancer."

The girl looked as though she wished to ask further questions, but a significant glance of Patricia's directed towards the Squire, who knew nothing about the Miko Dance, made Mara more prudent. She rose abruptly from the table, and shortly the rest followed her example. Akira went to see that his servant was packing his things properly, and Basil accompanied him. As for Theodore, he followed his uncle into the library and closed the door.

"What did Pentreddle say to you last night?" he asked anxiously.

"It's a long story," said Colpster, sitting down to look over his correspondence; "he will tell it to you himself. I am driving over to Hendle, and will bring him back with me. Akira I can drop at the station to catch the afternoon express."

"I should like to come also, uncle, as I am so anxious to hear Harry's story."

"There is no room in the brougham for you," said Colpster, coldly, and showed very plainly by this unnecessary lie that he did not wish for his nephew's company. Theodore frowned. He knew that he was no favourite.

"At least, uncle, give me a short account of what you heard."

The Squire at first refused, but Theodore was so persistent that in the end he was obliged to yield, and hastily ran through the story. "What do you think?" he asked, when he ended.

"I expect Harry is right, and that the priest with the scar murdered his mother.

No doubt the man learned why Harry was hanging round the Home of Art and laid his plans accordingly."

"But Martha did not possess the emerald!" insisted the Squire, doubtfully.

"The priest did not know that at the time," said Dane, grimly; "his accomplice watched Harry, apparently, while the man with the scar watched the Crook Street house. He must have induced Martha to let him in—she might have thought it was her son, you know. Then, when she grew frightened, and threatened him with her stiletto, he used it against her, and having murdered the poor old thing, finally searched the house."

Colpster nodded. He could see no other solution of the mystery. "Curious, though, that the priest did not get caught by the police."

"Oh, according to the evidence the fog was very bad, and one policeman confessed in print that he did not patrol the *cul de sac* carefully. Pity he did not catch the brute."

"Oh!" said Colpster, with a grim look, "Harry will see that the man is punished. He is going from Amsterdam in a tramp steamer to Japan for that very purpose."

"I can't understand," said Theodore, after a pause, and tapping the desk with his long fingers, "why Harry didn't give me the emerald when he met me. It would have saved all this trouble."

The Squire coughed in rather an embarrassed manner. He could scarcely tell Theodore that Harry, acting under his mother's instructions, wished particularly to prevent him from gaining possession of the jewel. He therefore shrugged his shoulders and evaded the question. "There are many things we cannot understand in connection with this case."

"Quite so," said Theodore, with an uneasy look at the safe; "particularly why the Mikado Jewel should have been sent to you. Uncle," he added, after a pause, "get rid of it. Sell it; pawn it; return it to Akira to take back to Japan, but send it out of the house, I beg of you."

"Why?" demanded Colpster, drawing his brows together; "are you mad?"

Theodore wiped the perspiration from his high, white forehead. "On the contrary, I am particularly sane. You heard what Akira said about the reverse power possibly bringing the cliff down on the house."

"Oh, rubbish," said the Squire, roughly; "Akira doesn't know that the gem is in this house."

"All the more reason for believing that he spoke truly," said Dane, with a desperate look. "I am sure the thing is evil. There is now an in-drawing power, as you know. Miss Carrol felt it."

"I don't believe in all this rubbish. Patricia is a fanciful girl," said Colpster coldly. "The emerald is in my possession, and I intend to keep it. If you dare to tell Akira about it, Theodore, I shall send you out of the house and will never recognize you again as my nephew."

"I am not so sure but what I would prefer to be out of the house, while that damned thing is in it," said Theodore between his teeth. "You are playing with fire, uncle. See that you don't get burnt," and with this warning he departed, leaving the old man looking after his back contemptuously. He was a very material man was the Squire, and considered that his nephew was an ass for believing in things which could not be proved by arithmetic.

Theodore was not happy in his mind when Akira and Colpster departed, for there were many matters which worried him. Basil, as usual, was following Patricia about the house, and that was one grievance. Now that Mara would not marry him he would certainly lose the chance of inheriting, through her, the desirable acres of Beckleigh, and that was another grievance. Finally, the presence of the charmed Mikado Jewel in the house troubled him very much indeed. He felt certain that Granny Lee's prophecy concerned it, since Akira had spoken of the occult powers of the stone. And Patricia had felt the reversion of the power, so Theodore uneasily considered that it was just possible that the cliff might be shaken down in ruins on the house.

He went out and looked at its mighty height, almost expecting to see signs of crumbling. But, of course, there were none. The red cliff stood up boldly and gigantically, as it had stood for centuries past. The sight of its massive grandeur rather reassured Theodore.

"It's all rubbish," he muttered to himself, coming in out of the rain, for all the morning there had been a downpour. "I daresay I am making a mountain out of a mole-hill. All the same"—his eyes fell on the safe in the library. In it he knew was the jewel safely locked away. To shift the Mikado emerald he would need to shift the safe, and that was impossible. "Oh, it is all rubbish!" he declared again, and then went to his own rooms.

On the way he passed the library, and saw Mara lying on the cushions of the sofa stringing beads: onyx, turquoise, malachite, pink coral and slivers of amethyst. They gleamed like a rainbow as they slid through her deft hands. Theodore wondered where she got them and entered to inquire.

"Count Akira gave them to me," said Mara, gaily, and tried the effect of the glittering chain against her pale golden hair; "aren't they lovely?"

"Yes, but your father won't like you taking presents from that infernal

Japanese, Mara," said Theodore, crossly. His nerves were so upset that he felt it would relieve him to vent his temper on someone.

Mara sprang to her feet like a small fury, and her face grew darkly red, as her pale eyes blazed with anger. "You have no right to speak in that way of Count Akira. I love him; I don't care who hears me. I love him!" She sat down again suddenly. "I wish he would take me to Japan," she ended viciously.

"Mara!" Theodore was horrified; "a Japanese?"

"Well. I was one ages ago," she retorted.

"I don't believe it."

"Yes, you do. You know too much about these occult things to disbelieve."

Theodore, as a matter of fact, did believe, but he did not intend to confess as much. "You can't be sure," he snapped, furiously.

"I can be sure, and I am sure," said Mara, mutinously; "since I danced the Round of the Divineress and heard the music, it all has come back to me. I remember the Temple of Kitzuki quite well, and the ceremonies. Oh, I wish I could go back there. It is my native land."

Theodore looked at her stealthily, and his eyes glittered as an idea struck him hard. "Would you go if Akira took you?"

"Yes." Mara wet her lips and stared at him. "Perhaps he will take me," she said softly; "he is coming back in his yacht, you know."

"If you went, your father would disown you."

"I don't care."

"You would lose Beckleigh."

"I don't care."

"You would be cut off from your own race."

"I don't care."

"You are a fool," shouted Theodore, savagely. "I'll tell your father."

Mara wreathed her many-hued beads artistically round her neck and admired herself in the mirror over the fireplace. But she also had a glimpse of her cousin's face, and spoke from what she read written thereon. "No, you won't, Theodore," she observed, coolly, and meaningly; "you would be glad to see me run off with Count Akira and give up everything."

"Why should I be glad?" demanded Dane, taken aback by this shrewd reading of his most secret thoughts.

"Because, as you say, my father would have nothing to do with me, and you would inherit Beckleigh. I am safe in your hands."

"There is no chance for me," said Theodore tartly. "Failing you, Basil would inherit."

"I don't think so if he marries Patricia."

"Uncle George likes Patricia."

"I know that: so do we all. But I don't think he would like Basil to marry her. In fact," Mara faced him, "I believe that father would like to make Patricia my step-mother."

"What!" Theodore was now really astonished. "It's absurd!"

"I don't see that. Father is still a young man for his years, and—"

"Oh, rubbish; nonsense!" Theodore broke furiously into her speech, and fairly ran out of the room to think over the problem thus presented to him.

He believed that what his cousin said was perfectly true, as Mara was an observant young person in spite of her dreamy ways. Then he remembered how Colpster always professed to admire Patricia, and did so loudly. He was always asking her if she liked the place and what he could do for her, and telling her that he hoped she would stay there for the rest of her life.

Theodore drew a long breath. "I see what the old man is up to," he considered. "As Mara won't marry either Basil or myself, he intends to marry Patricia in the hope of having an heir to the estate. That would be an end to everything. Not that I believe the girl would have him."

And yet of this Theodore could not be sure, as he judged Miss Carrol by his own greedy self. Could any girl, penniless, as he knew Patricia to be, resist the offer of so beautiful a home? Dane thought not, and set his wits to work to bar any possible chance of this very unexpected thing coming to pass. To do so, he had only to throw Patricia into Basil's arms and he believed that he knew how to do that.

"I'll ask her to marry me," thought Theodore with an evil smile; "and then Basil will be so furious that he'll ask her. She hates me and loves him, so in the end they will become engaged. Then Uncle George will kick them both out of the house. Mara evidently intends to elope with Akira when he returns in his yacht. The little beast said that the boat after leaving here was going straight to Japan. That will settle her. Ha! I shall be the only person left to console Uncle George, so he must as a reasonable man leave me the property. I can see it all."

Thus arranging his plans, he went away to find Patricia, and force her into

Basil's arms. He was sorry to lose the girl because of her psychic powers, but as she plainly hated him—he saw that easily—there was not any chance for him. Since he could not make use of her in one way, he therefore decided to make use of her in another. Through her, Basil could be got rid of, and then Mara would ruin herself by eloping with Akira. Dane rubbed his hands with delight, at the prospect thus opened out before him. He even forgot his uneasiness over the Mikado Jewel, and ceased for the moment to remember the sinister prophecy of Mrs. Brenda Lee.

Of course, it was necessary to act a comedy so as to accomplish his aims, and he suspected that he would suffer pain during his acting. If he insulted Patricia, which he intended to do, Basil would assuredly knock him down. But if the sailor did that he would be obliged to declare his love for Patricia, if only to prove his rights to be her champion. And what did a little pain matter to the prospective owner of Beckleigh Hall?

The schemer found the pair in the smoking-room, a cosy and somewhat modern apartment—for the house—which was in the west wing. It possessed a large plate-glass window which looked down the vista, where the trees were cut down, to the beach and the waters of the bay. Patricia, knitting a silk tie, sat on the sofa near the window, while Basil lounged in a deep arm-chair smoking his pipe. The two were laughing when Theodore entered, but suddenly became serious when they saw who had disturbed them. It was strange that the elder Dane should always produce a dull impression on the gayest of people. Perhaps it was owing to the uncanny and disagreeable atmosphere which he always carried about with him.

"What's the joke?" asked the new-comer, throwing himself into an arm-chair opposite to that in which his brother sat.

"Nothing," said Basil shortly, and his brow wrinkled. "What do you want?"

"To smoke a cigarette," replied Theodore, producing his case; "the room is free to all, isn't it?"

"Quite free," said Patricia colouring, for she did not like his tone. When the two brothers were together she was always apprehensive of trouble. For this reason, and because she hoped to throw oil on troubled fraternal waters, did she refrain from leaving the room. Yet Theodore's look was so insolent that she half rose to do so. "I must—"

"Don't go, Patricia," said the elder brother hastily.

"Mr. Dane, I do not like you to call me by my Christian name," she said, and her colour grew deeper than ever. She rose to her full height now, and made ready to go.

"Theodore doesn't know what he is saying," muttered Basil in a tone of suppressed rage; and his brother, looking at him mockingly, saw that his face was as crimson as that of Patricia's.

"Really, I seem to be like the Goddess of Discord," went on the intruder, intent upon bringing about a catastrophe; "you seemed jolly enough when I entered, laughing and talking and—"

"We'll be jolly, again, when you leave," snapped Basil savagely.

"I daresay. But you shan't have Miss Carrol all to yourself. No, don't go, Miss Carrol, you see that I am addressing you with all respect." He rose and slipped between her and the door as he spoke. "I want Basil to see that you like me as much as you do him."

Patricia looked nervous and her feelings were not soothed when Basil rose in his turn. "Go away, Miss Carrol," he said sternly, and the veins on his forehead stood out with rage. "I can deal with Theodore."

"Theodore can deal with himself," said that gentleman, turning on his brother with a black look on his face. "You are always taking up Patricia's time, and I have a right to it also. Yes"—he faced to the startled girl—"I intend to call you Patricia because I love you. I want you to marry me."

"Theodore, are you mad?" thundered Basil furiously.

"Is it mad to ask a girl's hand in marriage?" sneered Theodore.

Patricia stopped the further speech of Basil with an imperative gesture and looked at Theodore. "I am well able to take care of myself," she said quietly. "Mr. Dane, I thank you for your offer, but I decline it."

"Oh, I am not so handsome as Basil. I am not so rich as Uncle George!"

"Take care; take care!" breathed Basil savagely in his ear.

But Patricia again stopped him. Her temper rose, and her eyes sparkled in an angry fashion. "What do you mean by your reference to Mr. Colpster?"

"You want to marry him, and—ah! keep off!"

Theodore flung out his hands with a scream, as Basil hit out. The blow caught him fairly in his left eye, and he reeled towards the window to fall on the sofa. "You bully!" he fairly sobbed.

"Apologise to Miss Carrol, or, by Heaven! I'll break your neck!" raged Basil, standing over the flabby man with clenched fists.

Patricia, admiring her strong lover, came forward and laid her hand on his arm imploringly. "Leave him alone, Basil. He is not worth hitting."

Theodore struggled to his feet, and with his rapidly swelling eye presented a miserable spectacle. "Basil!" he screamed, and his rage was partly real; "so you call him Basil, and no doubt that that is for him you are knitting. Oh!" he burst into mocking laughter, and pointed a finger at them both; "so this is how you are carrying on! This is—"

He got no further. Basil, breaking from Patricia, sprang forward, and catching Theodore's bulky body in his powerful arms, fairly flung him through the window with a mighty heave. Patricia gasped with surprise and delight as the glass smashed and Theodore swung across the grass and down the slope like a stone fired from a catapult. "You devil!" roared Basil, shaking his fist through the broken window. "I'll kill you if you come near me or Patricia!"

"Oh, he's dead!" gasped the girl, clinging to the sailor.

"Not he! See!" and sure enough Theodore, with his face convulsed with impotent rage, rose heavily and limped out of sight. "I've settled him, the hound! and now—" he looked at her meaningly.

Patricia shrank back flushing like a sunset. "Mr. Dane!"

"You called me Basil just now, and you shall call me Basil for the rest of your life. You would not marry Theodore; but," he said masterfully, "you shall marry me."

"Yes," whispered Patricia, yielding to his embrace; "I always loved you."

"My darling! my darling! my darling!" cried the delighted sailor, straining her to his breast. "Theodore meant to part us, but he only succeeded in bringing us together!" and he kissed her again and again.

He little knew how Theodore had schemed to bring about that very kiss!

CHAPTER XVII

TROUBLE

Misfortunes rarely come singly. Theodore was so damaged by Basil that he was compelled to keep to his rooms, and had his meals sent up to him. Apart from his physical pain, the schemer was very satisfied with the result of the comedy he had played in the smoking-room. Lurking unseen at the corner of the house, he had beheld Patricia in his brother's arms, and could believe the evidence of his own eyes that the Rubicon had been crossed. Nevertheless, he felt a pang at losing the girl, for apart from her psychic powers, which would have been extremely useful to him in his studies, she was so pretty and charming that a less susceptible man than Dane would have regretted the success of another. But Theodore had by this time decided that he could not have his cake and eat it, so it was necessary to lose either Beckleigh or Patricia. It was characteristic of his greedy nature that he had sacrificed the girl for the estate.

No doubt Mara's hint that she might go with Akira to Japan had urged him to the course he had adopted, for with both his brother and his cousin out of the way, Dane did not see how he could lose Beckleigh. He was the only one save these two who had the Colpster blood in his veins, and even though his uncle disliked him, he could scarcely pass him over. With aching limbs Theodore lay snug in bed, building castles in the air. Next day he intended to arouse the old man's jealousy by telling him of the embrace, of the kisses, and of the probable engagement. Then the lovers would be turned out of the house. Later, when Akira came round in his yacht, Mara would go, and he would be lord of all he surveyed. No wonder Theodore chuckled.

But then came the second misfortune, and an even more unexpected one. Mr. Colpster was brought back from Hendle with a broken leg. He had duly driven Akira and his servant to the railway station, but had failed to find Harry Pentreddle at his lodgings. Rather annoyed, the old man had left a note, saying that the sailor was to come to Beckleigh and stay the night, so that he might repeat his story to the Danes, and then had turned homeward. But on the winding road which led down to the Hall, the horse had slipped on the rain-soaked ground, and Mr. Colpster, having foolishly tried to get out, had been thrown over the high bank. The coachman was uninjured, although, with the horse and vehicle, he had rolled down the slope. But the Squire had been picked up insensible by some labourers who had seen the accident, and had been carried into his own house with a broken leg.

Much concerned, Basil and Patricia had the Squire put to bed and sent for a doctor. Mara, in an indifferent way, expressed her sorrow, although she never offered to nurse her father. Instead of helping, she went up to her cousin's room to tell him of the accident. Not finding him in the sitting-room, she knocked at his bed-room door, and stood amazed to find that he—as she supposed—had gone to rest.

"Are you ill, Theo?" she asked, crossing to the bed.

Theodore groaned. "I had a row with Basil and he threw me out of the window."

Mara clapped her hands and her eyes sparkled. "How strong he is!" she said, which was not the sympathetic speech Theodore desired to hear. "Why did he fight you, Theo?"

"I asked Patricia to marry me and Basil cut up rough."

"No wonder!" said Mara disdainfully. "Why, any fool could have seen that Basil is in love with Patricia. He won't let anyone come near her. Oh!" she clapped her hands again and laughed gaily. "I should have liked to see you flying through the window."

"Little beast, you are," snarled Theodore. "I'm all aches and pains, and my eye is black where he struck me, damn him!"

"Would you like to see the doctor?"

"No. It's not worth sending to Hendle for the doctor. Besides, he'd only chatter. I know these local gossips."

"But the doctor is coming here. You had better let him examine you, Theo."

Theodore, from the shadow of the curtains, stared at the delicate face of his cousin. "Why is the doctor coming?"

"Oh, I quite forgot what I came up to tell you about," said Mara in a matter-of-fact tone. "Father has broken his leg."

"Broken his leg!" With a groan of pain Theodore hoisted himself on one elbow. "How did he do that?"

"The horse slipped coming down the winding road. Jarvis could not hold him up and they all fell over the bank. Father tried to get out, and broke his leg. But Jarvis and the horse are all right," ended Mara cheerfully.

"I don't believe you are sorry," said Theodore, angered at her indifference.

"I don't see what is the use of crying over spilt milk," replied the girl calmly. "If I cried my eyes out and tore my hair, it would do father no good."

"You might at least pretend to be sorry for him," growled Dane, sinking back.

"Well, I am. It's horrid to suffer pain. I'll tell him I'm sorry."

"If you tell him in that voice he'll box your ears," said Theodore grimly. "You don't display much sorrow for me, young lady."

"Because I don't feel any," said Mara coolly. "You brought it on yourself, for I told you that Basil loved Patricia. Besides, I don't like you."

"I'm not a Japanese. Eh?"

"No. You're not anything half so nice. Would you like Basil to come and see you?" she added maliciously. "I'm afraid Patricia can't, as she's attending to father."

"Oh, get out of the room and tell the cook to send up my dinner to me here as soon as she can. When I'm up again, I'll tell Uncle George everything."

"What do you mean?"

"I shall tell him that Basil and that infernal girl are engaged, and he'll give her notice to quit. And I shall tell him that you intend to run away with that beastly little Japanese."

"Oh, I haven't made up my mind what to do," said Mara, retreating to the door. "And if I decide to go with Akira, I shall do so, in spite of father or anyone else. But you won't tell, Theo; you're only too glad for me to go. You look like a great toad lying in bed."

Theodore caught up one of his slippers. "Will you clear out?"

"Mum! Mum! Mum!" jeered Mara, with an elfish laugh. "You can't do anything. And even if I do go, even if Basil does marry Patricia, you won't get Beckleigh. Mum! Mum! Mum!" And she closed the door just in time to escape the slipper which Theodore threw with all his strength.

The doctor duly arrived and put the Squire's leg in splints. The old man had recovered his senses, and considering his pain, behaved himself very well. The doctor approved of his patient's fine constitution and cheerfully said that he would soon be on his legs again. "You're not dead yet, sir," he remarked, when Colpster had been made comfortable for the night.

"I don't intend to die," said the Squire coolly. "Quite other plans are in my mind. But while I lie here I shan't have anything disturbed in the house. Patricia remember that. Should Akira's yacht arrive, you and Mara and Basil, together with Theodore and the servants, can go to his entertainment."

"Oh, we couldn't leave you like that, Mr. Colpster," said Patricia quickly.

"You can and you shall. I hate a lot of fuss." And then the doctor took Patricia out of the room to explain that the patient must be kept very quiet, else he would work himself into a fever.

"Humour him, Miss Carrol, humour him," said the doctor, as he took his leave. "To-morrow I shall come over and see him. Don't worry."

But Patricia did worry, not so much over the Squire, who was getting along fairly well considering his age, as over the fracas with Theodore. She dreaded lest he might speak to the Squire. "And then I should have to leave," said Patricia, much distressed.

"I don't see why, dearest," replied Basil, twining his brown fingers in her hair and wondering if God had ever created a more perfect woman.

The two were seated, as usual, in the smoking-room, deeming that the safest place, since Theodore since the quarrel had carefully avoided entering it. It was now three days since the accident, and since Basil had been driven to disclose his feelings. They had the house to themselves almost entirely, for Mara rarely troubled them. Theodore, although he had risen from his sick-bed with a more or less discoloured eye, kept to his own rooms, and did not even present himself at meals. He cherished a deep anger against Basil, and was sullen with Patricia as the original cause of his humiliation. The elder Dane had not a forgiving nature. Nor, indeed, did his brother feel inclined to welcome any advances. He was too much disgusted with Theodore to pardon him readily.

"I don't see why, dearest," said Basil again, and slipped his arm round Patricia's waist. "Uncle George can't kill us."

"He could turn me out of the house, and I have nowhere to go."

"There is no reason why he should turn you out. He loves you like a daughter. I'm certain of that."

Patricia sighed. "You are wrong, Basil. He loves me, certainly, but not like a daughter."

"What!" Basil scowled with a brow of thunder. "Does he dare to—"

"He dares nothing," interposed Patricia hurriedly, and placed her pink palm over his mouth to prevent further speech. "But I am certain that he wants to marry me."

"At his age. Ridiculous!"

"Why ridiculous? Older men than the Squire have married."

Basil's arm grew loose round her waist. "Do you admire him, then?"

"Of course. I both admire him and love him. Look how good he has been to me. I hadn't a shilling when he took me from The Home of Art."

"Patricia, do you mean to say—"

She stopped him again, and this time his mouth was closed with a kiss. "I mean to say that you are a dear old stupid thing, darling. I can't help myself if your uncle admires me."

"It shows his good taste. All the same—"

"All the same, I'm going to marry you, my dear. But we'll both be turned out of the house, I'm sure of that."

Basil hugged her again. "I knew you would never marry for money, dearest," he whispered.

"And if we are turned out we can live on my pay. I have to join the Mediterranean Fleet when my leave is up in a couple of months from now. My ship will be always at Malta—always calling in there, you know. We'll get a tiny flat, and you shall stay there when we're married."

"Oh, darling, that will be heaven!"

"It will be poverty," said Basil ruefully; "not what you're used to."

"My dear," she put her arm round his neck and looked into his hazel eyes, "what nonsense you talk. Since my father died I have been desperately hard up in every way, and if your uncle had not taken pity upon me, I really don't know what I should have done. I can cook and sew and look after a house splendidly. I'm just the wife for a hard-up sailor."

"You are, indeed," said Basil fervently, and would have embraced her, but that a knock came at the door. "Oh, hang it! here's Sims."

"I must attend to my duties," said Patricia, as Sims entered. "It's the butcher, of course. Go on, Sims. I'm coming to the kitchen." And Sims discreetly departed with a knowing smile, while Patricia remained for a last kiss.

The Beckleigh Hall servants saw very plainly what was taking place, and even although they were old and jealous retainers, did not resent it. Basil was an immense favourite with one and all, while Patricia during the short time she had acted as housekeeper had captured all hearts with great ease.

In the days which followed Patricia was kept closely in attendance on the Squire, since Mara would do nothing, and Colpster objected to being attended to wholly by the servants. She became rather pale and thin, which only made her the more adorable in Basil's eyes, and, unfortunately, in the eyes of her patient also. The Squire had made up his mind to ask Patricia to be his wife, notwithstanding the difference in their ages. Since Mara resolutely refused to marry either of her cousins, Colpster's pet scheme for the family to be re-established, now that the emerald had returned, fell to the ground. Failing this, he wished to make Miss Carrol his wife, and hoped that she would give him an heir in the direct line of descent. The more he thought of the scheme, the more he liked it, as he was extremely fond of Patricia, notwithstanding he had been so rude to her on the night when the Mikado Jewel had arrived so mysteriously. It never struck him that she might fall in love with a handsome young man like Basil.

Patricia saw how devoted the old man was becoming to her, and at times she was quite embarrassed by the youthful fire of his eyes. Colpster was now getting well rapidly, as it was a fortnight since the accident and the leg was mending. He remained, of course, in bed, and received various visits from the various members of his household. Theodore and Mara did not pay many visits, as the former knew that his uncle disliked him, and the latter was entirely without affection. The Squire never did expect much from Mara, as he looked upon her as weak-minded. She certainly was not, but her father never took the trouble to see what qualities she possessed. It was little wonder that Mara did not give affection, seeing that she never received any.

Mr. Colpster worried a great deal over the continued absence of Harry Pentreddle, and had frequently sent Jarvis to Hendle to inform him that he was wanted at the Hall. But Pentreddle had gone away from his lodgings without leaving any message behind, and no one—not even Isa Lee—knew where he was to be found. This absence and silence made the Squire quite uneasy, especially when he remembered that Harry had seen the emerald. He had stolen it before and—as the Squire, without any grounds to go upon, considered—he might steal it again. Haunted by this thought, Colpster gave Patricia the key of the safe and made her bring him the Jewel. He slept with it under his pillow and hugged it to his heart every day, talking meanwhile about the good luck it would bring.

"It has not brought any good luck yet, Mr. Colpster," said Patricia one evening, after her lovemaking with Basil in the smoking-room.

"How do you mean, my dear?"

"Well, in the first place, you have broken your leg; in the second, you have lost that lawsuit which—"

The Squire groaningly interrupted her: "Yes, I have lost it, worse luck, my dear. The land has gone, and my income will be diminished to eight hundred. Yes, I admit that bad luck. And the weather is really terrible too," he added, looking at the streaming window-pane. "It so rarely rains here, yet it has poured ever since my accident."

"And before then," Patricia reminded him. "The rain, by making the road slippery, caused your accident. If I were you, Mr. Colpster, I would send back the jewel to Japan with Count Akira. He is quite right: the good luck it brought to your family centuries ago has changed to bad."

"How can you believe in such rubbish!" groaned the Squire, hugging his gem.

"You believe in it," said Miss Carrol, wondering at his want of logic, "or you would let the Mikado Jewel go."

"The luck will change now," insisted Colpster, trying to persuade himself into a kindly belief. "Everything will come right."

"I hope so," said Patricia, poking the bedroom fire, before which she was kneeling. "You must write and tell me if it does."

The Squire sat up in bed and gasped. "Write and tell you?"

"Yes. I am going away."

"Nonsense! Why should you go away?"

"Mr. Colpster," said Patricia, who had brought the conversation round to this point that she might thoroughly explain herself, "you have been very good to me, and I have been very happy here. But your nephew Theodore has been rude to me; in fact, he has insulted me; so I cannot remain under the same roof with him."

"What?" the Squire's scanty hair bristled and he trembled with rage. "Has that dog of a Theodore been rude? He shall leave my house at once."

"No. That would not be fair. He is your nephew. I shall go."

"I shan't let you go, child. I love you too much to let you go. How did he insult you—what did he say? Tell me and I'll—I'll—" Rage choked his further utterance, and he sank back on his pillows.

His nurse came forward and smoothed the bedclothes. "Don't worry over the matter, Mr. Colpster. It's not worth it."

"It's worth everything when you want to leave. How did Theodore insult you?"

Patricia looked down and sketched out figures with the tip of her bronze shoe. "He is angry because I am engaged to Basil."

Colpster flung himself forward and caught her wrist. His sunken eyes filled with angry fire. "You are not engaged to Basil?" he said fiercely.

"But I am. Leave go my wrist, Mr. Colpster, or I shall go away at once."

He still held her tightly. "You shan't marry Basil. You shall marry me."

Patricia was greatly indebted to the old man, as she had admitted, and was sorry for his misplaced passion. But she was also a woman, with a woman's feeling, and did not intend to allow him to dictate to her. With a dexterous twist, she freed herself from his grip and retreated to a safe distance. "If you behave like this, I shall leave the room and never enter it again," she exclaimed, angry at his want of self-control.

The threat brought the Squire to his knees. "No! no! Don't go!" he cried in piteous tones. "I can't live without you. I wish to marry you. See, Patricia, dear, I shall settle Beckleigh on you, and when the emerald brings back the good luck you shall—"

"The emerald will only bring bad luck," said Patricia, interrupting coldly. "And if you had millions I would not marry you. I love you as a daughter, and I thought that you loved me in the same way. Basil and I are engaged and intend to get married in a few months."

"He has no money," wailed the Squire, clutching the sheets; "no money."

"I don't care. He is the man I love."

"He has no right to ask you to marry him."

"If he had not asked me, Mr. Colpster, I believe I should have asked him," was the girl's quick answer. "Can't you understand that he is the only man in the world for me? If you don't, then the sooner I leave this house the better. You have no right to dictate to me, and I won't allow it."

"I'll cut Basil out of my will. I shall leave the property to Theodore."

"That is a matter for your own consideration," said Patricia coldly. "Now it's time for your beef-tea, and I must go and get it."

"I shan't take it," cried the Squire childishly.

"Mr. Colpster, for a man of your years you are very silly."

"My years—my years; you reproach me with those!"

"I reproach you with nothing," said Miss Carrol, tired of the futile argument. "Can't you see that if you go on like this I must leave?"

"No, don't," he implored, with wild eyes. "I'll be good."

"Very well," she said, in a matter-of-fact tone. "Now I shall get your beef-tea," and for that purpose she left the room.

Left alone, Mr. Colpster whimpered a little. He was old, he was sick, and he was very sorry for himself. He had sought to woo a girl who was young enough to be his daughter, and his wooing had taken the fashion of trying to bribe her with house and land and money. To this insult she had retorted by showing him the mother that is hidden in every woman, married or unmarried. He felt like a naughty boy who had been put in the corner, and at his age he did not like the new experience. He could have kicked himself for having gone on his knees to be whipped, for that was what it amounted to. In the darkness—it was evening, and there was no light in the big bed-room save that of the fire—he flushed and burned with shame. How, indeed, could she, having found her mate in a young man of her own age, beautiful and ardent as she was, be expected to accept his Philistine offer of beeves and land?

The Squire, with all his oddities, was a gentleman, and as he came from a brave race he was a man. His age, his fantasy about refounding the family, his sickness, had all landed him in this slough. It behoved him, if he wished ever again to look his ancestors' portraits in the face, to get out of the quagmire and reassert his manhood as well as his good breeding. Patricia should marry Basil and become his niece-in-law. Mara could be given an income to indulge in her fantasies, and he could live at Beckleigh with Mr. and Mrs. Colpster, which was to be the married name of the young couple. In the middle of these visions, Patricia returned with the beef-tea and a lamp. The naughty boy came out of his corner to beg pardon.

"My dear," he said, in an apologetic voice, "I'm an old fool."

"Oh, no," said Patricia kindly; "you are just one who has cried for the moon."

"I give the moon to Basil," said the Squire, holding out his hand. "And he will be my heir. Forgive me."

"Willingly," said Miss Carrol, and they shook hands gravely.

"But I agree with you," sighed Colpster, ending the scene; "the jewel has brought bad luck."

CHAPTER XVIII

PLEASURE

Count Akira did not return so soon to Beckleigh as he had promised, for he wrote that official business still detained him in London. But during the third week after his departure, his yacht, *The Miko*, steamed into the fairy bay and cast anchor a quarter of a mile off shore. It was Basil who espied her first immediately after breakfast, and he ran up a flag on the pole erected on the lawn. *The Miko* dipped her ensign in reply, and shortly a boat put off, which doubtless was bringing Akira on his return visit. Basil walked down to the beach to meet him.

There was a tiny pier on the right of the beach which ran into deep water, and the boat made for this. Basil, with his hands in his pockets, stared at the yacht. She was a graceful boat of some two thousand tons, and her hull was painted white while her one funnel was darkly blue. The chrysanthemum flag of Japan streamed from one of her mast-heads, and she looked a singularly beautiful object as she rocked on the blue waters of the bay. Basil judged from her lines that she was swift. But he had little time to take in much, as the boat which approached at a furious pace was a small steam launch. She came alongside the pier in a few minutes.

"And how is my good friend Dane?" asked Akira, hoisting himself up like a monkey and removing his cap. "You see, I am here as promised."

They shook hands, and Basil thought that Akira looked very workmanlike in his smart blue yachting dress. A wiry brown lithe little man was the Japanese, keen-eyed and alert. The most casual observer could see that, if necessary, he could make himself very disagreeable.

"I am glad to see you again, Akira," said Basil; "come up to the house."

The Count gave a few directions to the officer in charge of the launch and then placed himself at his friend's disposal. "All are well in your family, I hope?" he remarked, as they strolled up through the woods.

"My uncle has broken his leg, I regret to say."

"Indeed!" Akira looked shocked. "I am very sorry. How did it happen?"

Basil gave him a hasty description of the accident. "In fact, Akira," he added, with a puzzled look, "since you went away everything has gone wrong."

"What do you mean?" asked the Japanese quietly, and his face became entirely devoid of emotion.

"What I say. My uncle broke his leg and has lost a lawsuit, which he hoped to gain. Theodore and I have quarrelled, and the house is as dull as tombs."

"I hope Miss Carrol is not dull?" observed Akira politely.

Dane turned swiftly to observe the expression of the little man's face. He had said more than he meant to say on the impulse of the moment, and now that he had said so much, he deliberately said more. Apparently Akira, who was very sharp, had noted, during his visit, symptoms of lovemaking. It was just as well to let him know how matters stood, for, after all, the Japanese was not a bad little fellow. "Miss Carrol is engaged to marry me," said Basil, drawing a deep breath.

"I congratulate you, but I am not surprised. I saw much when I was here on my visit"—he paused; then went on shrewdly, "I do not wonder that you have had a quarrel with your brother."

"Never mind that, Akira," said Basil hastily; "I really did not intend to tell you that. It slipped out."

Akira nodded. "You must permit me to send you and Miss Carrol a present from my own country when I reach it," he remarked, changing the subject.

"It is very good of you. I am sure Miss Carrol will be delighted. When do you sail for the East?"

"To-morrow. I have secured an excellent appointment at Tokio."

"It is very good of you to anchor here, and delay your journey," said Basil cordially; and Akira gave a little laugh as the young man spoke.

"Oh, I had a reason," he said coolly. "I never do anything without a reason, Dane. I shall tell my reason to Mr. Colpster, if he is to be seen."

"Oh, yes. He is out of bed, although he has not yet left his room. The leg is mending splendidly, and he lies mostly on the sofa in his bedroom. I am sure he will be delighted to see you."

"And Miss Mara? Will she be delighted?"

Basil again gave a side glance, but was far from suspecting why the remark had been made. "Don't you make her dance any more," said Dane, nervously.

"No, I promise you that I won't do that," answered Akira, his face again becoming so unemotional that Basil could not tell what he was thinking about; "but you have not answered my question."

"Here is Mara to answer for herself," said Dane, and he spoke truly, for as they advanced towards the front door of the house, it opened suddenly and Mara flew out with sparkling eyes.

"Count Akira. I am so glad to see you again. Is that your boat? What a nice boat she is. When did you arrive and what are—"

"Mara, Mara, Mara!" remonstrated Basil laughing, "how can the man answer so many questions all at once?"

"I would need Gargantua's mouth as your Shakespeare says," observed Akira with a quiet smile, and his eyes also sparkled at the sight of the girl.

"Come inside, Akira, and I will tell Miss Carrol," said Dane hospitably.

He stepped into the house, but Akira did not follow immediately. He lingered behind with Mara, and, after a glance at the many windows of the house, he gave her hand a friendly shake. But his words were warmer than his gesture, for they were meant for Mara's private ear, while the handshake was for the benefit of any onlooker.

"I have come, you see. You are glad?" and his black eyes looked volumes.

Mara nodded, and from being a pale lily became a dewy rose. "Of course. Did I not promise to love you for seven lives?"

"Your father will not understand that," said Akira dryly.

Mara started. "Will you tell him?" she asked anxiously.

The Count bowed stiffly. "I am a Japanese gentleman," he said in cool and high-bred tones, "and so I can do nothing against my honour. I cannot take you with me unless your father consents."

"But he will not," breathed Mara, becoming pale with emotion.

"He will. Already this morning he has received a long letter from me, which I sent from London. It explains how I love you, and asks for your hand."

"But you are not of my religion!" whispered Mara distressed; "he may object to that."

"I think not, as your father, from what I saw, is of no particular religion himself. I have a special license in my pocket. We can be married to-day in your own church and by your own priest. When we reach Japan we can be married according to Shinto rites."

"But your family?"

"I have my uncle in London. On hearing all about you, he has agreed. There will be no trouble with my family."

Mara, still nervous, would have asked further questions and would have put forward further objections, but that Patricia made her appearance at the door. She looked singularly beautiful, although she was not so in Akira's eyes. He preferred the small features and colourless looks of Mara. Patricia's face was too boldly cut and too highly coloured to be approved of by an Oriental.

"How are you, Count?" said Miss Carrol, shaking hands.

"Very well; and you? But I need not ask, Miss Carrol." Akira laughed in a very sympathetic way for him. "Dane has told me."

"Oh!" Patricia blushed.

"I wish you all happiness, and may you be united for seven lives."

"What does that mean?"

"I know! I know!" cried Mara, clapping her hands and jumping; "in Japan we all believe in reincarnation, and lovers promise each other to love during seven earth-seasons."

"But you are not a Japanese, Mara," said Patricia, wondering that the girl should so boldly couple herself with Akira.

"Yes, I am," Mara asserted decidedly; "my body is English, but my soul is Japanese. I know now that I was a Miko in the Temple of Kitzuki three hundred years ago, and that I loved him," she pointed to Akira, who smiled assentingly.

"Oh, what nonsense!" said Miss Carrol, rather crossly; "it is your imagination, you silly child!" and then, before Mara could contradict her, she turned to the Count. "Mr. Colpster wants to see you," she remarked. "Will you follow me?"

"I want to come also," said Mara; and grasping Akira's hand she went into the house. They looked at one another adoringly and smiled.

At the bedroom door Patricia left them, as the Squire had intimated that he wished to see Akira privately. Miss Carrol therefore desired to take Mara downstairs with her, but the girl refused to go. "I have to speak to my father also," she declared obstinately, "and I must do so while the Count is present."

"As you please," replied Miss Carrol, finding it impossible to move the girl, and knowing Mara's obstinate disposition of old, "you will find me in the library when you come down."

"With Basil!" cried out Mara mischievously; and Patricia looked back to give a smiling nod. Then the two entered the bedroom.

Mr. Colpster was lying on the sofa near a large fire, wrapped in his dressing-gown, and looked thin, since his illness had rather pulled him down. He also appeared to be somewhat cross, and shook at Akira several sheets of blue paper with an angry air.

"I received your letter this morning," he said sharply, and without greeting his visitor in any way.

"That is good," said Akira politely, "it will save me the trouble of an explanation, Mr. Colpster."

"I think not," growled the Squire. "I must know more, and in any case I do not intend to consent."

"Oh, father, you must!" cried Mara, indignantly.

"Go down stairs, child," said her father quickly; "I wish to speak alone with this—this gentleman."

But Mara stood her ground. "What the Count has to say concerns me," she declared obstinately. "I shan't go!"

Colpster stormed vainly, while Akira looked on passively. But nothing would move Mara from the position which she had taken up. She simply laughed at her father, and in the end he had to yield a grudging consent to her remaining in the room.

"And now, sir," he said, when this was settled and again shaking the sheets of blue paper at Akira. "I understand from this that you wish to marry my daughter Mara. Of course, it is quite impossible!"

"Why?" asked Akira calmly, and holding Mara's hand.

"Because you are not an Englishman," spluttered the Squire.

"If I was a Frenchman, or a German, you would not object!" retorted the Count coolly. "Why not say that it is because I am not a European!"

"Very good then, I say it. You are of the yellow race, and Mara is of the white. Marriage between you is ridiculous."

"I don't think so, sir."

Mara looked at her father disdainfully. "I don't know why you talk so," she said with a shrug. "I intend to marry Count Akira to-day, and go away with him to-morrow, to Japan in our yacht."

"Our yacht, indeed!" echoed the Squire angrily, and then stared at the pale obstinate face of his daughter, framed in a nimbus of feathery golden hair. "Oh you are a minx! You never loved me!"

"I can't help that," said Mara doggedly; "I never loved anyone until I met with the Count. I couldn't understand myself until I danced that night in the drawing-room. Danced the Miko-kagura."

"What is that? What is she talking about?" Colpster turned to Akira.

The Count explained politely. "When I came here, sir, I noticed that Miss Colpster was greatly interested in what I had to say about my own country. And often, when I told her of things, she said that she remembered them."

"How could that be when she has never been out of England?"

"That is what puzzled me, until I, one night—by way of an experiment and to convince myself—placed on the fire some incense used in the Temple of Kitzuki, and played on a flute the music of the Miko-kagura, which is a holy dance. Miss Colpster rose and performed it perfectly. Then all the past came back to her, as she told me later."

"What past?" demanded the Squire, much bewildered.

"The past of her life in Japan, three hundred years ago."

"Oh, that is rubbish!"

"It is true!" cried Mara in a thrilling voice, and raised her arms. "I was a Miko of the Kitzuki Temple three hundred years ago. That is why I remembered about the emerald, when Theodore sent me into a trance. And for the same reason I could describe the shrine. I loved the Count then, when we wore other bodies, and promised to love him for seven lives. This time I have been born in England, but he has come for me here, and I am going with him to my native land."

"Oh, you are quite mad!" said Colpster furiously.

"Mad or sane, let me marry her, Mr. Colpster!" pleaded Akira. "From my letter you can see that I am going to occupy an excellent official position at Tokio, and that I am of very high rank in Japan, besides being wealthy. I love your daughter, because, I truly believe—strange as it may seem to you—that we loved three hundred years ago. I have a special license in my pocket, and if you consent we can go to your church this day and get married according to your religion. When we reach Japan we shall be married according to mine. Do you consent?"

"No! It's ridiculous! You have only known Mara a few weeks."

"I have loved her for three hundred years!" insisted Akira, smiling.

"I don't believe in that rubbish."

Mara seized her lover's hand. "I am tired of all this," she said in her old fashion, "why can't you leave me alone. I marry the Count!"

Colpster saw that, whether he gave his consent or not, she would certainly do so. And, after all, as he asked himself, what did it matter? Mara had never displayed any affection for any single person, since she had always lived in a dream-world of her own. Now that he had decided to leave the property to Basil and Patricia on condition that they assumed the name of Colpster, Mara was unnecessary. Finally, it was certain that she would be happier in Japan than in England, since there was evidently no future for her in the West. The Squire did not believe in reincarnation. All the same, he admitted that Mara's many oddities suggested that she was a soul born out of time and place. But that his daughter should marry one of the yellow race offended the old man's pride. He was just about to open his mouth and refuse permission again when

Akira spoke blandly.

"If you consent," said Akira, "I will send you someone who can tell you who killed your housekeeper."

"How do you know?" asked Colpster, startled.

"I have been making inquiries in town. Consent, and you shall know all."

"And consent," said Mara, stepping up to her father and bending to whisper in his ear, "or I shall tell the Count that you have the emerald."

Colpster turned white. "How do you know?" he whispered back.

"I saw you slip it under your pillow one day. It is there now. If you don't let me marry the Count he shall take it from you now."

The Squire breathed heavily and dark circles appeared under his sunken eyes as Mara stepped back to stand beside her lover. He knew that his daughter did not love him, or anyone else, but he had never believed she would have spoken as she had done. Undoubtedly the theory of reincarnation was a correct one. She was an Eastern soul in a Western body. "I consent to the marriage," he said in cold, dry hard tones. "You can go to the church on the moor and get the affair settled. I cannot come myself, but Basil and Patricia can go with you. Mara, you had better tell your maid to pack your clothes, since you leave to-morrow."

"Everything is already packed," said Mara, turning at the door and looking cool and white and more shadowy than ever. "I shall come and say good-bye."

"No, don't!" shuddered the Squire, as she went out. "You go also, Akira."

The Count smiled blandly and walked to the door. "I shall keep my promise, sir, and to-night you will receive one who will be able to tell you the whole truth of what has puzzled you for so long."

When Akira disappeared, the Squire tore up the blue letter and threw the pieces into the fire. He had done with Mara: she was no longer any daughter of his. And, indeed, she never had been. Always cold: always indifferent: a very shadow of what a daughter should have been. He was well rid of her, this traitress, who would have surrendered the emerald. Colpster felt under his sofa pillow and pulled out the gem. It was wrapped in paper, and he unfolded this to gaze at it. A knock at the door made him hastily smuggle it away again. Basil entered immediately and looked worried.

"Is it true, uncle, that Akira and Mara are to be married?" he asked abruptly.

"Quite true. Akira has brought down a special license. Go with Patricia and see that all is shipshape."

"But, Uncle George, surely you don't want Mara to marry a Japanese?"

"What does it matter? Whether I give my consent or not, Mara will do what she wants to do. There is some rubbish about reincarnation between them— about loving for seven lives, or for three hundred years. I don't understand these things. But what I do understand," cried Colpster with cold fury, raising himself on his elbow, "is that Mara does not love me, and that I intend to cut her out of my will. Send Jarvis to Hendle and tell Curtis the lawyer to come over at once. You will have the property, Basil, and then can marry Patricia. Theodore can go away. I won't have him in the house after the way he has insulted your future wife. As to Mara, she can go to the devil! or to Japan. I never wish to set eyes on her again!"

"But what has she done?" asked Basil, bewildered.

The Squire could have told him, but did not intend to, since that would mean revealing that the Mikado Jewel was under the sofa pillow. "Never mind; I am well rid of her, and so are you, and so are we all. Only see that this Japanese marries her properly."

Dane argued, implored and stormed, but all to no purpose. His uncle vowed that if Mara remained, he would turn her penniless from the house, and Basil was sufficiently acquainted with his obstinate character to be certain that he would keep his word. Under the circumstances it seemed reasonable that Mara should lie on the bed she had made and the young man, making the best of a bad job, went away to get Patricia. He would act as Akira's best man, and Patricia could follow Mara as her solitary bridesmaid. Whatever might be the outcome of this sudden arrangement, Basil determined to see that the marriage was legal. And when he saw the joy and delight of Mara and the lover-like attentions of Akira, he began to think that his uncle had acted for the best. In the face of Mara's obstinacy, nothing else could be done, although Basil, being a true Englishman, did not relish the Japanese as a cousin-in-law. All the same, he approved of Akira's fine qualities, and knew that from a worldly point of view Mara was making a brilliant match.

Obeying instructions, he sent Jarvis for the Hendle lawyer, when, with the prospective bride and bridegroom, he and Patricia were on their way to the quaint old church on the moor, where so many Colpsters were buried. The clergyman could not disobey a special license, so that was all right, and he hoped to return later with the pair married. Indeed, had Basil possessed a special license himself, he also would have stood before the altar with Patricia, but such things were far beyond the means of a poor lieutenant of His Majesty's Navy.

Meanwhile, the Squire received Curtis and made a new will, which made no mention of Mara and Theodore, but left the entire Colpster estates to Basil, provided that he took the family name and married Patricia Carrol. When the testament had been duly signed, sealed and delivered, the Squire decided to keep it in his possession until the morrow, so that he could show it to the young couple. Curtis wished to take it with him, but Colpster refused, and finally departed without even a copy of the document. However, he promised to call the next day and take it with him for safety. Just as the lawyer departed, Theodore entered the bedroom.

"What's all this about?" he asked sharply.

His uncle looked at him with a frown. "What do you mean entering my room without knocking?" he demanded in his turn.

"I beg your pardon," said Theodore with forced politeness, "but everything seems at sixes and sevens since that infernal yacht came in. All the servants are getting themselves ready to go to the entertainment to-night, and I can't get anyone to answer my bell."

"Wait until Miss Carrol returns and she will see to things," said Colpster indifferently. "I can't be bothered."

"Where is Miss Carrol? I have been in my room all day, and when I came down I couldn't find anyone."

"Basil and Patricia have gone to attend the marriage of Mara and Akira."

Theodore stepped back and then stepped forward. He could scarcely believe his ears. "Have you allowed that?" he asked in consternation.

"Yes. Akira is a good match, and Mara loves him."

"But he's a Japanese?"

"What does that matter?"

"I don't believe in marriages between members of different races."

Colpster looked at him cynically. "What the devil does it matter what you believe! I agreed to the marriage for two, or rather, for three reasons. In the first place, Mara would have married in any case had I not consented. In the second, she threatened, if I did not agree, to tell Akira about the emerald, which he would then have taken from me. In the third place, Akira said that if I agreed, he would send someone to-night to tell me all about the murder of Martha and reveal the name of the person who did it."

"It was the priest with the scar on his cheek who did it," said Theodore in vigorous tones. "Will he—Akira that is—send him?"

"I don't know. Don't bother me!" said the Squire, turning over on his pillows. "I'll see him when you are all out of the house."

"I'm not going to that infernal entertainment," said Theodore snappishly, "as I don't approve of Mara marrying that yellow man. I shall stay here and listen to what this emissary of Akira's has to say."

"Oh, do what you like; do what you like; only don't bother me!" said Colpster again, and very sharply. "Clear out, please!"

"All right!" Theodore went towards the door; "only I want to say one thing. Curtis has been here. Have you cut Mara out of your will?"

"Yes; although it is no business of yours. When she marries Akira, she will have plenty of money."

"Well, then, I suppose," said Theodore, shooting his arrow, "you know that Patricia and Basil are engaged?"

"Yes, I am aware of that, and I wish them joy."

"Aren't you angry, uncle?" Theodore was astounded.

"No. Why should I be? I like Patricia."

"I fancied you loved her and wished to marry her."

Colpster rolled over and glared fiercely. He was annoyed that his secret should have been discovered by Theodore, of all people, since he hated him so ardently. "I never did wish to marry Patricia," he said furiously, and telling a smooth lie. "I look upon her as a daughter. I have always looked upon her as a daughter. When Basil told me that she had consented to be his wife, I was delighted. I am delighted."

"Oh!" growled Theodore, wincing and thrusting his hands deep into his pockets; "so you brought Curtis over to alter your will!"

"Yes! I have left everything to Basil and Patricia!"

"What about me?" Theodore by this time was ghastly pale.

"Oh, you can go to the devil!" said his uncle carelessly. "You insulted Miss Carrol, so I pay you out. The will cutting you off is here," he patted his pocket.

Before Theodore could express the rage which consumed him, there came the sound of advancing feet and the laughter of happy people. The door was suddenly thrown open by Basil, and Patricia entered, followed by the bridegroom and the bride, arm-in-arm English fashion.

"Allow me," said Patricia gaily, and in a ringing voice, "to present to you, Mr.

Colpster, the Count and Countess Akira."

CHAPTER XIX

THE TRUTH

With the early darkness of February came a spectacle to delight and astonish the home-staying folk of Beckleigh. Suddenly at eight o'clock, when the entire household were gathered on the beach for transport in the launch to the yacht, *The Miko* became outlined in coloured fire. Radiant and weird against the gloom in red and blue and yellow and green, she flashed into being like a spectral Flying Dutchman. Never before had such a sight been seen in that quiet Devonshire bay, and loudly sounded the amazed voices of the servants, praising the gorgeous illumination. It was like magic to them, and several were heard to express a hope that the devil was not on board the ship of light. However, the Japanese officer in charge of the launch which puffed up spoke sufficient English to reassure them, and they all embarked for an evening's revelry.

The bride and bridegroom, with the two who had witnessed the marriage, had long since gone on board. Mara did not intend to set foot on English soil again, and had taken a final leave of her father. Colpster had not been unkind, although his farewell had been rather cold. But then the newly-made Countess Akira was cold herself and rarely demonstrative, so she did not mind in the least. In fact, Patricia, being a warmhearted Irish girl, reproved her for the coolness with which she took leave both of her parent and of her childhood's home.

"Oh, nonsense!" said Mara with her usual cry. "I wish you'd leave me alone, Patricia. I can't make a fuss when I don't feel the least sorry to go away."

"But surely, Mara, you are sad. You leave your home, your father, your native land, for ever it may be."

"Certainly for ever. And now that I know all about the past, now that I am the Count's wife, I don't look upon England as my native land."

"Mara, you surely do not really believe that you lived at Kitzuki as a priestess centuries ago?" said Patricia, shaking her head.

"I am sure that I did. I was a Miko, which means The Darling of the Gods."

"Did Count Akira tell you that translation?"

"No; I remembered it. I spoke Japanese ages ago. I am beginning to recollect all manner of things. And Akira gave me a book of Lafcadio Hearn's, which contains a description of a Miko-kagura. It is exactly what I danced on that evening, and is precisely what I did when I was at the Temple."

Patricia asked no more questions. The problem was beyond her. She saw that Mara firmly believed in reincarnation, and on that belief based her sudden marriage with Akira. The little man had known her only for a few weeks, and in the ordinary course of things would not have fallen in love with her so rapidly, if indeed at all, seeing that he was East, while she was West. Therefore, it really seemed as if what Mara believed was true, and that she had met her husband before in the Province of Izumo. In no other way could the puzzled Patricia account for the unexpected which had happened so quickly.

And she agreed with Basil that it was just as well that Mara had obtained her heart's desire in this strange way. Had she not met Akira, she would have gone on living in an unhealthy dreamland, and perhaps as she grew older would have lost her reason. But now she seemed to be a different girl as her formerly pale face was rosy with colour; she looked less shadowy, and strangest of all, she took a profound interest in the entertainments provided for the Beckleigh servants. This was particularly odd, for Mara never, when she was single, troubled about pleasures of any kind, and certainly took no interest in the likes or dislikes of other people. But over this revelry she presided like a queen, and for the first time in her strange life she appeared to be thoroughly happy.

"After all," said Patricia, to her lover who stood by her, while a sailor was singing some legend to the music of the biwa, "the Count is a very charming and highly-bred man."

"Oh, yes," assented Basil heartily, for having taken everything into consideration, he now quite approved of the turn affairs had taken. "He is one of the best is Akira. As good and clever a chap as ever lived. If you do want courtesy and good breeding, you can find them to perfection in a Japanese gentleman. Mara is lucky to get such a husband, considering what a strange nature she has."

"It is that very nature which has brought such a husband to her," said Patricia. "I hope and trust and pray she will be happy."

"I think so. Akira adores her. Strange when he is East and she is West."

Patricia shook her head. "Mara would never admit that, my dear. Only her body is West according to her; her soul is Eastern."

"Well," remarked Basil, looking somewhat puzzled, "I don't know much about this occult rubbish of which we have had so much lately, but I should think that the soul was of no country at all. It comes on the stage of the world dressed as a native of different countries just as it is told."

"As its Karma calls it."

"What the deuce is Karma?"

"The accumulated result of good and evil and—"

"Look here, Patricia!" interrupted the young man, slipping his arm within her own. "I have had enough of this jargon and occult rubbish. I half believe in it, and I half don't. At all events, I don't think it is healthy for either you or I to indulge in such things. Let us live as two healthy people, my darling, as we have plenty of work to do in this world before we leave it. You agree, don't you?"

"Of course I do. I should agree if you proposed to cut off my head."

"I prefer to leave it on your shoulders," laughed Basil, and slyly stole a kiss, for they were standing in the shadow. "Look at old Sims, how amazed he is at those Japanese dresses!"

They pressed forward to look. Some of the sailors were arrayed as samurai in antique armour of the Middle Ages of Japan, and were fighting with huge swords. All round flashed the many-coloured lights, and the little group of Devonshire folk sat and stood in their homely dresses, looking delightedly at the fairyland which had been brought before their astonished eyes. The dresses, the music, the unusual food, and the brown faces of the foreign sailors, fascinated them greatly. And, indeed, the spectacle was as pleasant to Basil and Patricia as to them, in spite of the fact that they knew more of the world beyond Beckleigh. As to Mara, she was flushed with enjoyment and so deeply interested in the brilliant spectacle before her that she did not notice the absence of her husband.

But he had slipped away silently, and was standing at the stern of the yacht, speaking softly to an Englishman. The light of a near lantern would have shown anyone who knew him that the man was Harry Pentreddle, and he was just getting ready to lower himself by a rope into a rowing boat, which was fastened alongside.

"You can get ashore in that," whispered Akira softly; "and, later, I shall send the launch to fetch you."

154

"I can row back again," protested Pentreddle. "You won't be able to get away quick enough," said Akira mysteriously.

"Away from what?"

"Never mind. Do what I told you to do, and bring me what I told you to bring me. Obey my instructions implicitly, or there may be danger."

"But I don't understand, sir."

"You understand enough for my purpose," broke in the Japanese smooth voice; "and you know why I ask you to go ashore to the Hall to-night."

"Yes, I know," said Harry grimly, and spat on his hands as he prepared to grasp the rope.

"You needn't go unless you like. I can go myself. Well?"

For answer Pentreddle clambered over the taffrail and swung himself by the rope into the small craft below. As he took the oars, Akira's voice was heard again even softer than before as he leaned over the side. "The launch will be waiting for you at the pier when you come out," he said. "Lose no time."

The boat shot away into the gloom, while Harry Pentreddle wondered why the little man was so insistent about his getting away quickly from the Hall, after what had to be done was accomplished. However, the sailor being aware of certain facts, was prepared to obey implicitly, and rowed hard to reach the land. There was no time to be lost, as the entertainment would not last for ever, and it was necessary that Harry should come back to *The Miko* before those on board returned to Beckleigh Hall.

It was a calm night, but cloudy and threatening. The rain of the last few weeks had stopped, and fine weather prevailed. But no stars were visible, and the moon was veiled heavily. As Pentreddle beached his boat near the pier, and dug her anchor into the damp sand, he felt a breath of wind, and looked into the semi-gloom to see that already white crests were forming on the waves. Afar off, *The Miko* looked like a fairy ship with her coloured lights glittering against the darkness. The wind was distinctly rising, as Pentreddle felt when he passed up the path to the Hall, and on glancing overhead he noted that the clouds were beginning to move. Already a few stars were revealed, and there was an occasional glimpse of a haggard moon lying on her back.

"It's going to be a nasty night," said the sailor. "Bad for those folk on board that yacht. They'll be sea-sick."

He chuckled, although he felt far from merry. The errand he was on was too serious to be treated lightly, and he was even nervous as to what would be the outcome of the same. But he strode on resolutely, nevertheless, and was soon standing at the front door of the Hall. The building was in darkness save for one window on the second storey near the angle of the wall. Pentreddle, acquainted with the building ever since he could walk, knew very well that this was one of the windows of the Squire's bedroom; on the other side of the wall there were two more. For a moment Pentreddle looked up at the light and noted that the tough arms of the ancient ivy grew up to the very sill of the window, and afforded a ladder to anyone who wished to descend in that way. He smiled grimly when he recalled this fact, which might be useful, and then opened the door.

It had not been locked, as there were no robbers at Beckleigh, and bolts and bars were not attended to very particularly. The hall should have had the central lamp lighted, but Pentreddle found the place entirely dark. He did not mind this, as he knew every inch of the way up to Squire Colpster's bedroom. There he would find the old gentleman, and he presumed that Mr. Dane—who had refused to come to the entertainment on *The Miko*—would be in his rooms at the back of the house. He walked softly up the stairs, as he did not wish to arouse Theodore, for reasons which he intended to impart to the old Squire.

Feeling his way in the darkness along the walls, and wishing that he had brought a lantern, Pentreddle gained the second storey and walked along the corridor towards the line of light which shone from under the bedroom door. On arriving immediately outside, he paused for a moment to listen. A sound of struggling struck his ear, and he became aware with a thrill that there was a fight going on between uncle and nephew. Considering Colpster's age this was unfair, so Pentreddle dashed open the door and shot into the room intent upon taking side with the weaker party.

"What's all this?" he shouted.

"Help, Harry, help! He's strangling me!" gasped Colpster, recognizing the voice. "Oh! help me! Help!"

Pentreddle did not waste any time in words. He darted forward, and gripping the shoulders of Theodore, who was holding his uncle down on the floor, he spun him to one side. The Squire, struggling to his feet, clawed at the sofa to rise, on seeing which Dane, who was crazy with rage, tried to slip past the sailor and tackle the old man again.

"Ah! would you?" cried Harry, who hated Theodore fervently, as, indeed, everyone did. "I'll show you," and in a moment his sinewy arms were round the big man and they wrestled desperately.

Theodore was ghastly white and his blue eyes blazed with unholy fire, as between closed teeth he cursed his antagonist. Huge as he was, the man had only that strength which comes with furious anger. He was flabby, and not at all muscular, since he never exercised himself in any way. Half on the floor and half on the pillows of the sofa, Colpster watched the fight with breathless interest, grasping in his hands a large envelope. The two men swayed and swung round the apartment, and Theodore fought like a tiger. But the wiry sailor was too much for him, and gradually Dane was forced to the floor where he lay struggling and kicking, with Pentreddle kneeling on his big chest. Harry hailed the half-fainting old man.

"Pull down that curtain cord near you, Squire, and throw it over," he panted.

Dane gurgled and tried to curse, but could not, as Pentreddle's brown hands gripped his fat throat. Colpster struggled across to the window and took with feeble hands the silken rope which draped the curtains on one side at no great height from the floor. He crawled back with it to Harry, who at once proceeded to bind Theodore's arms behind his back, and rolled him over for this purpose. Dane was so sick and breathless with the struggle and in such a bad condition for holding his own, that he had to submit.

"Now the other rope, Squire," commanded Harry, but seeing that the old man's strength had given out, he darted across himself to the window and speedily brought back what he required. In a few minutes Theodore, trussed like a fowl, was lying on the floor, face uppermost, and regained his breath sufficiently to curse.

"I'll have you arrested for this, Pentreddle," he said viciously.

Harry deigned no reply, as he had to attend to Colpster. On a small table near the bed was a decanter of port, with some glasses and a dish of biscuits. The sailor poured out a glass of the generous vintage, and held it to the Squire's lips. He drank it eagerly and demanded more. A second glass brought the colour back into his wan cheeks, and the light of life into his sunken eyes. Shortly he was able to sit up on the sofa and Harry arranged the pillows at his back. But all the time Colpster held on to the large envelope. Also, he fished about feebly under the pillow and brought out the Mikado Jewel.

"Thank heaven!" panted the old man feebly; "he has got neither."

"I'll get them yet, you old beast," growled Theodore, trying to break his bonds, but vainly. "I'll have that will and burn it. I'll get the emerald and sell it. Curse you! And you too, Pentreddle! What the devil do you mean binding me in this way?"

"I'll explain that to you later, sir," retorted Pentreddle, wiping his brow, and taking a glass of port himself. "With your permission, Squire," he said in a polite tone when he drank it.

"You arrived just in time," said the Squire, in stronger tones. "That wicked wretch would have killed me."

"Why?" asked Pentreddle quickly.

"He came up here and insisted that I should destroy the will I made in favour of his brother and Miss Carrol. Here it is," and Colpster passed along the large envelope. "Take it, Harry, and give it to Basil when he returns. It is not safe here."

"Shall I take the emerald?" asked Harry, putting the envelope containing the will in the breast-pocket of his pea-jacket.

Colpster snatched the gem to his breast and nursed it there like a baby.

"No! no! no!" he cried vehemently. "I can't part with that. I'll die before anyone shall have it but me. Give me more wine."

Still clutching the jewel he drank another glass of port, and became quite strong again with the stimulant. Meanwhile Theodore lay stiffly on the carpet, cursing volubly. Harry kicked him.

"Shut your mouth," said the sailor, "or I'll gag you."

"I'll have you arrested for this," repeated Theodore, impotently scowling.

"That's all right," said Pentreddle, and drawing a chair near the sofa he turned to the Squire. "Now, sir, we must have a talk."

"What's the matter?" asked Colpster in some alarm. "Where have you been to, and where have you come from?"

"I'll tell you, sir, if you'll listen. On the night I left here that Japanese Akira followed me up the road, when I was making for my friend and the trap on the moors."

"Ah!" Theodore groaned. "That was why he went to bed early. I knew that he was up to some game. He pretended to go to bed and—"

"And followed me. Quite right, sir. He did, and he told me all about the murder of my poor mother."

"What?" Colpster gasped. "Are you the person Akira said he would send to tell me all that I wished to know?"

Pentreddle nodded grimly. "I am the person. I went to London next day with Count Akira, and he introduced me to a person who knew all about the murder. I got it written down, signed and witnessed in a proper manner. Then I came here with the Count in his yacht, and arrived just in time to save that devil," he pointed to Theodore, "from committing a second crime."

158

"A second crime," echoed the Squire, bewildered. "I don't understand."

"It's a lie; a lie," howled Theodore, straining at his bonds. "If I were free I'd dash the lie down your throat."

"And my teeth too, you murdering beast," said Harry, clenching his hands. "I owe you one for the murder of my mother."

Colpster sprang to his feet with surprising alacrity, considering his late exhaustion. "Murder! Did—did—did," he pointed a shaking finger at the mass on the floor, "did he murder Martha?"

"Yes," said Harry sadly.

"It's a lie; a lie!" muttered Theodore again and again, struggling fiercely.

"It's the truth. Sit down, Mr. Colpster, and I'll tell you all about it. I have the document of an eye-witness signed and witnessed here," he touched his breast-pocket.

"An eye-witness?" said Colpster, resuming his seat heavily.

"Yes. That priest with the scar on his cheek I told you about, who saw me watching The Home of Art."

"He did it himself, you fool," roared Theodore, defending his lost cause.

"So I thought, and I was going out to Japan to kill him. But I know that you were with my mother on that night, for the priest saw you enter the house by the window. You tapped there, and my mother let you in. The priest was watching the house, as he fancied the emerald might be there. He got on to the balcony and peeped through the window. He saw you struggle with my mother, you brute, and stab her. Then you left the room and hunted the house for the emerald. When you came out the priest, thinking you might have it, waited at the gate and tried to seize you. You escaped and he lost you in the fog. But he retained hold of the white silk scarf you wore round your throat. It is here." Pentreddle took a folded square of silk from his pocket and shook it out. "Your name is in the corner, your name in full, hang you! Look, Squire! look!" And Harry, his hands shaking with emotion, pointed out the name "Theodore Dane" marked on the silk, with blue thread. "You see, sir. He is guilty."

"Oh!" the Squire groaned, as he saw the evidence of his nephew's wickedness, and he laid the emerald on the table so that he could the more easily cover his face with his hands "It's terrible—terrible. That one of my blood should be an assassin! That one of my blood should be hanged!"

"Oh, he won't be hanged!" said Harry, refolding the silk scarf and replacing it in his pocket. "I am going to leave him to Akira."

"What—what do you mean?" quavered Theodore, with sudden terror.

The young sailor walked over to him and looked into his face. "Akira told me that he would attend to your punishment. What he means I don't know. But what I *do* know is that these Japanese can make things very unpleasant for you. I have heard of their ingenuity in torturing."

"Torturing!" Theodore shrieked.

"Yes. Hanging's too good for you, beast that you are."

"Oh, Harry, don't—don't let Akira get hold of me!" screamed Dane, all his nerve broken down. "The law won't let him; the law won't let him!"

"He won't trouble about the law. He will send sailors ashore this very night and have you taken on board his yacht. When you are on the high seas he'll deal with you."

"No! no!" Theodore tried to kiss the man's foot and rolled over to do so.

Harry spurned him. "You worse than devil, try and be a man. You murdered a poor, weak woman and now you're frightened of your skin. Beast!"

Outside the wind had risen to wild fury. The whole house was shaken by the gusts which came howling from the bay. Harry strode to the window and looked out. He saw by the swaying of the festival lights that *The Miko* was dragging at her moorings. There was no time to be lost, if he wanted to carry out his promise to the Count. Colpster was lying limply on the sofa, while Theodore moaned and groaned on the floor. On the small table beside the sofa gleamed the emerald which had brought about all the trouble.

"Let me be arrested and hanged. I don't want to be tortured," wailed the man on the floor.

"Did you kill my mother?"

"Give me some wine and I'll tell you."

"I shan't," said Harry; then thought better of it, and poured a glass of port down his enemy's throat. "Now tell!"

"I really didn't mean to kill her," said Theodore, and Colpster raised his head to listen. "I followed Martha up to London, intending when she got the Mikado Jewel to make her give it to me."

"Why?" asked the Squire, looking very old and grey.

"Because you said that the one who produced the jewel would be your heir, curse you!" shrieked Theodore savagely; "You are the cause of all the beastly trouble. I learned from Martha in an indirect way that Harry was coming, and then I met him."

"Yes," said the sailor bitterly. "And like a fool I told you too much."

"You told me nothing," said Dane, scowling. "Your mother wanted the emerald for Basil. But I got into your room at the boarding-house you lived in at Pimlico, and I read your mother's letters."

"You did."

"Yes. She said that she would be alone on that night and would come to get the emerald. I went to the house to see if she had left. I knocked at the door, but no one came, so I went to the window and saw her lying on the sofa near the fire. I called out to her, and asked her to let me in."

"She couldn't get off the sofa, you fool!" cried the Squire.

"She could and she did. I said that I had found out that Harry had been killed by the Japanese for the sake of the emerald. Then she crawled to the window and let me in."

"You beast!" said Pentreddle, gritting his teeth. "You told a lie."

"Martha would not have admitted me if I had not done so. She got me into the room, and then I insisted that she should give the emerald."

"She hadn't got it."

"She wouldn't confess that she hadn't. Perhaps she feared lest I should intercept her messenger, Miss Carrol, on the way home, and rob her of the jewel. At all events, she gave me to understand nothing, and I really believed that the emerald was in her pocket. I tried to get it; then she brought out that damned stiletto and stabbed at me. I wrested it from her and in the struggle somehow I drove it into her throat."

"You intended to!" shouted the Squire, rising to shake his two clenched hands over the criminal.

"I swear I did not," panted Dane; "it was really an accident. When I saw what I had done I grew afraid. I thought that I heard someone outside—"

"So you did," interrupted Harry sharply; "It was the watching priest."

"If I'd known," Theodore scowled, and his eyes gleamed in a most murderous manner. "But I didn't. I saw that Martha was dead or dying, and opened the window to throw the stiletto into the area. Then I searched her clothing for the emerald and afterwards the bedrooms."

"Oh! And you say you did not murder her?" raged the Squire.

"Not intentionally. I swear that I did not. But seeing that she was dead, it was just as well to hunt for what I wanted. I found nothing, so I came down and got out by the window. Just outside the gate someone—that infernal priest as I now know—snatched at my shoulder and grabbed my scarf. I slipped him in the fog and—and—that's all."

"Quite enough too. You shall hang," cried the Squire.

"No," said Pentreddle, rising and making for the window, "he shan't hang." He threw up the window and the fierce gale came howling into the room. "I shall call up Akira's sailors," shouted the young man.

"Don't; don't!" screamed Dane. "They'll torture me."

"Serve you right," said his uncle fiercely. "You have brought shame and disgrace upon the family."

"Mr. Colpster," the Squire turned as he heard his name mentioned and saw that Harry had picked up the Mikado Jewel, "I take this back to Akira."

"You shan't! you shan't! It's mine!" and the old man dashed forward with outstretched hands while the wind drove wildly into the rooms.

A roar of laughter came from the bound man on the floor. "Ha! ha! ha!" he screamed. "Uncle, you're done for! you're done for! Ha! ha! ha!"

"Give! give! give!" whimpered Colpster, trying to seize Pentreddle. "It is mine! it is mine!"

"It belongs to the Temple of Kitzuki," said Harry, backing towards the window. "I stole it and now I am going to return it. I promised to do so, if Akira told me who murdered my mother. Keep back, sir! keep back!"

Theodore roared with laughter and twisted himself round to see what would happen. Colpster, his eyes filled with mad anger, dashed at Pentreddle, who evaded him dexterously, and before the Squire knew his intention, slipped like an eel out of the window.

Harry clambered down the ivy with the cleverness of a sailor and saw above him the wild despairing face of the Squire, while he heard the loud ironical laughter of the bound man. The rain was coming down in torrents dashed here and there by the wind. The sailor slipped and fell on his back, but was up again in a moment and made for the beach. He heard high above the sound of wind and wave the thin lamentations of Colpster, who saw the luck of his family being carried away for ever.

Pentreddle raced for the beach through the furious weather. There he shouted as he stumbled towards the pier, and immediately two Japanese took him by the shoulders to tumble him bodily into the launch. They seemed to be in a desperate hurry, for scarcely had he got his breath when he found that the launch was plunging at full speed through the turbulent water.

"What the devil is the hurry!" gasped Harry, shaking the water from his eyes.

The answer did not come from the Japanese, who were driving the boat out to sea at high pressure but from the land. There was a low, moaning sound, which boomed like an organ note above the tumult of the elements. It grew louder and more insistent, and droned like a giant bee. The mere sound was terrifying, and Harry saw the bronze faces of the sailors blanch with fear. Suddenly the note grew shrill, like a cry of triumph, and then came a loud crash, which seemed to shake the earth. Far and wide he could hear, even through the tempest, the splashing of great fragments into the sea, and the crumbling of mighty masses on the land. Then came a stillness and the wind dropped gradually to low whimperings.

"The cliff has fallen," said the Japanese officer; "it is the Earth Spirit."

"This," said Harry, his face grey with terror, and showed the Mikado Jewel flashing in the light of the lamps.

The sailors fell on their faces before its sinister glare. Only the officer, unable to desert his post, although his face was ghastly white and his limbs shook, continued to steer the launch seaward.

CHAPTER XX

A FURTHER EXPLANATION

The morning dawned raw and bleak, to display the scene of the disaster in its most searching light. None of those who had come to the entertainment were allowed to go on shore during the hours of darkness. Basil, indeed, as soon as Akira informed him of the catastrophe—and Akira seemed to know positively what had taken place, even before the arrival of the steam-launch with the news—wished to see what had become of his uncle and brother. But the Japanese pointed out that fragments of the cliff were still falling, and that it would be dangerous to venture. As every hour or so the thunder of falling masses was heard, Dane considered that the advice was good, and possessed his soul in patience until the dawn. Frequently during the night he lamented that he had not the searchlight of his own ship to see what extent of damage was done. But, of course, such wishing was altogether vain.

As *The Miko* was large, there was plenty of accommodation, and the servants were persuaded to go below and sleep. The women were very hysterical, and the men greatly upset. Everyone was devoted to the Squire, and hoped against hope that he had been saved. But it was noticeable that no one troubled about Theodore. Until that night Basil had no idea how very unpopular his brother really was. But he had not much time to think, as the greater part of his time was spent in soothing Patricia. She felt the dreadful accident and its consequences much more than did Mara. That young lady neither wept nor expressed any great sorrow. With a rigid face she stared into the gloom which veiled the home of her childhood, and made scarcely any remark.

Akira, when Harry came on board, privately asked him if he thought that either Colpster or his nephew had escaped.

"I'm certain they have not," said Pentreddle emphatically. "Mr. Theodore was tied up, and the last I saw of the Squire he was at the window cursing me for taking away the Mikado Jewel."

"Ah, yes! You brought that away with you!" Akira held out his hand.

Harry produced the Jewel, which he had thrust carelessly into his pocket after his glimpse of it on the launch. "They all fell on their faces," he told the Japanese.

Akira smiled in a peculiar manner. "No wonder, when they saw the might of the Earth-Spirit."

"What do you mean exactly, sir?" asked the sailor, quite puzzled.

The Count handled the Jewel reverently, and producing a sandal-wood box, carefully wrapped up the emerald and its jade setting in fine silk before placing it therein. "I mean that this jewel holds the power of the Earth-Spirit, and pulled down the cliff on those who had to be punished," was his remark, as he locked the box and put it away safely.

"Is this the punishment you intended for Mr. Theodore for murdering my mother?" asked Pentreddle, with a faltering voice.

"Yes. Are you not satisfied?"

"I thought you would have taken him on board and tortured him."

Akira drew himself to his full height, which was not very great. Still in his indignation he contrived to look quite imperial. "I am a Japanese gentleman and do not torture anyone. I knew that the cliff would fall as soon as you left the house, and that those behind would be crushed."

"But how could you make the cliff fall?" persisted Harry.

"The Earth-Spirit brought the fall about through its power stored in the Jewel of Go Yojo. Do you understand?"

"No," said the bluff sailor, frankly bewildered.

"Well, then, I can explain no more. You must take it that there was an accident owing to the late rains. The earth fell for that reason. But you are revenged on your enemy. Now tell me all that took place."

Harry did not require much urging, and related everything. Akira listened in silence. "Hai!" said he, when the tale was ended. "This poor wretch was ready to commit a second murder. So much evil we have saved him. Have you the will he spoke of?"

"Yes." Pentreddle produced it from his pocket, but Akira did not offer to take it. In fact, he refused to touch it.

"Give it to Mr. Dane as you have been instructed. I am glad to hear that he will inherit the property. I have a great opinion of Mr. Dane and a better one of the charming young lady he is going to marry."

"I'll give it to him," said Pentreddle; "and now, sir, what is to become of me, if you please?"

"Well," said Akira quietly, "as you have restored the emerald, you are no longer in danger. I give you your life. Also, and because you obeyed my instructions so implicitly, you can have these," and he produced ten notes of ten pounds each. "One hundred pounds, my friend."

"I couldn't touch them, sir. It would look as though I wanted to take money for avenging my poor mother's death."

"That is very creditable to you, Pentreddle, but I don't think you need decline. You have been useful to me and deserve payment."

Thus persuaded, Harry gladly took the notes, but as he placed them in his pocket he observed gloomily that he thought Theodore Dane had died in too easy a manner. Akira shook his head and rebuked him.

"My friend, that Mr. Dane broke the Great Law, and when next he is born he will have to pay back to your mother all he owes her. By wishing to torture him, as you suggested to me, you are only preparing trouble for yourself. He has been partly punished. Leave him, as to the rest, to the Great Law."

"What is the Great Law?"

"As you sow, so shall you reap," said Akira quietly.

"I have heard that before, sir."

"It is in your sacred Book, my friend; but few of your people in the West understand its real meaning. They think that the Master who said it takes the reaping on His own shoulders, while they sit in happiness and see it done." Akira shrugged his shoulders. "A great many of these foolish ones will be undeceived when their Karma is ripe."

"Karma?"

The Count arose and shook his head. "We must not talk on these subjects, as I am no priest," he said with a smile; "all I tell you is, that you must obey the Great Law, or suffer according to your breaking of it. Now go and give the will to Mr. Dane."

Pentreddle did so, and when questioned as to how it came into his possession, related all that he knew, and how he had brought back the will to its rightful owner. Patricia was present when he explained, and both she and her lover were horrified to hear that Theodore had murdered the poor woman. They questioned and cross-questioned him until he was weary and excused himself so that he might get a little sleep. But there was none for the young couple.

"If Theodore is indeed dead, it is a mercy," said Basil thankfully.

"Oh, dearest! dead in his sin?"

"Oh!" said the young man rather cynically; "if one had to wait until Theodore, from what I knew of him, was fit to die, he would have become immortal. No, darling," he added quickly, catching sight of Patricia's pained face, "I don't mean to be flippant. God have mercy on his soul! I say, with all my heart. But he was a thoroughly bad man."

"Well, he is dead, so let us think no more about him."

So they said and so they felt, but throughout that weary night they continued to talk of the scamp. Also they referred regretfully to the death of the Squire, and Patricia wept for the old man who had been so kind to her. In the end, grief and anxiety wore her out, and she fell asleep on Basil's breast. They sat in a sheltered corner of the deck, for Miss Carrol refused to be parted from her lover.

In the grey, grim light they finally saw the ruin which had been wrought by the fall of the mighty cliff. There were vast rents in its breast, and it was by no means so high as it had been. Below was a tumbled mass of red rock, beneath which, not only the Hall but the greater part of the grounds were buried. That which had been Beckleigh was now a thing of the past, for in no way could that enormous quantity of rubble and rock, and sand and stone, be lifted. The whole formed a gigantic tumulus, such as of yore had been heaped over the body of some barbarous chief. Squire Colpster and his wicked nephew certainly had a magnificent monument to mark the place where they reposed. Amidst all that fallen rock it was impossible to rebuild the Hall, or to reconstruct the grounds.

"We have the income," said Basil, while he stood on deck with his arm round Patricia's waist, looking at the ruin, "but our home is gone for ever."

Patricia shuddered. "I am sorry, of course, for it is such a lovely place."

"*Was* such a lovely place, my dear."

"Yes! Yes! But I always felt afraid when in the Hall. I felt certain that some day the cliff would fall. It always seemed hostile to me."

"It was only hostile to two people," said the quiet voice of Akira behind them: "the man who murdered for the sake of the emerald, and the man who set in motion the causes which brought the emerald to Beckleigh. Both have paid for their sins."

"Whatever do you mean, Count?"

"I shall tell you and Dane when we go ashore," said the Japanese calmly; "in the meantime come down and have some breakfast. You look faint, Miss Carrol, and it is time that you restored your strength. Go down and see my wife, and she will look after you."

When Patricia descended the companion, Akira turned to Basil. "Excuse me, Dane," he said courteously, "but this fall of the cliff has robbed you of your home. You will want money. Allow me to be your banker."

"Thank you; but there is really no need," said Basil hastily. "I have five or six pounds in my pocket: enough to take myself and Miss Carrol to London. Once we are there, I shall see my uncle's lawyers about the will, and get them to advance what I require."

"But all these servants who are homeless?"

"They can go to their various relatives and friends. I shall get the lawyers to send money for them. Don't be afraid, Akira, I shan't neglect my people. For they are mine now, you know. Unless—" he cast a hopeful glance at the scarred face of the cliff.

"No. Both the Squire and your brother are dead. They will lie under that mighty pile of earth to the end of time, unless some high tide washes it away. Of course, I mean their sheaths will. Their souls are now reaping according to the sowing. Come to breakfast."

Basil descended, and with Patricia and the bridal couple had an excellent breakfast, which was much needed. It was useless to sorrow for the dead to the extent of starving for them, for Basil had seen very little of his uncle for many years, and certainly had no cause to mourn for Theodore. As for Mara, she was as cool and composed as ever, and ate so well that no one would ever have believed that she had just lost her father.

"It is no use crying over spilt milk," she said, making use of her favourite proverb; and although both her cousin and Patricia considered that she was decidedly heartless, they could not deny the good sense of the saying she invariably quoted as an excuse for her indifference.

But she was not sufficiently hard-hearted to remain behind—although her feeling may have been merely one of curiosity—for she came on deck cloaked and gloved, and with her hat on, ready to join the party. Akira promptly told her that he did not wish her to go, and as his slightest wish was law to her, she obeyed. The yacht was to sail somewhere about noon, so there would be no chance for Basil and Patricia to come on board again. Nor did they want to, seeing that at present they had so much to think about. So they said good-bye to the Countess Akira and departed along with the melancholy household that had now no home.

The launch took them ashore under what seemed an ironically sunny and blue sky. After the late rains and storms, it was cheerful to see the water of the bay sparkle in the sunlight. But, alas! Beckleigh was as ruined as ever was Pompeii, and in future the fairy bay would only be stretched out before a desolate scene. Patricia almost wept when she saw the ruin of the beauty spot. Not a vestige of the house was to be seen: it was crushed flat under tons of red earth, while nearly down to the water's edge great sandstone rocks and much rubble had smashed the trees and obliterated the flower-beds. And over the gigantic heaps of *débris*, the mighty cliff still soared, rent and scarred, although not to its original height. Early as the day was, many people, both men and women, were moving amongst the rubbish, seeing what they could pick up. But there was absolutely nothing to be found. The enormous fall of tons and tons of earth had pulverized Beckleigh into dust. It was like the ruins of a pre-historic world.

Many people came down when they saw the approaching launch, amongst them relatives of the servants, together with friends. These took charge of the homeless wanderers, and gradually the whole household disappeared up the winding road to find shelter. Before they departed Basil informed them that within a week he would return to Hendle and attend to their needs, as he had inherited the property. Although the young man was a favourite, the dispossessed were too miserable to raise a cheer, and departed with sad faces and hanging heads. Their world was in ruins, and save what they stood up in, all were without money or home. But the promise made by their new master that he would look after them cheered them not a little.

Akira, after he had walked round the desolation with Basil and Patricia, asked them to return to the pier. Here, he had seats brought up from the launch, and they sat down to hear what he had to say. His first speech rather surprised them, used as they were becoming to the happening of the unexpected.

"I am sorry that all this has occurred," he said seriously, waving his hand towards the ruins; "but I had to bring it about."

They looked at one another and then at the speaker, believing, and with some reason, that he was crazy. "How could you possibly bring it about?" asked Mr. Dane in a sceptical tone.

"The Mikado Jewel brought it about."

"Oh!" Patricia winced; "are you going to talk more of this occult nonsense?"

"Can you call it nonsense in the face of this, Miss Carrol?"

"That is an accident owing to the late rains."

"Quite so, and that is what the world will consider it. But I can tell you differently. It happened because the Mikado Jewel was in the house."

"It was not!" said Basil imperatively, and would have gone on talking, but that Patricia stopped him.

"It *was* in the house," she said quickly, "only Mr. Colpster—poor man!— asked Theodore and myself to say nothing about it."

Basil cast a glance at the red heaps. "Then it is buried under this rubbish," he said disdainfully; "for all its occult power, it couldn't look after itself!"

"I looked after it," said Akira quietly. "It is now on board the yacht, and I am taking it back to Japan to restore it to the Temple of Kitzuki."

"How did you get it, Akira?"

"Pentreddle, by my desire, took it from the Squire when he went last night to accuse Theodore, your brother, of murder."

"He did not tell me that," said Basil involuntarily.

"I asked him not to, as I wished to tell you myself. I am sorry to bore you with occult talk, Miss Carrol, but I think you would like to understand the reason for the Jewel being at Beckleigh at all."

"You sent it to Mr. Colpster?"

"Yes, I did. To punish him for daring to have it stolen from Kitzuki."

"But he didn't wish it stolen. He was angry that Harry should steal it."

Akira waved his hand. "Mr. Colpster was the original cause of setting in motion the causes which led to Mrs. Pentreddle's death, to his own death, and to that of his nephew. He believed that the Jewel would bring back luck.

170

Instead of that, it brought that," and he pointed to the ruins.

Basil looked helplessly at the speaker. "My dear fellow, I am quite in the dark as to what you are talking about."

"Listen, and I shall explain. Something of what I tell you has been told to you before, but something I now tell you is new." He drew a long breath and continued: "I don't expect you to believe all I say."

"We'll try," said Basil ironically. "Go on!"

"Mr. Colpster wished for the Mikado Jewel," said Akira deliberately, "and so he employed you, Dane, to offer money for it. Mrs. Pentreddle heard from her late master that he intended to give the property to the nephew who brought back the Jewel. She hated Theodore, and loved you, so, as her son was going to Japan, she asked him to get the Jewel. In a way which he told Mr. Colpster, but which I need not repeat, he stole it, and got away with it. But he was followed and watched. The priests of the temple told the Government at Tokio, and I was deputed to see if the Jewel could be recovered. I went to Kitzuki and saved your life when you came to offer money for the gem."

"And thank you for doing it, Akira," said Basil heartily.

"All right. I was only too pleased, since the information you gave me about the emerald having been presented to one of your queens, helped me to unravel the mystery. Several attempts were made to get the gem from Pentreddle while he was in Japan, but all failed. I therefore sent two men to watch for the arrival of his ship in London and followed myself. I knew that I had made you my friend, and intended to come to Beckleigh, if it was necessary. When I arrived in London I found that Pentreddle was trying to give the Jewel to his mother, and learned—through his hanging round the house—that the old lady was staying at The Home of Art, in Crook Street."

"And you had that watched, I suppose?"

"Of course," replied Akira serenely. "A man with a scar on his cheek, who was an attendant in the Temple of Kitzuki, watched that house. Then I learned where Pentreddle was boarding in Pimlico, and my second man gained access to his room. His letters, which he left about, were read, and I learned that his mother intended to meet him at the Serpentine in the way we know of. I followed him when he went to keep the appointment."

"What?" cried Patricia. "Was it you, Count, who snatched the jewel from me?"

"Yes. I noticed that Pentreddle passed you the box, and followed you. I fancied you would take the box home, but you sat down to examine it."

"It was the strange drawing-power which made me open the box. I wanted to see what caused the power."

"I fear," answered Akira, rather ironically, "that your curiosity was not gratified. However, as the power still radiated from the stone, keeping off all things that would hurt it, I reversed the power, or rather, stopped it altogether."

"How did you manage that?" asked Basil doubtfully.

Akira shook his head. "I cannot tell you. I dare not. It is a secret. And even if I did, you would only laugh, since you do not believe in these sort of things. I knew the necessary mantra to say and said it." He looked at Patricia with a smile. "You felt the difference."

"Yes," she nodded, with a look of something like awe. "Then you snatched it."

"Of course, and the jewel being recovered, I would then and there have taken it back to Japan, but for the murder of Mrs. Pentreddle."

"Theodore *did* murder her, then?" said Basil in a low, shamed voice.

"Oh, yes, and in the way her son told you. My man with the scar saw the crime committed, and secured the scarf, as evidence, with the name of your brother marked in the corner."

"Bad as Theodore was," said Basil, drawing a deep breath, "I am glad that you did not shame the family by denouncing him."

Akira smiled at him in a friendly way. "Of course, you are my friend," he observed. "Also, I wished to find young Pentreddle. I came down to Beckleigh, as you know, and left instructions to my two men to send down the Jewel to Mr. Colpster. But before leaving London I reversed the power."

"But I don't see—-"

"I do not expect you to see, my dear man," interrupted Akira quickly; "but the jewel arrived with the power reversed."

"Yes," Patricia nodded again. "I felt it," and she shivered.

"Well, then," Akira glanced at his watch, "there is little more to tell. I simply waited while the Jewel did its work of loosening the cliff. All the time it was in the house it was drawing those tons of earth down on the place. I heard in the drawing-room that night that Mr. Colpster was going to speak to Pentreddle, and pretended to go to bed. Instead of doing so, I got out of the window and intercepted him on the winding road. I then told him that I could prove who killed his mother, and sent him to wait for my arrival in London.

He went the next morning. I came on later, and then I made my man with the scar tell him everything. Pentreddle left me with a full statement, signed by my man and witnessed. As your brother is dead and it is useless to make a scandal," said Akira, glancing at Basil, "I got that document from him last night and burned it."

Dane leaned forward and shook the hand of the Japanese. "I am greatly obliged to you," he said with emotion.

"Why," said Akira, in a friendly manner, "there is no reason that you should suffer for the sins of others. That would not be fair. Besides, I wish you to give Miss Carrol a clean name. Now, then, do you wish to know any more, as I must up anchor and steam for the East?"

"How many people know that my brother committed this murder?"

"I do and my two men. As we are going away for ever and will hold our tongues, you need not fear us. Harry Pentreddle will say nothing, as he respects you and Miss Carrol too much. Besides, I gave him one hundred pounds to get married on, so when he is happy himself he will not wish to make others unhappy. The Squire was the only other person who knew, and he is dead. Your name is quite safe."

"Thank God for that!" said Basil reverently, and took off his hat.

"One question more," said Patricia, rising. "What did you mean when you told me that you now knew why you had come to Beckleigh?"

"It was because of Mara," explained Akira gravely. "She was formerly a priestess in the Temple of Kitzuki, and for some reason the Spirit of the Earth, whose spell was on the emerald, wished to bring her to my arms. We had promised to love for seven lives, you know. For this reason the theft of the Mikado Jewel was permitted. But for that, Pentreddle would have been kept back by the radiating power. Even I, with no ill-intent, had to reverse, or rather break, the power, before I could take the gem from you. But, then, I know the spell."

"And what is the power contained in the stone now?"

Akira hesitated. "I told you that the Jewel was left on board," he said, "but that was not true. I brought it with me." He produced the box from his pocket and took from it the Jewel. The great stone blazed with green lustre in the sunlight. "Take it in your hands, Miss Carrol."

Patricia did so, while Basil looked at the gem curiously. He had never seen it before. Suddenly Patricia cried out with delight. "Oh, yes, I feel the warmth and the light, and the power streaming out from every petal."

"Imagination," said Basil impatiently, and took the stone. "I can feel nothing of what you describe."

The Count carefully replaced the Jewel in its box. "You are not psychic."

"I never wish to hear that word again," said Basil fervently.

"I don't think you will," replied Akira dryly, and slipped the box into his pocket. "Well, now I shall say good-bye, and from Japan I shall send you my wedding-present."

"Be kind to Mara," said Patricia imploringly.

"Be sure of that. She is a sacred thing to me. Was she not the Miko of Kitzuki, and did not the Earth-Spirit bring her to my arms?" He changed his reverent tone for a matter-of-fact one. "Good-bye, Dane!"

Akira held out his hand, then suddenly drew it back. "There is one thing I should like to add, so that you may guess that I am not in favour of killing innocent people. I gave my entertainment so as to lure you, Dane, and you, Miss Carrol, together with all your servants, on board the yacht out of harm's way. Therefore Mr. Colpster and the assassin were left to their fate alone in the house."

"But Pentreddle?" asked Basil, shuddering.

Akira looked towards the winding road up which Harry was slowly climbing. "I had to send him to get the Jewel," he remarked, "but I warned him of the danger and he escaped. Now that is all I have to tell," he added quickly, seeing that Patricia was about to ask another question. "Good-bye, both of you, once more."

They shook hands gravely all round, then Akira jumped into his launch and it steamed away in a great hurry, as usual. Basil and Patricia set their faces landward and picked their way over the loose rocks. In a short time, and walking above the grave of uncle and cousin, they gained the clear space of the winding road. Here they came face to face with Mrs. Lee, who was toiling down all alone.

"Ah!" she said, with a chuckle. "So it's you, Mr. Basil." The old creature nodded. "I told him he would be crushed as flat as a pancake if he allowed It to come into the house. He did, like a silly fool, and now he is buried under all that rubbish." She pointed her staff disdainfully downwards.

"Who did you tell this to, Granny?" asked Basil, who knew her well.

"To your brother Theodore. Bless you, deary, he often came to consult me. I didn't like him, though, as he brought such bad Ones with him."

"What is the It you meant?" questioned Patricia, wondering if Mrs. Lee had any knowledge of the fatal Jewel.

It appeared that she had not. "Ah, lovey! They didn't tell me that. All I knew and all I told him was that It would crush him as flat as a pancake." She looked at the tumbled red earth and chuckled maliciously. "And it has, deary; it has. A grave for an emperor that is."

"I don't believe these things, Granny," said Basil, placing Patricia's arm within his own. "Here's a shilling."

"Bless you, deary; may you never want bread," croaked the old crone, biting the shilling before tying it up in a corner of her apron. Then she faced them and waved a circle thrice, which she crossed once. "The sign of power to bring you luck, my dears," she explained, wagging her head. "But, bless you both, you ain't wicked to the marrow as he was, drat him! I can see your future bright and fair." Her eyes became fixed as she spoke, and she looked into the viewless air. "You'll both be happy all your lives, for sorrow is ended and the debts of Fate are paid. Money and children and rank and lots of good, staunch friends. All that you desire will come to you and the poor will bless you evermore. So be it and let it be." After which weird speech the old creature toddled down the hill with a senile laugh.

"What do you make of that, Basil?" asked Patricia, when they reached the top of the winding road and came in sight of the carriage which was to take them to Hendle railway station.

"Well," said the young man reflectively, "after what has taken place I dare not disbelieve in many things."

"I hope that what Granny says will come true."

"My dear," Basil amidst all his trouble turned to catch her in his arms, "I am sure that with such a darling as you are for my wife everything is entirely feasible and possible. If the emerald of Amyas Colpster brought luck to no one, it certainly has done so to me. And now let us drive to Hendle and catch the evening train to London. To-morrow we must get married."

"It seems heartless when your uncle is just dead," sighed Patricia, "but I have no home to go to, and no one but you."

"You shall stay at The Home of Art, and when I marry you, my dear, Mrs. Sellars shall be the bridesmaid. Come, my darling!"

The sound of a gun stopped them before they could take a single step towards the new life, which spread out so brightly before them. They turned to see *The Miko* standing out to sea, with the black smoke pouring from her funnel. As they waved their handkerchiefs, the yacht dipped her ensign, and fired a second gun. Then they saw her turn her nose seaward and steam direct for Japan. And the boat was carrying the Mikado Jewel, after it had fulfilled its mission in the West, back to its shrine in the Temple of Kitzuki, in the Province of Izumo.

FINIS.

Lightning Source UK Ltd.
Milton Keynes UK
UKHW042011060820
367798UK00002BA/455